THE WAGNERIAN
ASSIGNMENT
Second Edition

By
Alan Starforth

info@straightfacedpublications.com
www.straightfacedpublications.com

Published by **Straightfaced Publications**
© Straightfaced Publication
Kehlsteinhaus Image © Corporal Wesley E. Jackson

Dedicated to my wife Dawn,
and my sons Stuart and Daniel for all their help and support.

MONDAY, MARCH 12TH 1945

***

The passing of each tortured second ticks slowly toward the inevitable destruction of the self-proclaimed German Führer, Adolf Hitler's National Socialist Third Reich. Twelve years into what the Nazis had proclaimed would last a thousand and a mere twenty-six since the founding of the Nationalsozialistische Deutsche Arbeiterpartei (NSDAP), the Red Armies of Marshal Georgy Zhukov's 1st Belarusian front and Marshal Ivan Konev's 1st Ukrainian front bear down on Berlin in the fight for the tributes of being the first to conquer the once imposing German capital. Thunderous explosions can be heard from far-off artillery, breaking the cold, wet spring morning that hours earlier had calmed after a devastating night bombing raid by the Royal Air Force.

***

Flying the flags of general and state, a battered, dirty Mercedes Benz G4 sedan staff car drives through the destroyed city, passing destitute and starving civilians scratching through the rubble for any resemblance of the life that had been torn from them. Terrified that the occupants have the power of life or death over them, the civilians and military personnel stop and come to rigid attention with arms outstretched giving the Nazi salute. Fearful for the future, the terrified German people are well aware of the crimes fellow citizens had committed in their name and that revenge and rape will be foremost on the mind of the Red Army soldier preparing to conquer their capital. Through a cloud of dust, the Mercedes turns onto Wilhelm Strasse past the Reich Chancellery and into the heart of the Berlin government sector that Hitler had pretentiously renamed Germania and whose plans were laid out by Albert Speer, his chief architect. Only a small portion of the grand project had been built before the onset of the war that now lies in ruins.

***

Due to carpet bombing carried out at night by the Royal Air Force and day by the United States Army Air Force, Hitler had been driven below the Reich Chancellery gardens into a bunker complex that at the onset of war had not been thought of as an option that may be required for the future. The building work was started in 1943 and was completed in late 1944. The Allies undertaking to destroy the industrial potential of an enemy through terror bombing had seen two million tons of high explosives dropped onto Germany during the ill-conceived strategic bombing offensive designed to bring the German nation to its knees. Killing six hundred thousand Germans in the process.

In September 1939, after Great Britain and France had declared war on Germany, Reichsmarschall Hermann Göring had bombastically boasted to the National Socialist elite, "No enemy bomber can reach the Ruhr. If one reaches the Ruhr, my name is not Göring. You may call me Meyer."
After such an arrogant, self-aggrandising statement, many ordinary Germans called Göring Meyer.

***

In the rear of the Mercedes, wearing the rank of SS standartenführer for the first time, Otto Skorzeny hardly ventures to gaze at the devastation that informs him his war is ending in inevitable defeat. Closing his eyes, his mind returns to better times, bringing a slight smirk to his battle-hardened face, but this is quickly broken when his second in command, SS Sturmbannführer Karl Radl, turns to him, showing his exasperation at all that beholds them.
"Are you alright, Otto?" Radl questioned, making Skorzeny's eyes flicker and then open to see they had arrived at their destination. "You seem a little distracted."
Not needing to explain, Skorzeny ignores his friend and comrade as he looks at the devastation outside. Hauptfeldwebel Hans Bergdorf, an impressively dressed Wehrmacht non-commissioned officer showing medals and battle honours gained during the war on his tunic, alights the driver's seat and opens the rear door before standing aside and coming rigidly to attention. Showing the effects of a long-drawn-out war which of late had been one of dismal retreat and a long, tedious journey fraught with the dangers from prowling Allied fighters, Skorzeny alights followed by Radl to stretch out their aching bodies. Looking at the wasted desolation he had attempted to avoid during the journey, Skorzeny shows no emotion as his eyes shift to the once grand Reich Chancellery, which shows the marks the heavy bombing had left. The stonework is heavily scarred, and the grounds and gardens are pitted with varying sizes of bomb craters. Soldiers and civilians clear the debris in a ridiculous show of Germanic efficiency as they attempt to keep normality. Waffen SS officers and soldiers from countries conquered by the Germans and who elected to betray their own and serve the fatherland in the fight against communism find themselves

constructing defensive structures as they anxiously await the Red Army onslaught. The last of the millions of highly trained soldiers of the once massive German army that had conquered large swaths of Europe, Russia and North Africa stand ready to protect a Führer who is alien to them as they fight against the odds as if protecting their homeland capitals from invaders well aware that in their own countries, they are traitors to their own.

***

Born on June 12th 1908, in Vienna, Austria, SS Standartenführer Otto Skorzeny stands six foot four inches tall with broad shoulders and a handsome Germanic demeanour. A large duelling schmiss received during his Burschenschaft University days in Vienna runs across the left side of his face, from his chin to the tip of the left corner of his mouth, across his cheek, almost reaching his ear lobe. His uniform bears a single oak leaf on both collars indicating the rank of colonel, the Iron Cross first and second class, and the Knights Cross of the iron cross on his chest., His swift rise to notoriety and the attention of the Allies had come when on July 26th 1943, Hitler gave him the task of rescuing his friend, the Italian dictator, Il Duce (the Leader) Benito Mussolini. Code-named Unternehmen Eiche (Operation Oak) Mussolini had been overthrown and imprisoned on the orders of the Italian King, Victor Emmanuel III, who had seen the wind of change and had approached the Allies to save himself. This mission was carried out with great finesse on September 12th 1943, by Skorzeny, the men of Jagdverbande 502 and General Karl Student's Fallschirmjäger who assaulted the Gran Sasso Italy to rescue the dictator with minimal casualties that propelled the once unknown soldier into worldwide infamy with the help of Josef Goebbels' propaganda machine which needed a hero desperately. His military career was then catapulted to greater heights when Unternehmen Panzerfaust (Operation Armoured Fist) was devised, and he successfully kidnapped the wayward son of the Hungarian President, Admiral Miklos Horthy, on October 15th 1944, after he was found to be negotiating the surrender of all Hungarian forces in the east. The surrender of the Hungarians would have caused a catastrophic collapse on several of the Russian fronts and would have left the German army vulnerable to encirclement and annihilation. Due to his actions, Hungary fought to the end of the war, saving the lives of tens of thousands of German soldiers and Airmen. The Russian Premier, Joseph Stalin, had a bounty placed on his head for his death. In late

1944 Unternehmen Griffin (Operation Grief) was devised as the ultimate task to disrupt the American lines of communication and their ability to fight during the Ardennes offensive. Known to the Germans as Unternehmen Wacht am Rhein (Operation Watch on the Rhine) and to the Allies as the Ardennes counteroffensive or the Battle of the Bulge, his English-speaking men were hastily trained to infiltrate American lines and cause as much disruption as possible which allowed the German army to push the Americans back between December 16th 1944 and January 25th 1945. After a minor setback, it was thwarted by overwhelming American forces. Known as Germany's last gamble in the West, their plan, although nonsensical, was to separate the British and American armies recapture the Belgian port of Antwerp, and disrupt the Allies' military expansion into the Western European theatre. Discerning German generals knew this wouldn't win the war but had hoped it would bring the Allies to the table where they could negotiate the cessation of hostilities in the west to defeat the Red Army in the east. Skorzeny's men caused minimal disruption, and most were executed after their capture in American uniforms, contravening the 1907 Hague Convention. The most significant disruption caused to the Allies was when word was put about that Skorzeny's mission was to assassinate high-ranking officers, including General Eisenhower, which kept them under maximum security and thus away from their command. The use of German soldiers in American uniforms and the accusation of assassinating the Allied Commander would come back to haunt him when the Allies added him to their most wanted list of war criminals.

**

Small, stocky but powerful, Sturmbannführer Karl Radl was born on November 12th 1911, in Gloggnitz, Austria, and was a comrade of Skorzeny's since their days together at the University of Vienna. When Skorzeny received orders to set up a school to mimic that of the British Commandos, he was the first to be approached. He hadn't been a soldier by profession but had proved himself in the field for Skorzeny to make him his second in command. Being Skorzeny's adjutant, he was involved in all actions taken by his commander and stood with pride by his side throughout.

**

Air raid sirens sound their impending danger, informing the terrified Berliners that their short-lived period of calm was ultimately ending and scattering them in all directions in the hunt for shelters that litter the surrounding area. Skorzeny and Radl look into the bright sunlight that blinds them momentarily as they scan for enemy planes. Anti-aircraft guns open up and blast their ordnance blindly upwards to shoot their enemy down as the first bombs land, adding to the panic and devastation. Not needing a reason but taking the air raid as one, they hasten their entrance through large grey steel doors into the bunker complex and descend into the semi-lit darkness below. Their boots echo with an uneasy sense of safety and security, which gets louder the deeper they get into the bunker.

As the doors close behind them, Radl feels an instant foreboding as the cold and darkness fall over him. Claustrophobia had never been a problem he had suffered from, but this day was different. Was it the guilt of being in the safety of the bunker as the people left on the surface were being obliterated? Having taken more than his fair share of the fighting over the years, his nerves were coming to an untimely end. "How much more punishment can the people take?" he mutters solemnly, forcing Skorzeny to grab his arm and pull him off balance down several stairs bringing him around from his melancholy moment. "We don't have time for sentiment, Karl. Remember where we are." Lights flicker, and dust falls as the land above takes a direct hit shaking their sensibilities.

"Come, Karl, let's get this over with."

They go through the dimly lit concrete corridors as soldiers and civilians scurry about, frantically sensing the doom that beholds them. Ahead, two immaculately dressed black uniformed SS bodyguards of the Führerbegleitkommando stand alert as they guard the large mahogany doors to the conference room where their beloved Führer is in session with his general staff.

"Looks like there's a meeting in progress, Otto," Radl said coyly.

Not wanting to be caught up in the politics of war, Skorzeny draws an anxious breath as he and Radl move to pass, but the doors crash open to knock the SS bodyguards aside as the newly promoted Field Marshal Robert Ritter von Greim exits, limping off aided by two of his lieutenants. Without a word of excuse or apology, they barge past Skorzeny and Radl, forcing them against the wall and annoying the SS colonel with the overbearing arrogance of the Luftwaffe officers. Stooped and shaking uncontrollably, Hitler exits behind, his face red, twisted with rage, and looking decidedly older than his fifty-five years.

Turning to see their beloved Führer, Skorzeny and Radl come rapidly to attention forcing their bodies rigidly erect as they click their heels and give the Nazi salute with a united shout. "Heil Führer." Hitler's face mellows momentarily as the sight of his favourite soldier comes into focus. His left hand, uselessly hidden behind his back, trembles uncontrollably as he reaches out with his right to take Skorzeny's. "Colonel Skorzeny," he mumbles with delight. "I have not yet thanked you for your stand on the Oder. Day after day, it was the one bright spot in my reports. For your National Socialist heroism, I have awarded you the oak leaves to your Knights Cross, and I mean to hand it to you myself. Then you can give me a full account. For the future, I have other work for you."

An overriding sense of pride overcomes Skorzeny as he digests what he had been informed and forces his body even more erect. "Yes, my Führer."

***

Born on April 20th 1889, in Braunau am Inn on the Austrian German border, Adolf Hitler left school at 16 and moved to Vienna then Linz, where his racial and political views intensified by what he believed he had witnessed in his short life. Living in hostels and on the streets, he watched the rich and powerful, whom he thought were of Jewish origin and unprepared to help the vulnerable and weak as he was at the time. At the onset of World War One, to avoid being conscripted into the Austrian army, he crossed into Germany to enlist in the 1st company of the List regiment of the Bavarian reserve infantry, which he felt more akin to. Decorated for bravery in the field, he was awarded the Iron Cross first class and served throughout the four years of war in and around the trenches of the western front as a runner, conveying orders given by others. After being injured and temporarily blinded in 1918, he was hospitalised before the armistice was signed. He was furious in the belief that the military had been stabbed in the back by the politicians and bankers, once again mistakenly believing it to be a Jewish conspiracy. After the war, Germany was in turmoil, and he was sent by the army to spy on the Nationalsozialistische Deutsche Arbeiterpartei (NSDAP) (National Socialist German Workers Party) and was so taken by their politics that he began speaking at their meetings, joined in 1919 and by 1921 was their leader. In 1923, the National Socialists attempted a putsch to overthrow the Bavarian government, which was unsuccessful and resulted in several party members' deaths by the army he had mistakenly thought would stand aside but instead chose to obey the orders of the Bavarian government and oppose them. After running from the scene, he was captured and put on trial, which proved to be his first propaganda victory in the cause of national socialism, and he was sentenced to five years imprisonment in Landsburg, where with the help of his deputy Rudolf Hess, he wrote the book Mein Kampf (My Struggle) which became a best seller and showed the world his intentions on war and his hatred of the Jewish people, which in 1939 took him and the German people on the road to war and mass genocide. The royalties from Mein Kampf made him a millionaire in his own right, and he bought a chalet named Haus Wachenfeld with the proceeds, which was later renamed 'the Berghof' and was situated outside Berchtesgaden, Bavaria. A large residence in Munich was also bought and was used as the National Socialist's headquarters and became known as the Brown House.

***

Hitler gave Skorzeny a wretched smile and nods as his body stoops, and he shuffles off, giving Radl a stupefied glance in passing. Waiting until the two SS bodyguards have passed, Skorzeny and Radl watch their Führer with sadness at the noticeable demise in his stature.

Having witnessed his Führer for the first time in person, Radl speaks with sorrow. "Not the man who took us to war all those years ago." Without replying, Skorzeny turns to walk off, only to be confronted by the menacing figure of Reichsführer Heinrich Himmler as he exits the conference room behind.

***

A leading National Socialist, Heinrich Luitpold Himmler, was born on October 7th 1900, in Munich. His anti-Semitic ideals and fastidious attention to detail helped get him noticed, and he rose rapidly through the ranks from a lowly clerk and standard bearer at the unsuccessful beer hall putsch to the pinnacle of his career, commander of all armies on the eastern front. After Hitler's imprisonment, he went into hiding and had a short stint as a chicken farmer. On Hitler's release, he re-entered the National Socialist hierarchy, where his rise up the chain of command was enhanced through deceit and deception. Obsessed with racial purity and hatred of all things Jewish, he oversaw the final solution to the Jewish question and eradicate all Jews and Nazi-dictated racially impure people through forced labour and extermination. A task he almost succeeded in with the mass murder of millions of innocents as he committed heinous crimes against humanity from a remote safe, clean environment where his involvement was his hand on the death orders and cowardly used others to commit the offences on his behalf.

***

Skorzeny gives a Nazi salute, followed by Radl, who turns into the staring eyes of the narcissistic psychopath.

"Good morning, Reichsführer."

Intrigued by the presence of the chief of special troops, Himmler glares through his pince-nez glasses before taking them off and cleaning them with a crisp, clean cotton handkerchief. "Colonel Skorzeny," he said in his dark demonic tone that has most who hear it frightened for their lives. "What brings you here this day?"

Skorzeny and Radl look into the crazed eyes of the methodical madman who stares back, searching for the intelligence he constantly craves to use against his many increasing enemies and give him the self-gratifying laudation he can't live without from his beloved Führer.

"We've been ordered here by General von Stiffel, Reichsführer."

Himmler's mistrusting glance shifts several times between the two protagonists. "And you can tell me for what reason, Colonel?"

Unaware of the answer, Skorzeny attempts to duck the question, but Himmler's evil eyes insist on a reply.

"He hasn't informed us, Reichsführer."

"Is that so, Colonel?" Himmler said with a grin of mistrust.

Although Himmler is Skorzeny's superior as the head of the SS, he could so easily put a bullet in his head without a moment's compunction rather than spend one more second in the obnoxious man's presence.

"He'll no doubt enlighten me at a later hour," Himmler said, then added to the uneasy quiet with haste in his voice. "Well, carry on, gentlemen. We still have a war to win."

Unnerved by the stupidity of Himmler's words, Skorzeny and Radl give the Nazi salute and then move off as Himmler reluctantly salutes back. Puzzled by their meeting, Radl looked to find that the Reichsführer had lost interest and had moved in the opposite direction. "A war to win," he said with a laugh. "That man is severely mad and gives me the creeps."

Shocked, Skorzeny grabs Radl's arm firmly as he looks around to make sure they haven't been overheard. "Voices resonate in these hollow corridors, Karl," he whispers. "He is still dangerous." He looks to

confirm that the despotic man has gone. "Probably even more now that his back is firmly against the wall."
"Surely he's no threat to you, Otto?" Radl mutters with a cynical smile which Skorzeny sees as another idiotic comment.
"Need I remind you of the many generals who have died by the wire on that man's orders. I've seen the film, and it's not something you want as a memory."
Fearful of why he would have been a part of such an action, Radl questions his commander's reasoning. "Why have you seen the film?"
"No doubt shown to me as a warning not to go against the Führer." Understanding Skorzeny's unwavering loyalty to Führer and fatherland is beyond reproach, Radl shakes his head and laughs. "As if you would, Otto… I hope General von Stiffel has ordered us here to discharge us," he adds with a haughty laugh, and Skorzeny grins, amused.
Skorzeny turns his look solemnly into the distance to see Hanna, a striking woman making her way along the corridor and his stare fixes on her in amazement, and he waves with delight focusing on her beauty.

***

An aviator extraordinaire, Hanna Reitsch was born on March 29th 1912, in Hirschberg, Silesia, and is the only German woman to win the Iron Cross first class. A fervent National Socialist with unswerving loyalty to Führer and fatherland, yet she never joined the Nazi party. Blessed with excellent flying skills, she set numerous aviation and endurance records, making her a favourite of Hitler and a constant within his circle. She test-piloted numerous Luftwaffe and captured Allied aeroplanes, and due to her photogenic qualities, became a star of the National Socialist propaganda machine.

***

Having believed she would never see Skorzeny again, Hanna beams with delight as he takes her hand with great relief to kiss affectionately. Selfishly wanting the moment alone, Skorzeny turns to Radl, who recognises the look and backs off, neither wanting nor concerned to know about their private business. Skorzeny grabs Hanna's other hand and pulls her in for a quick loving embrace, and kisses her neck tenderly before they separate anxiously, not wanting to be seen as lovers.
Concerned that she is in Berlin as it is about to be swallowed up by the Red Army, Skorzeny's voice quivers as he whispers. "What are you doing here?"

Feeling she is still of service to the fatherland, which allows her to carry on her love of flying, she answers with pride. "I flew Field Marshal von Greim here for a meeting with the Führer."

"How the hell did you get a plane into Berlin?"

"On a Fieseler Storch. It's small enough to get over the rooftops and nimble enough to land on a short rudimentary runway."

Skorzeny thinks back to von Greim's exit from the conference room and grins. "I don't think the meeting went well."

"He was promoted field marshal and given command of the Luftwaffe," she said with pride.

He smiles amusedly, aware of the great honour even if there wasn't an air force left flying for him to command.

"We were peppered with small arms fire all the way in. The field marshal got hit several times but still showed great spirit in meeting the Führer."

Skorzeny fears the dangers of flying this late in the war. "Promise me this will be your last flight," he said, taking a tighter hold of her hands and staring ominously into her eyes.

Shocked at a statement she never thought to hear from the man she loves, she turns away as she replies. "I can't do that, Otto."

Having underestimated her love and desire to keep flying, his smile turns to one of despair.

"You know I can't," she adds, unnerved. "I have to go." She attempts to break free, but he keeps a tight hold preventing her from moving.

"I'm not joking, Hanna," he said, determined, but she jerked her arm away and moved off a few paces, showing her equally strong determination not to be intimidated.

"Neither am I, Otto."

Concerned she has no consideration for her safety and knowing how upsetting his words have been, he adds sincerely. "I can't implore you enough, Hanna. Stay away before all this madness comes down around us. This isn't a safe place to be."

Not enjoying the unwarranted attention conferred on her sworn duty, she turns away as tears well up in her eyes and roll down her cheeks. "I can't do that, Otto."

He attempts to wipe her tears, but she moves further off.

"I can't believe you asked that of me," she adds, turning to glare back. "You, of all people, should understand that." Visibly shocked and shaken that what had been a wonderful chance meeting had not ended well, she gives Skorzeny a sorrowful smile and then walks off as he looks around in guiltless innocence.

Shaking his head in disbelief, Radl moves back over. "I can't believe you asked that of her."

Shocked that his private conversation had been overheard, Skorzeny turns angrily to face his old friend.

"Voices resonate in these corridors," Radl adds with a grin of irony. "You of all people should know that."

Desperate to defend his actions, Skorzeny walks off dejected, with Radl following, amused.

***

The Führerbunker complex consists of thirty small rooms distributed over two levels. It sits twelve metres below the old Reich Chancellery gardens on Wilhelm Strasse, north of the new Reich Chancellery building at Vossstrasse 6. Four metres of reinforced concrete protect them from the bombs above, as secure and safe a place anywhere within the entire Reich.

***

General von Stiffel sits in his dimly lit office within the Vor bunker, which is located above the Führerbunker and is connected by a single stairway. Born in Konigsberg, East Prussia, in 1895, Lieutenant General Erich von Stiffel is the last of a long line of Prussian generals that date his lineage to well before the battle of Waterloo and the Napoleonic war against France. Having served throughout the Great War with distinction, he rose to the rank of captain but received a shrapnel wound in the second battle of the Somme on April 4th 1918, which left him with a constant ache in the left side of his pelvis and forced him to be sent home for recuperation that kept him out of front-line action for the rest of the war. After the Versailles Treaty of 1919 and the decimation of the German Imperial Army, he was lucky enough to continue his career within the newly formed Reichswehr. One of the hundred thousand strong military that the treaty permitted. Having retained his wartime rank, he stagnated in the ranking system of the post-war German military, where promotion was almost non-existent, and he had considered a career change that would have made him the first in six generations of his family not to reach the rank of general. The shame and sense of loyalty instilled in him as a child prevented him from requesting release from his sworn service, and he carried on in his duty in the Reichswehr, then Wehrmacht before being transferred to the Abwehr (German military intelligence) in 1932 and was promoted to the rank of lieutenant colonel. When the National Socialists gained power through the electorate in 1933, the military was increased substantially under Hitler's orders, him wanting the high command on his side, and he facilitated promotion within the ranking system which resulted in him achieving a subservient loyalty within the officer class of the Reichswehr and its predecessor, the Wehrmacht. Like many decent German officers, he was never a Nazi but had ridden the National Socialist tide and ignored the signs that showed they were without honour. Not all Wehrmacht officers were politically minded or Nazi party members; however, most were willing to turn a blind eye to the impending evil to gain the power and recognition they craved. At the onset of the war, he carried the rank of colonel within the Abwehr and throughout the advances in Poland, France, Ukraine and Russia, he witnessed horrors that reminded him of his time in the trenches of the Great War and crimes his mind would never be able to erase. Luckily for him and no doubt saving his life, he was transferred to a desk in Berlin in 1942 on the orders of the head of the Abwehr, Admiral Wilhelm Canaris, and at last promoted to major general, but sadly, his son, Lieutenant Wolfgang von Stiffel, was lost on the Steppes of Russia never to be found or receive the Christian burial his mother so desperately wanted. As the bombs explode on the city above, he sits terrified as the reinforced concrete shakes and the lights flicker, making him grimace at every blast. Nervous and broken after five years of war, he shakes uncontrollably as he takes frequent sips of whisky from a flask he had carried throughout both world wars and takes great comfort from. Of late, the strong alcohol content of the whisky had been the only thing to help dull the pain of his loss and the orders his position within the Abwehr had to give daily, sending operatives on missions he knew they had little chance of coming back from. Leaning back in his chair, he looks at the ceiling, lifts the flask in salute, then brings it slowly to his lips, ready to drink, when a soft tap on the door gives him a start that makes him spill some of the irreplaceable liquid. Angered at the whisky's loss and aware that supplies of such a delicacy were at an extreme low that even a general would find it impossible to come across, he wipes his uniform and then takes a sizeable lingering drink before putting the flask onto his desk. Feeling the excessive amount of alcohol consumed, he stands unsteadily, then moves precariously to the door and pauses for several anxious seconds, unsure as to who is on the other side until several more taps hasten his anxiety, and he tentatively opens it to reveal Skorzeny and Radl standing patiently bringing a relieved smile to his forlorn face in recognition of his old friends and comrades. Skorzeny and Radl give military salutes, which von Stiffel returns with glee, never having liked the arm-outstretched salute of the Nazis.

"A welcome sight on a day full of trials," von Stiffel said as he stood aside. "Come in."

Skorzeny and Radl enter as von Stiffel shakes their hands in turn.

"I hope there's some hospitality left," Skorzeny said with joviality to the general's intoxicated demeanour.

Von Stiffel glances back at his flask, and aware of the limited contents, he decides to spitefully ignore his subordinate's words as he closes the door and stands to face it for several tense seconds before speaking with increased volume. "I've awaited your arrival in anticipation, gentlemen! I have a critical mission for you to take the fight against the Russians!"

Apprehensive about any mission at this late date in the war that can only be one of suicide, Skorzeny's glance shifts ominously between Radl and von Stiffel as the general rounds his desk.

"I believe it will give them a bloody nose they won't forget." Lifting a pen and a piece of paper, von Stiffel pauses, deep in thought.

Concerned by the general's unusual behaviour, Skorzeny enquires. "Is everything alright, sir?"

Von Stiffel nods apprehensively as he scribbles several shaky lines onto the paper, which he lowers onto his desk and taps on several times before walking off. "Yes, Colonel! A great deal will depend on you!" he carries on.

Curiously, Skorzeny picks up the paper to read the almost illegible lines.

***

The paper reads: -

Ignore my chatter which is for the ears of the Reichsführer and his agents. I have a plan to save the Führer, but we need to speak in private.

***

Skorzeny looks around the room for listening devices as von Stiffel lifts a box of cigars which he opens to reveal three left inside. He turns to Radl and offers one, but the major declines as Skorzeny, knowing of their rarity, takes in its delicate aroma before placing it in his inside jacket pocket.

"If you don't mind, I will keep this for later, General."

Von Stiffel takes a cigar and lights it to take a long lingering draw before exhaling a large cloud of smoke that remains in the already stale air. "The Russian front is as we speak, not far off!" he adds in a loud bounding voice for the benefit of the Sicherheitsdienst officer sitting in a room several doors down, taking the minutes of every word being said.

Skorzeny hands the paper to Radl to read intently before looking back, bemused.

"What I have devised is a way to halt them in their tracks!" von Stiffel carries on as he moves to Radl taking the paper off him and setting it alight, then dropping it to the floor to singe into the well-worn carpet. "Or at least give them a bloody nose they won't forget while we recoup our forces and push them all the way back to their god-forsaken motherland!"

An unnerving calm comes over the room as the bombing ceases, and von Stiffel looks anxiously at the ceiling as he awaits the next explosion before realising it has ended. "At last, we have calm. Now, I believe we can go," he adds as he lifts his briefcase and exits in haste, leaving Skorzeny and Radl watching in bewilderment.

"What's going on, Otto?" Radl mutters showing his concern.

"That I don't know, Karl, but if we follow him, we may find out."

***

The steel doors to the Führerbunker creak open, allowing a desperately needed rush of light and air inside. Von Stiffel exits into the Reich Chancellery Garden for the bright sunshine to blind him momentarily, but this is quickly overshadowed by acrid black smoke billowing from the burning buildings around and darkening the area with its doom. The air raid sirens sound the all-clear as calm descends only to be interrupted by the moronic boom of the Red Army artillery firing in the distance.

Elated to be out of what he considers to be his hell, von Stiffel takes in a long lingering breath of fresh air. "I never thought I would breathe again."

Like claustrophobic men taking their first anxious breaths, Skorzeny and Radl exit behind, but neither gives the devastation of the air raid a second thought as they enjoy the freedom the outside beholds.

Von Stiffel takes another long lingering draw on his cigar, showing his preference for the smoke over the fresh air he so vigorously craved moments earlier. "I'd rather be out here facing the Red Army than in the so-called safety of the bunker," he mutters to Skorzeny's agreement. "Even with the acrid smoke, I can't get enough fresh air." Skorzeny and Radl look at each other in bewilderment at the general puffing on his cigar. A Mercedes Benz W31 staff car drives up and then stops in front of Sergeant Bergdorf, von Stiffel's long-term driver leaps out and opens the rear door with a salute as he comes to attention.

"Where are we going, General?" Skorzeny enquires as von Stiffel looks around, mistrusting the officers and soldiers who exit the bunker behind.

"I thought we should eat, gentlemen."

Von Stiffel gets into the rear as Skorzeny and Radl stare at each other, concerned at the manner the general is conducting himself, which is alien to their experiences of him over the years.

"What's going on, Otto?" Radl reiterates.

Aware that von Stiffel is suffering the effects of excessive alcohol, Skorzeny shakes his head; considering the pressure his friend is under, he has a good reason to be intoxicated. Skorzeny and Radl get into the rear of the Mercedes, and Bergdorf closes the door, then gets into the driver's seat and looks through the rear-view mirror awaiting instruction.

"Litzen café, Hans," von Stiffel said with a large grin.

"Yes, sir."

"My favourite place to eat while in Berlin," von Stiffel carries on with great enthusiasm as he slaps his leg several times in anticipation of the treat to come. "It has been since I was first posted to Berlin in twenty-nine."

Sitting in silence, no one wants to discuss the futility of carrying on the war as they witness the passing devastation on their short drive.

"We are being followed, sir," Bergdorf said, but von Stiffel didn't hazard a look and remains unnervingly calm.

Radl looks out the rear window to see an Opel Kadett K38 saloon a short distance off, showing all the signs of being in clandestine pursuit.

"Don't worry, Karl," von Stiffel said calmly as he drew heavily on his cigar.

Wondering why he shouldn't worry about something he knows nothing about, Radl frowns as his stare moves slowly to Skorzeny.

"What's going on, General?" Skorzeny enquires.

Von Stiffel pulls his briefcase protectively into his chest but doesn't answer.

"Sir," Skorzeny said, insistent on an answer.

"Don't worry, Otto. It's just the inevitable Gestapo tail."

Shocked by von Stiffel's nonchalant statement, Radl turns his stare back onto the Opel and the shadowy figures of two occupants inside.

"They're no threat to us," von Stiffel said nervously. "We're not meant to know they are there, so don't give the game away, Karl."

"Why would anyone want to follow us, General?" Radl enquires naively.

"Since the July plot to kill the Führer, all top-ranking officers have been under suspicion of treason against the state."

"With good reason, General."

"You think so, Otto? Not all are traitors, but all are suspected of such."

"What about Otto, General?" Radl jokes to Skorzeny's ire.

***

The July 20th bomb plot was an attempt by German officers, politicians and religious leaders to assassinate Hitler. Code-named Unternehmen Walküre (Operation Valkyrie), Lieutenant Colonel Claus Shenk Graf von Stauffenberg, a seriously injured Wehrmacht officer, planted a bomb in a conference room within Hitler's front-line headquarters, the Wolfsschanze (Wolf's lair) near Rastenburg in East Prussia but the bomb failed to do its job, and Hitler survived to take revenge on the conspirators. Hitler's propaganda machine had proclaimed he was at the front with his men, but during the early stages of Unternehmen Barbarossa (the invasion of Russia), the wolf's lair was well behind the fighting in the relative comfort and safety of the East Prussian countryside. The meeting was scheduled to be held in a concrete bunker, but due to the heat and humidity, at the last moment, it was changed to a wooden building that had windows which were opened to allow ventilation. The bomb was planted with only half the explosives due to Stauffenburg's inability to set them and placed not far from Hitler's side. Still, it was moved behind a heavy table leg and the explosion was deflected with the energy dispelled through the open windows. Hitler survived with only minor injuries making his right arm useless with severe shaking paralysis. Four men were killed, including two generals and a colonel and twenty were injured in the failed attempt. This was the sixth attempt to kill him, adding to his belief that he was protected and had been chosen to lead Germany by divine providence. Hitler immediately ordered Himmler's Gestapo to round up all believed to be involved, but the Reichsführer used his orders as an excuse not just to get rid of the conspirators but to seek retribution against his many enemies. Tortured to breaking point, the resistance members were put on a show trial in front of maniac judge Roland Freisler and the Volksgerichtshof (the people's court), where they were humiliated into giving a confession and naming other conspirators, mainly through the threat of violence against their families. Over five thousand suspects were executed with many of their families being sent to concentration camps. Hitler ordered the executions by hanging with piano wire and wanted them filmed for future entertainment, which he watched with glee. Several conspirators, including Stauffenberg were lucky enough to escape the wire, having been executed by firing squad as other complicit officers attempted to conceal their involvement. Others chose suicide in the naïve hope that it would save their families. Operation Valkyries' main designations were to assassinate Hitler and arrest all SS officers and National Socialist officials so the conspirators would be free to negotiate the immediate cessation of hostilities with the Allies. All to save the lives of Axis soldiers whom they knew would die with the continuation of the war.

***

Skorzeny believes that all who had sworn loyalty to Hitler should retain that loyalty no matter how bad things were. It was a matter of honour to him and even a necessity of war, but Germans killing Germans he finds abhorrent, and the thought of what had happened to several of the conspirators whom he knew sends a cold shiver down his spine.

Wondering if he had also been suspected or accused of involvement in the plot, Radl looks curiously at Skorzeny. "Some are obviously above suspicion," he said, amused, and von Stiffel wheezed with mirth.

"Otto's a favourite of the Führer, right?"

"The Führer knows I am loyal and above reproach," Skorzeny replied with pride.

"Not all are above suspicion. Many innocents were also sent to the gallows and guillotine," von Stiffel explains. Conscious of what he had said to be treasonous, he lowers his tone. "And the biggest traitor of them all is the Reichsführer."

Skorzeny and Radl stare in stunned disbelief of a statement that could only be said privately.

"That can't be right, sir," Radl interjects.

"Reports from my agents is that the Reichsführer has or is about to betray the Führer by negotiating a surrender with the Western Allies.

Of course, he's only after saving himself," von Stiffel blusters. "I don't know what world he lives in, but in mine, mass murderers would die a terrible death." Realising he had spoken in a second unguarded moment, he shuffles uncomfortably with no intention of backing down from his words.

"Have you reported this, sir?" Radl adds naively, making Skorzeny and von Stiffel laugh.

"Who in their right mind would try and darken the so-called good name of the Reichsführer," von Stiffel explains uneasily.

"But you've just said."

"Never mind, Karl," von Stiffel interrupts, annoyed with himself for speaking without thought. "Please, forget I said anything."

"If the Reichsführer is a traitor, the Führer needs to know," Radl mutters urgently.

"The Führer needs to be informed of his treason by someone other than myself," von Stiffel said with a sigh of inevitability. "Someone with their own agenda. I have more pressing issues at hand."

***

Believing he is imperative to the future of Germany and out to save himself, Himmler had contacted Count Folke Bernadotte, a Swedish diplomat and nobleman at Lubeck on the Danish border. Being delusional and assuming that Hitler would soon die, he believed the Allies would see him as Germany's legitimate successor and represented himself as just. He asked Count Bernadotte to act as a go-between with General Eisenhower and that he would surrender Germany to the Western Allies but not the Russians in the hope they would join together in the fight against communism.

***

Von Stiffel knows Himmler's treachery would soon come to the attention of Hitler and would be reported by one of the many sycophants in dire competition for his favour. "The Führer wouldn't hear a bad word against his old friend and comrade. He still believes he's a great National Socialist."

"I'd like to put a bullet between the bastard's eyes," Skorzeny snarls with venom even though he doesn't need another reason to kill the bespectacled madman.

"These are things beyond our control, Otto, and as I have said, it is for others and another day," von Stiffel interrupts. "Now, let's return to more important and patriotic things and why I asked you here today." He places his cigar into his mouth to allow him to open the briefcase, which he fumbles around inside before producing an envelope and gripping it tightly in his palm. His glance shifts slowly between Skorzeny and Radl, then out of the window at the lines of old soldiers and Volkssturm marching in determined well-disciplined lines toward the advancing Red Army. "Madness," he mutters to himself when his eyes fix on Bergdorf, who is looking through the rear-view mirror. "I believe some of them fought against Napoleon Bonaparte."

***

The Volkssturm (People's Storm) was founded on October 8th 1944, on the orders of Hitler to conscript men between the ages of sixteen and sixty who were initially thought too old or too young for military service. Many who volunteered were young boys indoctrinated in Nazi ideology since 1933, soldiers from the Great War and some who had been disabled from military service due to injuries in the field. They all volunteered with the full backing of the National Socialist party as the last bastion against the revengeful Mongol hoards coming from the east. On their arms they wear a band with Deutscher Volkssturm Wehrmacht stitched on. Their uniforms are whatever they can muster or just their everyday clothes. Armed and trained on numerous diverse weapons, they are hastily sent to the front after taking an oath of allegiance to their Führer to halt the might of an invading army. Invariably they are annihilated in many ill-thought-out battles where they were lured to their slaughter under the command of regular army units. Their only choices were to die in battle or be shot or captured by a vengeance-seeking Red Army and be sent to the Siberian Gulags, and if they deserted, they had the vengeance of the state against them as the SS and Gestapo would hunt them down and set an example with their executions.

***

Realising he isn't enjoying the cigar, von Stiffel stubs it out in the ashtray, to everyone's relief. "Far too many are boys too young to fight. If only they knew what awaits them," he adds after reflection. Disillusioned at how bad things are, Skorzeny and Radl stare out the window, maddened at the senseless sending of old men, boys and the infirm against a massive mechanised murdering machine.

Von Stiffel gazes at his reflection in the window, equally dismayed, to see how withdrawn he looks before turning away to hide his true feelings. "Well, to business. As you know Germany has lost this war." Skorzeny and Radl don't react to a statement that isn't news to them. Anyone with the slightest intelligence had known for years that

Germany had taken on too big of a burden but had only discussed such things in private circles. Countless Gestapo informers thirsted for such knowledge to inform on their neighbours and family, believing it would increase their standing within the National Socialist regime. With great tentativeness, von Stiffel hands the envelope to Skorzeny, who reads the handwritten title on the cover.

"The Wagnerian Assignment," he said, taken by the Germanic title.

"We cannot allow the Führer to go down with the rest of Germany. I have devised a plan to get him out of Berlin to the Obersalzberg, where we can protect him. I was overseeing the project myself until my premature recall back to Berlin a few weeks ago."

Skorzeny straightens out the envelope and opens it, but von Stiffel prevents him.

"Leave your reading for later, Otto," he said. "Why I called you here is because I need a man to take temporary command while I remain here." He looks into Skorzeny's eyes. "Are you that man, Otto?" he enquires, then adds without waiting for an answer. "I believe you are, and as such, my last order to you, as a commanding general, is for you to fortify and protect the Berghof until I arrive with the Führer."

Relieved the order is not the suicidal one expected, Skorzeny sighs as he looks at the envelope, desperate to read the secret it contains.

In the hope this will give his friends a reason to evade capture, von Stiffel adds thoughtfully. "If I don't make it, I order you and Karl to take off into the hills and save yourselves."

Not knowing what the Wagnerian Assignment truly entails, Skorzeny questions with concern. "What do you mean, don't make it, General?"

"Berlin will fall soon. Probably within eight to ten weeks. I intend to remain with the Führer awaiting the right moment to approach him with my intentions."

"Why not do that now, sir, while there is more time?" Radl enquired again with a naïve question he should have kept to himself.

Von Stiffel shuffles uncomfortably. "You don't understand the implications of diplomacy and government, Karl. If I don't get the timing right, the Führer will have me shot for defeatism. I'm afraid it needs to be timed to perfection. Not even his most trusted advisors, which I can assure you I am not, could approach him with such a delicate subject at this late hour. He still believes we can win and stands in the conference room surrounded by sycophantic field marshals, generals and lackeys moving long defunct armies around as if they existed. Ranting and raving all the time as all in the room stand like sheep too frightened or equally delusional to understand the truth and bow to his every word instead of advising him of what is truly happening."

"Why don't the generals inform him of the true situation?" Radl said, annoying Skorzeny with his ill-thought-out remarks.

"Weren't you listening, Karl? The Führer trusts no one."

"Maybe you should do it, Otto," Radl snipes to Skorzeny's increased annoyance. "With you being one of his favourites."

Oblivious to Skorzeny and Radl's petty conversation, von Stiffel contemplates his plan. "I hope to get the Führer to the Berghof before the end of April. That gives you six weeks, Otto."

"What about orders, sir?"

Believing his planning and foresight had covered every eventuality, von Stiffel answers with pleasure. "Everything you require is in the envelope."

Enthusiastically, Skorzeny opens the envelope, to von Stiffel's dismay and pulls out maps and handwritten statements that show what is expected of him. "One thousand men. Where do you hope to get these from, sir?"

"They are already there," von Stiffel said with pride in his accomplishments. "I had them posted several months ago."

Believing that taking soldiers from the front where they are desperately needed is madness saddens Skorzeny and shows on his forlorn face.

"I see by your expression you disapprove, Otto."

Skorzeny doesn't want to be seen as disrespectful and forces out an indignant smile. "It's not that, sir."

Having an excellent knowledge of all the aspects of warfare, von Stiffel answers with what should be Skorzeny's words. "I understand. What sort of a madman would transfer battle hardened men from the front to a quiet idyll untouched by war?"

"I wasn't thinking that, sir," Skorzeny pleads, not wanting to question the orders of a man he respects greatly.

"Of course, you were. I would think the same if I didn't know why."

"Obviously to protect the Führer, sir," Radl interrupts, attempting to make amends for his previous ill-thought-out remarks.

"To protect the Führer, I would have transferred the entire army," von Stiffel adds. "But I had to do it covertly, not to arouse suspicion. A company here and a company there. It all took time."

Skorzeny believes that with the end of the third Reich, the fourth will still require his beloved Führer. "I can understand that, sir."

"When you get to the Berghof, you will find an Obersturmbannführer Shint there. He's an extremely trustworthy officer. I handpicked him and left him in command when I was recalled to Berlin. I don't trust many officers these days, most are out to save their necks, but Lieutenant Colonel Shint is a man of honour. Just as an afterthought, don't allow his age or boyish good looks to fool you. He's a very capable officer and has proven himself many times in the field."

"Does he know about the Wagnerian Assignment, sir?" Radl enquired.

"A good question," von Stiffel answers, bringing a large smile to Radl's redeemed face. "No, he doesn't. The only people that know are in this car, but he's an intelligent officer and I would be amazed if he didn't suspect something."

Wondering why a mere sergeant would know such an important secret, Skorzeny looks at Bergdorf.

"There are very few people I would trust with my life," von Stiffel said on noticing Skorzeny's curiosity. "There's you and Karl, but Bergdorf is my dearest confident and aware of what I know. Not all, though," he adds with a mocking laugh that receives a giggle from the sergeant. "This car is probably the only place I feel I am not being listened to by the SD."

"He could be a Gestapo agent," Radl said, angering Bergdorf by the apparent slur to his honour.

"You're not, are you, Hans?" von Stiffel questions in total seriousness before bursting into exaggerated fits of laughter. "Hans is my most loyal and trusted confidant. He has witnessed more than his fair share of intelligence nastiness since being transferred to my command as my driver."

"Thank you, General," Bergdorf said with pride.

"No, Hans, I thank you," von Stiffel said, then continued. "I need the help of an officer in the Führerbegleitkommando, then the next to be informed will be the Führer himself, but only when and if the time is right." Apprehension of what that outcome may be makes him shuffle ill at ease. "Until then, nobody else must find out what we intend to do."

Radl glances out the rear window to see the Opel Kadett still following. "What about the Gestapo? They are sure to follow."

"That I believe I will leave to you," von Stiffel said reservedly to distance himself from what is sure to be a distasteful action.

Skorzeny considers von Stiffel's words. "What should I do to stop them from reporting back to the Reichsführer, sir?"

"What I would like to do with all the bastards," von Stiffel utters in a third unguarded moment to Skorzeny's shock. Him having never heard the proud officer swear or lose his temper during their years of friendship. "Kill them, Otto, kill them all," he adds, showing his venomous hatred towards Himmler and his state-sanctioned murderous machine. "They deserve no less than what they have done to others."

Skorzeny replaces the paper and maps into the envelope, then places it inside his jacket.

Boarded up and run down, the Litzen café shows signs of going out of business a long time ago. The Mercedes pulls over, and they look at the devastation as numerous Berliners out looting, exit the building and run off in fright of the official-looking car.

"When was the last time you were here, sir?" Radl enquired, amused by the general's expression.

Showing visible sadness at the plight of his favourite eatery, von Stiffel shivers as his mind races over the inevitability of his life crumbling around him. "Obviously, a lot longer than I thought… Well, gentlemen, I don't believe we had the time to eat anyway."

Having believed he was in for the first decent meal in days, Skorzeny drew a deep breath of sadness.

"Alright, Hans, back to the Reich Chancellery."

Bergdorf turns the car in the road, drives off as the Opel nears from the opposite direction, and passes with Skorzeny glaring at the two Gestapo men inside.

"The real face of the enemy," von Stiffel adds without hazarding a look.

"I've seen it before, General, in many different guises," Skorzeny said, recollecting the time he was in command on the Oder front when he ordered the execution of two Gestapo men for cowardice in the face of the enemy. This had angered Himmler, who ordered his arrest and execution but underestimating his importance to Hitler and the regime, no action was taken against him. Even though Himmler was in overall command of all armies in the east, his power was in the early stages of waning.

**

The Geheime Staatspolizei (Gestapo) is the secret state police of Nazi Germany. The National Socialist-sanctioned killing machine was established on April 26th 1933, on the orders of Hitler. Its first commander was Göring, who, on April 20th 1934, agreed to transfer its immense power to Himmler because of their mutual hatred of the Sturmabteilung (Storm detachment) (the National Socialist party's brown-shirted brutal paramilitary wing), which both believed was too formidable a power and needed to be kept under observation. Himmler then made his second in command, SS Obergruppenführer Reinhard Heydrich, commander on 22nd April 1934. From then on, the Gestapo became the most feared organisation within the Nazi state, increasing Himmler's dominance and power over his many enemies, both social and domestic.

***

WEDNESDAY, MARCH 14TH 1945

***

After a harrowing nine-hour journey over three hundred and sixty miles, Skorzeny, having used von Stiffel's Mercedes staff car that still carries the general's flags of rank and state, drives into the beautiful town of Berchtesgaden in the Bavarian Alps on the German Austrian-border. Having left out the autobahns and using more minor roads to avoid detection by Allied fighters roaming and shooting up everything that moves could have saved his life. All houses, buildings and lamp posts within the small-town show flags and bunting in honour of their beloved Führer and the National Socialist cause. Paying little attention to the scenery, he takes the tranquillity in his stride. All he wants is some food, a wash and a soft bed to rest in safety from the threat of an air attack that had focused his every move during the drive. Waffen SS soldiers, based in the area for the protection of their Führer, run amok, drinking and fighting amongst themselves between the bars and hotels as they let out the anger they had ruthlessly used to great effect on the battlefields of Europe and Russia. He pulls over outside the Berchtesgaden Hof hotel and stares, angered at the ill-discipline he is witnessing. His glance shifts into the rear-view mirror as the Opel, which had followed him from Berlin, stops some distance behind to sober him to why he had travelled such a long distance. Keeping his stare for several minutes, nothing moves before he drives off at speed, almost running over two SS soldiers who step drunkenly onto the road in front and force him to break into a skidded stop. The SS soldiers shout and swear at the car even though it blatantly carries the rank of general before giving half-hearted Nazi salutes and walking off, giggling at their total indiscipline, which angers him even more. Driving the narrow winding roads through the Obersalzberg, he frequently checks his rear-view mirror to find the Gestapo car hadn't followed. As he nears the Berghof, he passes all manner of militaria and machinery littering the roadside, not in place, enraging him more as he is aware the men to carry out the defences had been in place for some time. He drives through the gates of the Berghof, stops at the base of the stairs to the terrace, and alights, glaring at the soldiers milling around doing nothing constructive. Swearing under his breath, he moves to a wall overlooking the Obersalzberg Mountains as his glance shifts from their beauty to the half-finished camouflage netting hanging all around.

Standing on the terrace above, Hauptmann Wilder notices Skorzeny and makes his way down the steps as the SS colonel makes his way up. Meeting in the middle, the captain salutes and forces his body erect as he comes to attention. "Welcome to the Berghof, sir."

"Where is Colonel Shint, Captain?" Skorzeny shouts furiously without returning the salute.

As Skorzeny's ordering tone takes effect, Wilder steps back and lowers his hand. "I believe he's in the great room, sir."

Skorzeny carries on up the stairs, two at a time and onto the terrace to cross it at speed into the Berghof through an open door.

Inside the great room, wearing the dress uniform of the first SS Panzer Division Leibstandarte Adolf Hitler, Shint sits at the head of the table, looking around at his fellow warriors as they reminisce with pride in their service. Numerous empty bottles of schnapps litter the table.

***

To look at him, there was nothing to show the horrors he had witnessed throughout his time on the Eastern and Western fronts. His mother would still recognise the innocent cherubic face she knew before the war but would never understand the desolation it had done to his soul. Born in Upper Silesia in 1916, SS Obersturmbannführer Rutger Shint joined the SA at 16 in 1932 and fought many battles against the communists on the streets of Germany. After showing enthusiasm for the National Socialist cause, he was transferred to the SS, where in 1936, he joined the first SS Leibstandarte Adolf Hitler Division as a private soldier. Due to heavy losses, he was commissioned in 1941 and rapidly climbed the chain of command to his present rank. Late in 1944, a British Hawker Typhoon fighter bomber attacked his convoy during the retreat through Falaise to take him out of the war for several months to recuperate and leaving him with a permanent aching limp in his right leg that no matter how painful or incapacitating had never prevented him from carrying out his duty.

***

The door to the great room opens with a loud crash, and Skorzeny bursts in as his ire shifts rapidly between the inebriated officers unmoved by his presence.

Seeing a fellow SS officer, Shint lifts his glass in salute as he stands. "Come in, Colonel, have a drink."

"On the terrace now!" Skorzeny yells, angered at the casual manner of the officers who still aren't rising to attention. "Now!" The anger in his voice quickly takes effect and forces the officers to get to their feet before exiting, followed by Shint. "Not you, Colonel!" he shouts, and after the last of the officers have left, he kicks the door closed. "What were your orders, Colonel?"

Knowing his answer won't be the one expected, Shint forces his body erect and shuffles nervously. "To fortify and protect the Berghof, sir." "And is it fortified and protected?"

Not having the positive answer Skorzeny requires, Shint forces his body tighter.

"I understand men need to let off steam and relax. That they can't spend all their time locked up, but I can see tanks and artillery at the side of the road rusting. Machinery not in place, and men of the Waffen SS were fighting in the town like undisciplined monkeys. Then I get here, and there are men sitting on their arses as if on holiday with nothing better to do. And all this with the camouflaged netting unfinished, trenches half dug and all easily seen from above."

Not understanding, Shint looks up through his bloodshot, alcohol-fuelled eyes.

"This building is vulnerable to attack from the air!" Skorzeny shouts with frustration as he moves to the window and looks out at the inebriated officers on the terrace. "The discipline is a disgrace. I want all men returned to barracks immediately and the fortifications and defences finished at the earliest." He turns his demanding stare on Shint, then adds in a deep, determined, menacing tone. "Do you understand, Colonel?"

Shint understands a good soldier never questions his orders but decides after a moment's thought that he needs to know what von Stiffel had pained not to tell him. "What is this all about, sir?"

"This, Colonel!" Skorzeny growls aggressively. "Is about you carrying out General von Stiffel's orders!"

Shint steps back and salutes. "Sorry, sir. I will get straight to it." He turns to exit, but Skorzeny calls out, stopping him.

"Colonel, I want all the men back to barracks within the hour. I want the villagers of Berchtesgaden to believe we have left, never to return."

Shint nods his understanding and then exits. Skorzeny walks to the map table and leans on it as he studies the plans for the fortifications. Knowing von Stiffel had pained to prepare them, he now wonders what he had let himself in for.

***

Located in the centre of Berchtesgaden, the Berchtesgadener Hof Hotel is a superior-class hotel and restaurant that has wined and dined the elite of the National Socialist movement since Hitler had set up home in the surrounding mountains in 1928.

Retaining its pre-war glory, Nazi regalia hang from all the walls, with a large bust of the Führer in the centre of the reception dominating. Serving two boisterous SS officers, the agitated landlord stands behind the bar and notices Skorzeny enter. "Can I help you, sir?" he enquired, making the SS officers turn nonchalantly to look.

"You are recalled to barracks!" Skorzeny barks his ire at the SS officers, whose glances shift tentatively to the drinks they desperately want to finish. "That means now, gentlemen!" he adds decidedly more menacing as he unclips his Luger's leather holster.

Instinctively understanding the threat, the SS officers jump to attention, click their heels and salute while reluctantly exiting and leaving their drinks untouched.

"Schnapps, make it large," Skorzeny adds as he moves toward the counter.

Obligingly, the nervous landlord produces a new bottle and breaks the seal to fill a glass and place it on the bar in front of Skorzeny, who downs it in one noticing, the landlord's terrified stare had shifted with terror towards the door.

With a nervous stutter, the landlord speaks. "What can I do for you, gentlemen?"

Skorzeny turns slowly to see two stereotypical Gestapo officers standing menacingly in the doorway, wearing long leather coats with matching fedora hats that cast shadows over their faces in a vain attempt to make them look more intimidating to those they threaten.

"Sturmbannführer Mencken and this is Hauptsturmführer Behr of the Geheime Staatspolizei," Mencken said in a tone expectant that people will be attentive to.

With a nod at each in recognition of the men who had followed him on the journey to the Litzen café and to where they stand, Skorzeny speaks cordially. "Major, Captain. We meet again."

"So, we do, Colonel."

Unable to control his amusement, Skorzeny laughs to the Gestapo men's annoyance. "You've followed me from Berlin. Now, why would that be?"

"We are here at the request of Reichsführer Himmler, Colonel. He wants to know what your business is here."

"That's no concern of his or yours," Skorzeny adds, turning to the counter and tapping on the empty glass for the landlord to refill.

Behr speaks, carrying an arrogant air of self-importance beyond his mediocre rank and standing. "What I want to know is what the illustrious hero of Gran Sasso is doing here while the fighting is elsewhere?"

Skorzeny downs the schnapps and then replies without taking his eyes off the landlord. "I could ask the same of them for the entire war."

Not daring to show his obvious amusement, the landlord looks away as he wipes down the counter.

"Maybe he's plotting against the Führer?" Behr adds foolishly, and Skorzeny grabs the schnapps bottle and turns fast to throw it for the two Gestapo men to duck as it flies over their heads to smash off the wall behind, showering them in ceramic and the contents.

Skorzeny draws his Luger rapidly to aim at both as they recompose themselves. "Accuse me of treason again, and it will be the last words you utter."

"You accused us of not helping in the war effort," Behr retorts childishly, having never faced the fear of fighting in open battle himself.

"No offence was intended, Colonel," Mencken mediates to placate Skorzeny. "The captain here just got a little overzealous."

"You'd better keep a tighter rein on your dog before I put him down, Major!" Skorzeny snarls, then adds flippantly. "If you are looking for traitors, you couldn't do any worse than start with the man who sent you here."

"Now I take offence!" Mencken shouts, losing his calm as he takes hold of the Walther P38 pistol in his pocket.

"You won't make it," Skorzeny said confidently, and Mencken lifted his hand slowly in submission.

"The Reichsführer would never betray the fatherland."

"Is that so?" Skorzeny adds in a mocking tone that annoys the Gestapo men further.

"Next to the Führer, he is the greatest National Socialist," Mencken interjects with pride in a man he had only met on one occasion, making Skorzeny laugh uproariously. "Well, Captain," he adds vindictively as he turns to Behr. "I'm going to take great pleasure informing the Reichsführer of the allegation made against him by the colonel."

Skorzeny realises he had made a mistake in provoking the leather-clad brutes into reporting back to Berlin and the Wagnerian Assignment's greatest enemy.

"We'll detain you no longer, Colonel," Mencken adds, then exits, leaving Behr staring menacingly before following.

The landlord grabs another bottle of schnapps from under the counter and fills a glass for himself to down in one and help stop his shaking and regain his composure. "Didn't you know who they were, Colonel?"

Skorzeny throws a handful of notes onto the counter and looks confidently at the landlord as he holsters his Luger. "They are only little men under those silly hats, Herr Landlord. Don't allow them to intimidate you."

The landlord stares his distress at the thought of going against the Gestapo as the SS colonel makes his way to the door.

Skorzeny exits but keeps in the shadow of the doorway just out of sight as he watches Mencken and Behr cross the desolate street to the Kaiser Wilhelm Hotel directly opposite.

Having expected the Gestapo men's return, the landlord stands behind the hotel's reception counter, which also retains the pre-war glory and Teutonic efficiency as he trembles in fright on hearing the door open for them to enter straightens himself out, forcing a feigned smile of welcome.

"What about my call to Berlin, Herr Landlord?" Behr shouts in a cold, shallow voice intended to intimidate.

Knowing what he has to say will inspire irrational anger, the landlord's heart skips a beat as he nervously tenses in fright. "I haven't been able to make the call, sir."

The words are hardly out of his mouth when Behr grabs the terrified man harshly around the neck and slaps him several times across the face making his nose and mouth bleed.

"Get me, Berlin," Behr whispers menacingly, expectant to be obeyed. "I am unable to, sir."

Tightening his grip, Behr laughs, making it harder for the landlord to breathe. "That wasn't a request, Herr Landlord." He loosens his grip, and the landlord drops to the floor, wheezing for breath.

Anticipating his next option, Skorzeny moves into the doorway out of sight.

Mencken grabs Behr's arm. "Come, Behr; you have had your fun. We don't have the time for this. We need to report to Berlin at the earliest."

Having the landlord at his mercy enlivens Behr as he lashes out to kick the frail elderly man harshly in the stomach to knock him over. "Get our cases together and bring them down here." He turns to his superior officer. "We can telephone from Munich, sir."

Always entertained at their persecution of the feeble, Mencken and Behr head off upstairs and instantly change back to their laughing, jovial manner as they make light of the brutal treatment of the landlord. Trembling in pain, the landlord straightens himself out as he rubs his throat and aching head. Skorzeny moves the Luger behind his back and enters slowly as he scans the area for a threat. The landlord catches sight of him and backs off in terrified intimidation of the prominent scar faced SS officer standing in the doorway.

"Don't be worried, Herr Landlord. What are the intentions of those two?"

The landlord's stare shifts nervously between the stairs and Skorzeny as he ponders the relevance of a question that may have dire consequences for him.

"This is very important," Skorzeny adds impatiently.

The landlord notices Skorzeny's Luger making him holster and lifts his hands submissively to show he isn't a threat.

Conscious that every word will resonate throughout the building, the landlord whispers as he keeps his terrified stare on the stairs. "I believe they are going to Munich to use the telephone, sir. The phones here are down."

Skorzeny's glance shifts rapidly between the phone at the landlord's side and the landlord himself. "When do they intend to leave?"

"They didn't inform me," the landlord whispers even quieter. "But they want me to get their cases now."

Skorzeny backs off to the door. "Keep this to yourself, Herr Landlord," he mutters as the landlord grins with no intention of conversing with the Gestapo any longer than needed.

***

Skorzeny drives into the surrounding Obersalzberg Mountains looking for an ideal vantage point before swinging his car across both road lanes and stopping. He alights carrying an MP40 machine pistol and then stares over the mountains toward the Berghof, which is in clear view to his annoyance. Conscious the only way across the hills to Munich is past his present position, he looks at the surrounding area for cover, then checks the MP40s magazine to see it full, then replaces and cocks it as he makes his way to the tree line to settle out of sight amongst the foliage for what he believes may be a long wait. Sitting in the cold and damp, his anxious mind switches between the better days of pre-war Vienna and how good life was, but he is quickly brought back to the task at hand and what the future will hold for a soldier if he was to survive with the sound of a car approaching. He straightens out his cold, aching body but keeps his back against a tree out of sight. As darkness falls, the Opel carrying Mencken and Behr struggles up the mountain before stopping because Skorzeny's Mercedes is ideally positioned to prevent them from passing. Staring through the windscreen at what they believe is an abandoned car, they alight as Skorzeny steps out of the tree line into view, but it takes a short while for the Gestapo men to see the SS colonel through the Opel's lights. Still, his presence doesn't threaten them; it just intrigues their bemusement.

"What's the problem, Colonel?" Mencken said naively as Skorzeny brings the MP40 to bear.

"I can't allow you to report to the Reichsführer, Major."

The realisation of their predicament dawns on the Gestapo men as they glance at each other in recognition they are trapped and outgunned.

"I knew he was a bloody traitor, Wolfgang!" Behr shouts, attempting to draw his Luger, but Skorzeny opens fire, hitting him several times in the chest and knocking him back against the car and then onto the ground as the bullets smash across the windscreen to hit Mencken, who buckles into a crumpled heap. The MP40 clicks empty, and Skorzeny drops it and quickly draws his Luger as he moves over to see Mencken dead. He turns to Behr lying in a pool of blood and staring at his Luger, which lies to his side just out of reach, and painfully grabs it when Skorzeny puts a bullet in his head to make sure he is never going to report their findings. Saddened at having to kill fellow nationals, the thought of giving a coup de grace doesn't fit Skorzeny's psyche, but he consoles himself that his actions are a necessary evil to keep the secret of the Wagnerian Assignment from all enemies, including domestic. He lifts the lifeless bodies of Mencken and Behr, which bleed heavily onto his crisp, clean uniform, as he places them in the rear of their car. Taking the hand break off, he pushes the 750kg vehicle with a great deal of effort across the road and over to the side before giving one last push for it to disappear out of sight as it crashes through the trees and foliage, turning several times as it disintegrates into smaller parts and lands in a stream below to settle between the large glacial boulders that litter the area.

***

Standing in the great room, Shint scrutinises the plans for the Berghof and Bunker complex when Skorzeny enters, and he comes to attention with a salute.

"What happened, sir?" Shint said in shock on noticing the dried blood on Skorzeny's uniform.

Bemused by the colonel's words, Skorzeny stares at Shint until he motions to the blood.

"Are you injured, sir?"

Skorzeny quickly plays down the significance of his soiled uniform. "Don't worry about it; I've just killed some Gestapo men," he said, making Shint laugh awkwardly. "Well done in bringing the men back to barracks, Colonel. From now on, we need to keep a low profile. I want all the men at work preparing the fortifications twenty-four hours a day."

"I've already seen to that, sir," Shint said to impress, aware his commanding officer's first impression of him was not good, but Skorzeny ignored his sycophantic attempt to make amends as he moved to the table and scrutinises the plans as he flicks back and forth through the pages.

"The times I've been in this building and didn't know about the bunker complex."

"Reichsleiter Bormann had them added, sir," Shint explains. "He even had a nearby mountain hollowed out to make a tea house for the Führer's birthday."

"The Kehlsteinhaus," Skorzeny mutters with a knowing grin of disapproval. "More stupidity."

"I heard the Führer hated it."

"With good reason. It's just another odious monstrosity from a hateful self-appreciating man," Skorzeny said, showing his dislike of Bormann as he moved to the door. "I want the fortifications fully operational within forty-eight hours, Colonel."

Shint goes to question the order but holds back as Skorzeny exits.

***

FRIDAY, APRIL 13TH 1945

***

Relaxing in his room, Skorzeny enjoys his first cigarette of the day as he listens to the radio stating Vienna had fallen to the Red Army. He vaults to the side of the bunk, disturbed his family are in enemy-occupied territory. Overcome with despondency, he leans forward and stubs the cigarette in an overfilled ashtray. Had they escaped to the safety of the West, or had they been captured by the revengeful wickedness he knew was coming from the East? The thoughts ravage his mind. Conscious of the atrocities his countrymen had carried out at the expense of the people of the Soviet Union and that now his family are in the firing line becomes too much to bear, and he begins to pace. He questioned himself if he had done enough for Führer and his fatherland. He knows he will have to rid himself of the Berghof and its unwelcome command to get them to safety but he had never disobeyed an order. Determined, he switches the radio off and moves for the door when a loud knock brings him out of his melancholy, and he opens it to find Shint standing outside, coming to attention with a salute.

"Sorry to disturb you, sir, but we captured this man," Shint said, moving aside to reveal a dishevelled and worn-out Radl guarded by two soldiers who have him covered by MP40s. "He says you are expecting him."

"You know me, Otto, I always like to make the grand entrance," Radl said with a giant smile that didn't befit the situation.

Pleased to see his old friend safe and well, Skorzeny orders. "Where are the men of the Jagdverbande, Karl?"

With the realisation they are acquainted, Shint's puzzled glance shifts between Skorzeny and Radl.

"Out of sight in the valley, awaiting your order to come up. I brought 300 and left the rest at Friedenthal to carry on as ordered."

Pleased his friend has arrived without any complications, Skorzeny shakes Radl's hand.

"Colonel Shint, may I introduce Major Karl Radl, my second in command."

Shint motions for the soldiers to leave then nods at Radl and salutes Skorzeny before walking off.

"Colonel!" Skorzeny calls out, and Shint turns back. "You'd better come in." Standing aside, they enter, and he closes the door behind him and moves to a cabinet to produce a bottle of schnapps and three glasses. "How far did you get, Karl?"

"The front trenches. I was crawling along when one of the guards noticed me."

"He was lucky you gave orders not to shoot first, sir." Shint interrupts with an amused grin, but Skorzeny doesn't see the humour.

"That's why you were given the order, Colonel," Skorzeny adds as he pours a fair measure of the schnapps for each of them to down.

"I checked all around and approached the trenches on numerous occasions but only got spotted at the last moment before I had to give myself up."

"Then we need to tighten the defences," Skorzeny said, turning to Shint, who was still waiting for why he had been called back. "See to that, Colonel."

Believing he had been dismissed, Shint salutes and moves, ready to exit.

"Hold on, Colonel; it's time we informed you of what is going on." With pride, Shint forces his body erect and clicks his heels in anticipation to Radl's amusement.

"If everything goes to plan, we can expect the arrival of the Führer." Shint forces his body tighter, making Radl snigger.

"Is there a problem, Major?" Shint said aggressively, and Radl shook his head as he recomposed himself. "Then what is so humorous?"

"It's just so long since I've witnessed the spit and polish of Prussian discipline."

"Never mind that!" Skorzeny snipes with venom. "We must be ready to protect the Führer from all enemies when Berlin falls."

Having been ordered to keep radio silence by von Stiffel, who hadn't wanted the men at the Berghof to find out the truth about Berlin's imminent fall and desert, Shint looks genuinely shocked.

"We need everywhere cleaned to the highest standards before his arrival."

"I will see to that myself, sir," Shint interrupts. "Then it will be my honour to protect the Führer."

"Hopefully, you won't need to do it all yourself," Radl said to Shint's irritation.

"I've never met the Führer personally," Shint carries on with disappointment and then adds with excitement. "It has been my lifelong ambition."

"I've read your file," Skorzeny adds. "You were a soldier of the Führerbegleitkommando?"

"I was, sir."

"Then who awarded you your Knights Cross?" Skorzeny enquires with genuine admiration.

"It was parachuted to me at Kursk."

"I thought the Führerbegleitkommando were saved from harm so they couldn't be captured and give away the Führer's protection secrets," Radl snipes in the belief they had wished to be kept from active duty.

"I was only a small cog in a large protective machine, and I only saw the Führer from afar. I requested a transfer to frontline duties before that order was implemented. Probably because of my small role in his protection, I was allowed to slip through the loop. I couldn't have told the enemy anything even if I had wanted to."

Skorzeny stares at Shint's youthfulness in disbelief at how such a young man has been through so much. "Not good times, Colonel."

Overcome with pride, Shint goes to force his body erect but stops just in time to give Radl a scornful look.

"That's enough of that," Skorzeny rants. "You'll find the enemy is outside, closing in on us as we speak."

"I relive every battle every day, sir," Shint adds. "I'm proud to say I have fought in many theatres of operation."

"Haven't we all!" Radl interrupts.

Shint shuffles uncomfortably as he revisits the many battlefields in his mind before turning to the door and pausing. "Don't get me wrong. I'm not putting myself forward as a hero, but I think my rank and battle honours should command more respect from a junior officer."

"So do I," Skorzeny scowls turning his angry stare on Radl.

"I will get straight on with the cleaning, sir," Shint adds, then salutes before limping to the door. "You will find I am not above myself and will do anything for Führer and fatherland. Will that be all, sir?"

Skorzeny nods as Shint exits.

"What has gotten into you, Karl?" Skorzeny rants disturbed.

"What?" Radl answered innocently.

"Your attitude toward the colonel!"

Bemused as to why Skorzeny was concerned for Shint's feelings, Radl pauses and then grins. "I don't like his kind, Otto."

"His kind? What about his kind?"

"Prussian heel clickers!"

Skorzeny laughs. "You mean like General von Stiffel?"

"Not the general. He's a true soldier."

"So is the colonel. You've made a rash opinion without knowing anything about him. Maybe you should read the file General von Stiffel gave me on him."

Skorzeny hands Radl Shint's file, which he grips tightly. "General von Stiffel gave that to me to study," he explains. "Maybe he could foresee the attitude you have shown here today."

"You have no liking for his type, Otto."

"Not for Prussian heel clickers but for a young man who has been through hell I have the utmost respect for."

"Haven't we all been through hell?"

"Yes, we have, Karl, but everyone who has should have a great deal of admiration for bravery, no matter who carried it out. Read it. You may be surprised."

Showing signs of disinterest, Radl nods, placing the file down.

"Just for the record, Karl. Colonel Shint isn't from Prussia. He's Bavarian by birth and an SS officer also."

Radl nods as he sarcastically comes to rigid attention and salutes. "Doesn't mean I have to like the man."

"I suppose you don't, but he's right about one thing. He is your superior officer, so act accordingly."

"Yes, sir," Radl said, feeling dismissed for the first time by his friend, then exited.

***

Located in the Trianon Palace Hotel, Versailles, since December 1944, Supreme Headquarters Allied Expeditionary Force (SHAEF) has been in uproar as they wait to relocate to Frankfurt. Boxes, crates and all manner of goods litter the hallways, and military and civilian personnel scurry about, hastily apprehensive of the move.

***

His feet stretched out over his rickety old desk; Major Robertson sits bored with the lack of anything constructive to do. His office is an oversized exclusive bedroom set within the hotel that resembles a Victorian whorehouse with decoration abhorrently not to his liking. The room is in chaos, with boxes and papers strewn all over his desk and floor, but he shows little inclination to sort it out and end his long day.

***

Born in the Highlands of Scotland, a confident, ruggedly handsome, privately educated man, Major William Angus Robertson, having believed the recruiting posters that promised travel and excitement for all, enlisted in the Coldstream Guards in 1933 at the age of eighteen as a private soldier. Affluent in several languages, including German, he was soon picked up by SIS (Secret Intelligence Service) to assume the role of a German staff officer in the Oberkommando des Heeres (OKH) and gain intelligence against the long-foreseen enemy of the future. Considering all he had achieved in the field of intelligence, he bears no medals on his uniform, which irks him at the sight of others who had them awarded in abundance for a lot less. Thriving in the role military intelligence had given him in 1936, he infiltrated the OKH and sent information back to London through contacts at the British Embassy in Berlin. Proving proficiency in the role he had undertaken for the Germans, he quickly rose through the ranks putting him closer to the more delicate intelligence that his MI6 pay masters hungered for. In 1937, he was attached to Hitler's staff and promoted colonel and became a close friend to the Führer as they met about intelligence matters weekly. Betrayed to the Gestapo in early 1944, he was arrested and sent to Prinz Albrecht Strasse in Berlin, where he was tortured and then sent to Buchenwald concentration camp near Weimar in Germany to await execution. Professing his innocence to his SS torturers and jailers who were unable to confirm the intelligence against him ultimately kept him alive as they dared not execute a close friend of Hitler's without concrete evidence against him and without the Führer's orders which he was reluctant to give. Enduring terrible hardship, he awaited his execution which he believed was inevitable, unaware of the protection he was under. When his execution didn't come, he concocted an audacious escape plan where he dressed as an SS officer and, using his knowledge of military procedures, he walked off without being asked to show any form of identification. Over several weeks living off the land and his wits, he made his way through enemy lines into Normandy and was captured by the advancing American Third Army and placed in an internment camp until he was able to prove his identity and was repatriated back to Scotland to convalesce at his grandmother's house in Ballater. On returning to SIS headquarters in Broadway, London, he was assigned to SHAEF to work counterintelligence by using the knowledge he had acquired of the OKH command structure and operating procedures. To his relief, he was taken off the active register and put behind a desk as acting intelligence liaison between the British and her Allies, but of late; the role had become increasingly odious to him.

***

The Secret Intelligence Service (SIS) started as the Secret Intelligence Bureau in 1909. It was a joint initiative between the Admiralty and the War Office to control intelligence operations within the British Empire and foreign countries but was split into Navy and Army sections. These two sections underwent many changes, and the foreign section became the directorate of Military Intelligence, known as Section 6M of MI6.

***

The Oberkommando des Heeres (OKH) is the supreme high command of the German army and was founded in 1935 as part of the remilitarisation of the Third Reich's military structuring and commanded all military actions carried out during the War.

***

Several light raps on the door are preceded by Lieutenant General Waverley entering, giving Robertson a start, and hastily moving his feet off the desk.

"How are things going, Will?" Waverley says with a jovial American drawl, amused by Robertson's discomfort as he recovers his poise and stands to salute.

"Great, General. I'm just bored with a sore arse."

"Never mind all that crap. Are you ready for the move?"

Mindful, he doesn't get a visit from the American general unless there was an ulterior motive, Robertson answers. "I was."

Waverley moves to the window and looks out over the busy courtyard below. "Are you sure you are alright?" he adds without turning back.

Curious about his interest, Robertson stares at the back of Waverley's head.

"It's just that when I entered, I thought you were looking a little peaky."

Robertson straightens himself out and throws the papers onto his desk.

"Peaky! What has peaky got to do with anything, sir?"

"You are looking a little off-colour, my friend."

"The only thing discoloured is my arse. I am hardly bathed in sunlight sitting at that desk, sir."

Waverley turns to Robertson smiling amusedly. "I suppose not. Look, Will, I have a job for a real soldier, but as everyone is busy with the move, I suppose you will have to do."

Robertson laughs, then sighs heavily as he waits for Waverley's punch line.

"Are you up for it?"

"Well, as I don't know what you are talking about, how can I answer such a loaded question?"

Waverley laughs at the Scotsman's candour.

"Why don't you use your men, General?"

"I would, but you tick all the boxes for what I have in mind."

Pleased to escape the turmoil that comes with the move to Frankfurt, Robertson sits at his desk. "Then you'd better explain in greater detail, sir."

***

Lieutenant General Robert Leslie Waverley was born at Fort Stockton, Texas, in 1890. The son of a master sergeant and a sixth-generation Scottish immigrant who had escaped the land of his birth after the battle of Culloden in 1746, he had a sometimes harsh but generally comfortable upbringing in the outdoors of the American wild west. A career officer, he joined West Point military academy in 1912 and graduated in 1916 to finish in the top half of his class onto the horse. Climbing the promotion ladder, he rode into Mexico in the same year under the command of General Black Jack Pershing, along with four thousand eight hundred men of the punitive expedition force to capture the Mexican guerrilla commander, Pancho Villa. During World War One and the killing fields of France and Belgium, he had shown extreme valour on numerous occasions and rose to the lofty rank of lieutenant colonel before being demoted to his pre-war rank of captain after the armistice. Staying in the army, he served in Hawaii and the Philippines but mainly around the hot dusty forts of the American South, where his many experiences were put to training recruits. Transferred into army intelligence in 1929, and after the entry of America into World War Two, he played a small part in the setting up of OSS in 1942, rising to the rank of major general. Due to his role as an intelligence chief, he travelled with President Roosevelt to Casablanca and Yalta, where his pre-war admiration for the Russians waned with the reality of their intentions for world domination. His warnings were ignored, and he caused quite a stir with his remarks but still reached the rank of lieutenant general before D-Day and the invasion of Normandy on June 6th 1944.

***

The Office of Strategic Services (OSS) was formed on June 13th 1942, by order of President Roosevelt to collect and analyse intelligence and conduct espionage, propaganda and subversion behind enemy lines. Its first commander was the charismatic Major General William Joseph Donovan.

***

"I want you to locate the Berghof for me."

"Adolf Hitler's Mountain retreat?" Robertson questioned with an awkward laugh. "Isn't that still in German hands?"

"What's that to a man like you?" Waverley adds with sarcasm. "I'm not sensing hostility, am I? I've come all the way from the American sector to visit you."

Robertson grins, amused by Waverley's attempt at humour. "American sector. You're in the bordello two doors down."

"That may be, but I don't like to be seen associating with limeys, so I took a risk coming here today."

Relating a limey as an English sailor, Robertson retorts with pride in his Scottish heritage. "I'm no limey, General."

Although not a friend of the British military, Waverley had taken a keen liking to Robertson, not only because he reminded him of his younger self, but he also had great pride in his Scottish heritage and their kinship as fellow Highlanders.

"Joking aside, Will. A little assignment will get you out of this shit hole and stop you from getting bored."

The thought of going back into the field concerns the nervous twitching Robertson as the memory of the concentration camp and torture he endured comes racing back to plunder his mind. "Back to my original question, General. Why not use your men?"

"Your experience of working with the Germans is required one more time. If you can't decide, consider it is for King and country."

Although a devout Royalist, Robertson, like all other soldiers, isn't fighting for his King but his kith and kin and takes a piece of paper off his desk to fiddle nervously with it. "I'm off the active register since." He pauses for several tense seconds. "You are aware of that, sir?"

"Because you were found out?" Waverley adds with a laugh. "You've been riding that desk way too long. No wonder your ass is red and sore. Anyway, the mountain air will do you good."

"I'm sure it would, sir," Robertson said as his mind slipped momentarily back to his arrest by the Gestapo, making him shiver at the thought of the mistreatment he had endured and is noticed by Waverley.

"There won't be any problems, Will. Intelligence shows there's no military build-up in the area of the Obersalzberg so it will be a walk in the park."

"We've all heard that one before, sir."

"Well, because I'm in intelligence, I believe I am in a good position to confirm this."

"I always play the game, General, and confirmation the intelligence is correct make the prospect of going there worse, and you saying that with a straight face sends a shiver down my spine."

"It will be a breeze for a man like you. Plus, it will get you out of this office."

"That, General, is probably the only good that can come out of this."

"You've been to the Berghof many times. You understand the layout."

Robertson nods his agreement. "You'll have to clear it with my boss." Waverley winks as he moves back to the door. "Already done," he said with arrogant glee.

"I take it I'm the last to know?" Robertson adds sardonically. "Well, I suppose it's nice to be asked."

Waverley waves then salutes with animation as he exits. Robertson takes in a deep anxious breath and reaches for a drawer that conceals a bottle of Glenfiddich whisky and pours himself a large one and downing it as the prospect of being captured again and all the horrors that come with that haunt him.

***

SATURDAY, APRIL 28TH 1945

***

BBC radio broadcasts a Reuter's news agency report stating Himmler's attempt to negotiate the surrender of all German forces with the Western Allies. Days earlier, Göring had radioed the Reich Chancellery for permission to take over the Reich because Berlin and the Führer would soon fall to the Red Army, and Hitler wouldn't be capable of carrying on command. Himmler hadn't even asked for permission. On hearing this, Hitler flew into a rage, believing he had been betrayed by two of his closest friends and comrades at his most vulnerable time. Hitler recognised Himmler and Göring's actions as treachery and instantly dismissed them both from the National Socialist party, stripped them of all titles, and ordered their immediate arrest and execution.

***

Sitting in his office within the Vor bunker, von Stiffel is pleased Himmler's treachery was at last out in the open and exhales the burden from his trembling chest. He lifted his hip flask to take a lingering drink as the last drops dripped onto his tongue, then placed it down with a heavily distressed thud. Under the heavy shelling of the advancing Red Army, the room shakes, unnerving him to his feet before coming around his desk to a cabinet to open revealing an empty bottle of Himbeergeist Schnapps he had finished earlier that morning but had slipped his mind. Sighing hollow and heavy, he is saddened more by the empty bottles than that of the Red Army advancing rapidly through the Berlin suburbs toward him. In the shock from an exploding shell, a loud knock on the door buckles him to the floor as he trembles. Showing the signs of nervous tension and imminent breaking point, he clutches his jacket and pulls it in tight as he hunches his head into his shoulders and shuffles to the cover of his desk. Unable to distinguish between several more knocks and being under fire, he keeps his head down as he mutters, his thoughts and visions of the barbaric fighting on the Eastern front flashing through his mind to take him deeper into cover. After a short pause, the door opens slowly for an immaculately dressed SS Hauptsturmführer to step in and pause in shock at the sight that beholds him. Not wanting to embarrass the general, he calls out his name and looks away as von Stiffel stands as if nothing had happened and dusts down his uniform.

"Sir, the Führer will see you now," the SS captain says as he comes to attention with a majestic salute.

"Thank you, Hauptsturmführer."

Having awaited orders from von Stiffel, the SS captain enquires as if hastening him to decide. "How are things going, General?"

Nervous and apprehensive of his best course of action, von Stiffel replies without giving anything away. "I'm afraid you will have to wait a little longer, Captain, but hopefully not too much more."

The SS captain salutes, coming to attention, then backing off to allow the general to exit into the corridor.

***

Tensely sitting upright in easy chairs, Hitler and Eva Braun sit in the Führer's sparsely furnished private quarters within the Führerbunker. Their eyes are fixed on an SS Sturmbannführer who holds the Führer's German shepherd dog Blondi in a tight grip. She is in mid-convulsions with foam coming out of her mouth. On a table by Hitler's side lie a small calibre gun, a sealed envelope and an opened poison capsule. The poison had been supplied by the traitor Himmler, who Hitler believed may try to render him unconscious to use as a bargaining chip with the Allies. There is a light tap on the door then the SS captain enters, followed by von Stiffel. The scene inside the room makes them stop in the doorway as Blondi takes her last agonising breath, followed by a final convulsion before her body becomes completely still.

Solemn and dejected, Hitler looks around the room until his stare fixes on von Stiffel, whom he recognises as a friendly face. "I had to see if the poison worked, General," he said disconsolate.

The SS major and SS captain lift Blondi's lifeless body and head for the door. As they pass Hitler, he gives the dog a last loving pat explaining to von Stiffel. "I didn't want her to fall to the Russians."

Von Stiffel's glance shifts rapidly between the SS captain, who nods confidently, Hitler and the gun on the table. "You wanted to see me, my Führer?"

"Yes, General, please come in," Hitler said calmly.

Von Stiffel enters, giving the Nazi salute, and remains rigidly to attention. Hitler stands unsteady; his emancipated hand tremors vigorously as he outstretches it for von Stiffel to shake.

"My thousand-year Reich lies in ruins, General. Destroyed by treachery and international Jewry," Hitler said, saddened that his world was falling in around him. "Subhumans are at this moment overrunning our beloved capital." He looks solemnly at Eva, who stares back without any expression. "I'm afraid the end has come, my love." He walks to the table and stares at the gun and envelope. "I've been betrayed by those who were once loyal."

Believing he is under suspicion of treachery and is about to be arrested, von Stiffel scans the room for the men there to arrest him, but none can be seen.

"I've completed my personal will and testament, which Fräulein Junge has typed for me and which I intend to leave in your capable hands," Hitler said, tapping on the envelope and then walking off a short distance. Coming around on Eva, he takes a comforting hold of her shoulders.

Nervously apprehensive about how to put what he wants to say into words without the stigma of defeatism, von Stiffel picks up the envelope to place in his jacket pocket before speaking. "I have a plane waiting to fly you to the Berghof, my Führer."

"There's nowhere for me to go now, General."

"From there, you will be able to carry on the defence of Germania, my Führer," von Stiffel carries on with a bluster and nervous stammer as he plays to his Führer's vanity.

Hitler's eyes give away a slight glint of elation that there may be a way out of his self-inflicted hell as he murmurs to himself, and his stare fixes on Eva.

"I would dearly love to see the views from the Berghof terrace again, Adolf," Eva says with enthusiasm she hadn't felt in a long time. The thought of leaving the dingy, stale-aired bunker she had voluntarily entered against Hitler's wishes and getting out into the beautiful Bavarian countryside again proves too much for her as she looks to her lover to free her from her self-inflicted hell. "It will do your health a world of good," she adds, increasing Hitler's excitement.

Hitler digested what he had been told as his stare turned vacantly into the distance. "Where is your plane, General?" he said as he turned at the smiling faces waiting on his every word.

"I have a car waiting, my Führer," von Stiffel said, relieved he won't face a firing squad after all. He walks to the door and opens it to reveal the SS captain waiting patiently outside. "You know what to do, Captain."

The SS captain salutes and clicks his heels before walking off at speed.

Instantly feeling the haste required to get his Führer out of the besieged capital, Von Stiffel looks at his watch. "We had better leave, my Führer."

Silence descends on the room as Hitler looks confused at how fast he is to leave. Several seconds pass then he holds out his slightly calmer hand for Eva to help her stand. Not being privy to their love affair brings a grin to von Stiffel's face at seeing their affection.

Enthused with an overwhelming sense of impending victory he hadn't felt for a long time, Hitler speaks with animation. "Come, General; we still have a war to win."

Gallantly, Hitler leads Eva to the door, and they exit into the corridor to be confronted by Dr Bergman, who patiently stands sweating profusely for what he nervously knows is to come. Hitler doesn't give the doctor a second glance as he walks off, but von Stiffel beckons him to follow with a tilt of his head.

***

Born on February 6th 1912, in Munich, Bavaria, Eva Braun met Hitler in 1929 while working as a model for Heinrich Hoffman, the Führer's photographer. By 1934 she was his muse until the onset of World War two when his attention was taken by his despotic attempt to take over and rule the world. Believing all the maidens in Germany would be heartbroken that their Führer had a love in his life other than the German people, their relationship had been kept a national secret to the point that even the likes of von Stiffel had been unaware of it. Whether they had been lovers had constantly stirred conjecture with those who knew of her existence, but he treated her with contempt and indifference, making her into a sad and lonely woman in a world tinged with lethargy and boredom.

***

Born into an affluent family of Berlin bankers in 1892, a small thin, bespectacled unkempt man, Dr Alfred Bergman, had gone into medicine instead of the banking business to his parents' despair. The Bergman family had backed the Nazis, so after they came to power, their son was honoured with a minor medical role on Hitler's staff which incensed pride and bragging rights of the patriarch. This was why von Stiffel considered him for the Wagnerian Assignment, the doctor being a man who could look after Hitler and wouldn't be missed if he wasn't around.

***

Bergdorf and the SS captain stand patiently in the Führerbunker underground car park beside Hitler's Mercedes Benz 770 from his personal fleet as its engine runs. Bergdorf fearfully expects to get rebuked for wasting petrol as he had been ordered by von Stiffel in the past to under no circumstances leave the engine running as at that late stage in the war, the fuel was more valuable than gold, but as the general enters followed by Hitler, Eva and Dr Bergman, no rebuke was forthcoming.

Having expected an entourage to wish him a good journey which had always been etiquette in the past, Hitler looks around in bemusement at how quiet and empty the area is. "Where is everyone, General?"

Von Stiffel had ordered the area cleared to get Hitler away without being noticed. "Fighting the Russians, my Führer," he answers, placating Hitler enough to nod, pleased his loyal subjects were still fighting hard for him.

As if playing to the large audience of admirers who frequented his every move, Hitler glances around, delusional. "Thank you, gentlemen, for your loyalty. You are all heroes to the National Socialist cause." He gets into the rear of the Mercedes, followed by Dr Bergman and Eva, before Bergdorf closes the door and enters the driver's seat. Von Stiffel and the SS captain shake hands with a deep admiration for each other's resolve in carrying out their duty.

"Good luck, sir," the SS captain said with immense pride in the small part he had played in helping his Führer escape.

"Thank you, Captain," Von Stiffel said aware of what he had asked the officer. "You know what to do?"

"Yes, sir."

"Good luck."

The SS captain salutes, clicking his heels that echo around the empty concrete structure. Von Stiffel gets into the front of the Mercedes, drives off up the ramp onto Hermann Göring Strasse, and then turns north toward the Tier Garden.

***

The SS captain exits through the steel bunker doors at the rear of the Reich Chancellery into the severely destroyed gardens. Several SS men follow, carrying two bodies cloaked in blankets before dumping them unceremoniously into a shallow shell hole. Under orders, the SS men pour the contents of petrol cans over the bodies, and the SS captain lights a taper, throws it on top, and then stands back as the fumes ignite in a blast of flames that burn with acrid black smoke billowing off.

"That will do. Get back inside," the SS captain orders and the SS men re-enter the bunker leaving the bodies burning. Aware there isn't enough fuel to destroy them, he takes a last look at the bodies, gives the Nazi salute, and follows. He closes the steel doors with an ear-piercing clatter to shroud the stairwell in darkness before pulling two stick grenades out of his belt to prime before dropping them onto the concrete stairs and forcing the SS men who recognise the sound into a life-and-death panic as they roll down in impending doom before exploding, decimating them in a vainglorious attempt to keep a secret. Certain of capture, the fanatical SS captain knew the only way to keep the secret plan of his Führer's escape was for all involved to sacrifice their lives under an idiotic loyalty to Führer and his fatherland.

***

Avoiding the debris, Bergdorf drives the Mercedes cautiously through the devastated streets and then turns onto the grass of the Tier Garden for a short, uncomfortable distance before coming to a halt in a well-rehearsed show of German efficiency. Von Stiffel alights hastily as his glance shifts anxiously between his watch, the sky and the surrounding area as he searches for the threat of a Red Army breakthrough. Dr Bergman and Eva follow, terrified at the sights and sounds of war that beholds them, before helping Hitler out of the car. As if witnessing the war for the first time, Hitler breaks free and moves forward several paces, perplexed by the carnage. Having been a soldier in the Great War, the smells of the devastation momentarily take him back to the trenches of the western front, making Dr Bergman take his arm and lead him to a burnt-out vehicle, followed by Eva to cower in terror. Bergdorf attempts to alight, but von Stiffel prevents him from opening the door.

"Your journey ends here, Sergeant."

Unsure what to do or say, Bergdorf shifts awkwardly as he winds the window down for von Stiffel to hand him a sealed envelope. "What's this, sir?"

"Your discharge papers, Hans."

Believing he is still helpful to his general, Bergdorf doesn't want to be dismissed and goes to plead, but von Stiffel speaks first.

"I've already asked too much of you, old friend. I thank you for your years of loyal service. Now please go find your family and live."

A shell explodes a short distance off, forcing von Stiffel to duck for cover and Bergdorf to cower into the vehicle as debris covers the area and smashes off the Mercedes as it returns to earth.

Von Stiffel straightens himself out, then slaps the car's roof several times. "Hans, you must go while you still can."

Bergdorf smiles and then salutes to show his general great warmth and pride. "Thank you, sir. Good luck."

The Mercedes skids off churning up the grass as von Stiffel returns the salute, then gives a light, concerned wave. "Stay alive, old friend," he mumbles with a heavy heart.

The Mercedes drives a short distance when a T34 exits a side street adjacent and rakes the area with 7.62mm machine gun fire before firing an 85mm shell which strikes the car throwing it into the air in a ball of flames turning several times to land in a burning heap with no signs of life. German soldiers attack the Red Army tank with little effect as their bullets ricochet off as it moves forward, raking everything with devastating machine gun fire. Several civilians, proudly wearing their Volkssturm Wehrmacht armbands, exit an adjacent building carrying Panzerfausts and attack, firing the portable anti-tank rockets to smash into the T34's armour and destroy it and the Red Army crew inside to burn into oblivion. Having witnessed the death of his old friend, von Stiffel moves forward with the thought of helping, but Dr Bergman shouts through the noise and chaos to catch his attention.

"We have more important issues at hand, General!"

Tears roll down von Stiffel's face as his stare shifts between Hitler and the burning Mercedes. Desperately wanting to escape his hell, he knows the assignment he had set in motion must take precedence, and the sound of an approaching aeroplane's engines brings him out of his despondency as his attention quickly focuses on the sky. He looks at his watch, smiles and then draws a flare gun from his briefcase.

"What are you doing, General?" Dr Bergman shouts in panic.

"Now we get out of here," von Stiffel explains, firing the flare into the sky and watching it soar.

"What if it's Russian, General?"

"Don't worry, Doctor," von Stiffel adds confidently. "I guarantee you it isn't."

***

The T34 Soviet medium-sized tank was first produced in 1940. Often credited as the most effective tank of World War Two, it was continuously refined to enhance its battle effectiveness and fought efficiently throughout the Great Patriotic War. Possessing an unprecedented combination of firepower, mobility and being produced in massive numbers, it became a favourite of the Red Army and the scourge of the Axis soldiers that came up against it.

***

Flying high above the devastation of Berlin below, Hanna sits at the controls of a Junkers 52 of the Führer's transport fleet, knowing time is running out for a successful airlift before the capital is overrun. Her nerves at breaking point, having carried out the flight several times at the same time over the last few days, her stare shifts from side to side on the lookout for predators. One mile ahead, the flare explodes to illuminate the sky as it slowly drops to the rooftops bringing her strained face into a smile as she banks in the direction of the Tier Garden.

***

A German transport plane designed by Ernst Zindel of the Junkers company works at Dessau, the JU 52 saw both civilian and military service during the 1930s and 40s. Manufactured between 1932 to 1945 and powered by three radial engines, it proved to be one of the most resourceful German air force aeroplanes, having served in all theatres of occupation and formed the backbone of the Luftwaffe's transport fleet.

***

Panicked by the thought of a plane landing amongst the chaos of the Tier Garden, Dr Bergman's stare shifts to the sky. "You can't expect an aeroplane to land here, General."
Von Stiffel has great pride and confidence in the bravery of the Luftwaffe pilots who carry out such dangerous missions daily to keep the city supplied. "They land here all the time, Doctor. You look after the Führer and leave the rest to me."

***

Pushing the controls forward, Hanna takes the Junkers into a steep dive as she aims with determination toward the Tier Garden. With every yard closing toward the ground, Red Army soldiers take pot-shots with small arms hoping to shoot down such a prize as it races over their heads. Almost hitting columns of free-standing ruins, the Junkers comes over the rooftops onto the Tier Garden to bounce across the grass, skidding to a halt and spinning 180 degrees to set their course for escape. Keeping the engine revs, she opens the cockpit window and shouts. "Quick, General! We need to leave now."

Eva and Dr Bergman help Hitler to his feet as von Stiffel opens the fuselage doors and pulls out the step to drop it to the ground.

Hanna looks into the fuselage as her passengers get on and quickly take seats. "Fasten up, my Führer. This is going to be bumpy."

Hardly giving von Stiffel time to take his seat, Hanna pushes the throttle forward, and the Junkers engines roar into life as it accelerates across the grass. Advancing onto the Tier Garden, a KV1 heavy tank stops as its turret turns to aim at the landed Junkers as it speeds toward it on a collision course. Hanna stares out of the windscreen and pulls hard on the controls for the Junkers to lift into the air as a 76.2mm shell exits the barrel of the KV1, only missing by inches to explode into one of the adjacent buildings to send death and debris all over. Desperately aware height is her greatest ally, she pulls back on the stick, but one of its fixed wheels hits a free-standing chimney pot leaving the wheel hanging precariously below as the Junkers struggles to gain altitude.

**

The Kilment Voroshilov, KV1 heavy tank, was named after a Russian Commissar and Politician. Weighing 45 tonnes with a crew of five, it was a formidable fighting vehicle and was in service throughout the Great Patriotic War with many variations built.

**

As Hanna levels out, a Russian Yak 3 fighter exits from the sun with its machine guns riddling the Junkers with bullets that smash through the windscreen and fuselage, forcing her to duck inanely to one side as glass and debris cut into her body.

**

A robust Soviet fighter, the Yakovlev 3 has origins dating back to 1941 and the beginning of the Great Patriotic War. A 20-millimetre ShVAK cannon fires through the propeller spinner and also has one in each wing and twin 7.62 ShKAS machine guns that show enemy fighters that they are up against a formidable enemy.

**

Regaining control, Hanna brings the Junkers onto a straight heading as she hunts for the threat she knows won't go until its job is done and they are downed. Concerned for her Führer's safety, she turns into the fuselage, but her eyes instantly fix in shock on von Stiffel slumped over with blood trickling from his mouth. "Herr Doctor!" she shouts, pointing at the general.

Dr Bergman sees von Stiffel and then goes to assist but finds no signs of life. He slumps over and takes several deep breaths before turning solemnly to Hanna and shaking his head with the confirmation she had dreaded. Saddened at the loss of a man she admired dearly, Hanna momentarily forgets the perils they are still in and turns her stare out of the smashed windscreen as the cold air blasts into her cut, bleeding face. Hitler's hard, unfeeling stare shifts between Dr Bergman and von Stiffel.

"I'm afraid he's dead, my Führer."

Unconcerned by another death that adds to the countless millions of soldiers and civilians that had fallen on the battlefields or bombed out cities worldwide on his behalf, Hitler explains as he keeps his stare on the airspeed indicator on the bulkhead directly in front of his armoured seat. "The general gave his life in the cause of National Socialism." Hitler's compassion had only ever been to those he believed loyal to him, like his beloved German shepherd dog, Blondi, who in the end had only received his coldness in testing the poison he had intended to use on himself and Eva. Unconvinced by such a ridiculous statement, all Dr Bergman can only nod his agreement. He looks back at the gene, sees the envelope containing Hitler's last will and testament sticking out of his pocket, and scoops it up to place it in his safety. Hanna looks around when her stare stops rigidly on the right-side cockpit window, seeing the Yak pilot waving with enthused confidence that his prey was to die.

His voice trembling in fright, Dr Bergman fastens himself back into his seat. "What's he doing, Flight Captain?"

Worried about alarming her passengers, Hanna mutters to herself. "He's eyeing his kill." Not intending to go down without a fight, she banks the Junkers to the right to dwarf the Yak with its massive size as it nears, which panics the Russian pilot into a decisive life or death decision as he believes they are about to collide and puts the Yak into a dive that takes it devastatingly into the rooftops to crash in a massive explosion and cover the advancing Red Army soldiers with fire, debris and death. She brings the Junkers back to level flight and then pulls back on the controls to quickly gain the altitude required to escape from the small arms fire constantly ricocheting off the underside of the fuselage.

Dr Bergman takes several anxious breaths as he looks back at the flames escalating from the Yak and the burning building behind. "What happened, Flight Captain?" he shouts with great relief and elation.

Only just coming to terms with the highly heroic outcome herself, Hanna replies with the modesty she was born with. "I remembered we were still low, Doctor. Luckily for us, he forgot."

***

Overlooking Berchtesgaden Valley, Skorzeny and Radl stand on the Berghof terrace, enjoying the anonymity the camouflage net above gives them. The noise of a failing engine captures their attention, but it takes them several moments to locate the Junkers through the bright sunlight as it flies over with smoke billowing from the failing right wings mounted engine.

"At last," Skorzeny said with a breath of relief.

In a prearranged signal, Hanna rocks the Junkers from side to side before disappearing behind Mount Kehlstein. Shint exits the Berghof and comes up behind.

"That's our guest, Colonel," Skorzeny said. "Get down into the valley and get the Führer back here as fast and safely as possible."

Shint salutes and then turns to walk off, but Skorzeny grabs his arm, stopping him.

"As discreetly as possible, Colonel."

Aware of the need for secrecy, Shint gives a second salute and then heads off at speed.

"General von Stiffel's done it," Skorzeny adds in disbelief.

"Yes, Otto, thank God. Now you can take off into the hills and never be seen again."

Bemused by words he doesn't understand, Skorzeny turns to Radl until the irony of them makes him remember what von Stiffel had said to him back in Berlin. "If only, but for whatever reason, I don't think I will get off so lightly. The general will no doubt have a role for me, for us."

"You think so?" Radl said as he moved off a few paces. "I thought he made it plain you would be relieved of your temporary command as soon as he arrived."

"Then what would I do?" Skorzeny blusters, believing he is still vital to the Wagnerian Assignment. "We still have a fight on our hands, and the Führer will need as many men as possible to protect him."

***

The Junkers descends slowly with smoke and flames billowing from its failing engine. Unaware of the damaged wheel, Hanna brings the 19 metres, 6,500Kg aeroplane onto the valley floor as gently as she can. Bumping across the uneven ground for a short distance, the broken wheel buckles making the wing tip hit the ground and dig in tight to send them into a spin before stopping violently in a crumpled heap as the second wheel crumples under strain, taking both propellers into the ground to churn up the earth and disintegrate as they burst into flames.

Hanna exits the cockpit into the fuselage and hastily moves to Hitler's side. "Are you alright, my Führer?" she enquired deeply about his well-being.

Without a word, Hitler stares vacantly past her at the flames licking the outside to take her stare to follow his.

"We need to get the Führer out!" she shouts, opening the fuselage door.

Eva unclips herself, and Hanna pulls her out of her seat and pushes her unceremoniously toward the door before turning to Dr Bergman, who had moved Hitler to the door for Hanna to help them alight. Two Mercedes Grosse 770 sedans from the Führer's fleet race across the valley toward the Junkers and skid to a halt. Shint and several soldiers alight in shock at the sight of the aeroplane, now well ablaze and without ceremony; they bundle Hitler into the first Mercedes away from danger, followed by Eva and Dr Bergman and heading off at speed.

"Quick, I need a hand!" Hanna cries out on noticing Shint. She moves to the doorway of the Junkers and looks inside, unaware that the flames are closing in on her fast. Wanting to save the body of von Stiffel for burial, she attempts to climb on board, but Shint drags her away from the danger. Unaware he had saved her life, she turns angrily on him as he points at the aeroplane for her to look at its inferno.

***

Concerned by the black smoke billowing into the air, Skorzeny and Radl stare into the valley.

"That doesn't bode well, Karl."

Radl nods as the first Mercedes drives up and then stops at the foot of the stairs. Smartening himself out, Skorzeny races down the steps two at a time and stands expectantly to one side as Dr Bergman and Eva alight, followed by a soldier who helps his Führer out. Saluting and clicking his heels, Skorzeny comes to rigid attention as Hitler stares delusionally into the distance, unable to recognise his loyal subordinate or his surroundings.

"Welcome, my Führer," Skorzeny said obediently.

The soldier helps Hitler up the stairs, one shuffling step at a time, as Skorzeny's glance shifts to Eva, who smiles with delight at being back in the relative safety of the Berghof.

"Welcome, Frauline Braun."

"Thank you, Colonel, but my name is Frau Hitler."

Skorzeny grins, amused by her blasé statement. "Congratulations, Frau Hitler," he mutters and then turns to congratulate his Führer, only to find he has already cleared the stairs and is crossing the terrace into the Berghof. He turns back to Eva, but she is already at the top chasing her husband into the Berghof.

"Not the way the Führer would have wished to return, Colonel," Dr Bergman adds with irony as he outstretches his hand for Skorzeny to shake before making his way up the stairs, elated his terrifying journey fraught with danger is over.

The second Mercedes drives up and then stops for Shint and Hanna to alight, bringing a relieved smile to Skorzeny's face.

Her face reddened, cut and heavily blistered due to the ice-cold air battering her through the long flight; Hanna gave a pained smile as she turned to Shint. "Thank you, Colonel. I apologise for my actions in the valley."

Pleased to have been of use, Shint nods modestly, then walks off at pace.

"Good to see you again, Otto," Hanna says as her glance shifts to Radl standing on the terrace, looking down and gives him a cheery wave. "How are you, Karl?"

"Good for seeing you safe and well, Hanna."

Skorzeny looks inside the second Mercedes to find it empty. "Where's General von Stiffel?" he enquires, bringing tears to Hanna's eyes, which quickly rolled down her face.

"I'm afraid he didn't make it, Otto."

Skorzeny steps back, stunned.

"We were attacked as we left Berlin, and he was killed."

Unable to take the death that adds to a long list of friends and comrades lost throughout the war, Skorzeny moves off a few paces to stare into the distance.

Having heard Hanna's words, Radl shouts ironically before walking off. "Now you can't take off into the hills, Otto."

Hanna's bemusement turns to Skorzeny. "What does Karl mean?" she mutters delicately, aware of the tension.

"It's his subtle way of telling me I am still in command," he announces, turning with concern. "What happened to your face?"

Unaware of her injuries, she reaches up only to feel the sharpness of her touch. "I'm afraid it's the result of a long cold flight without the protection of a windscreen."

Aware Skorzeny is weary of command and yearns for others to be giving the orders, Hanna makes her way to his side and embraces him with affection before they part and stroll up the stairs onto the terrace and then over to the parapet to look into the valley below.

"I never thought I would take in this view again," she said sentimentally, overtaken by the Obersalzberg's magnificence.

"It's more beautiful with you in the frame."

Elated at words from a man she loves and deeply respects, she smiles. "I could, but only for a second, forget our predicament."

With the hope of forgetting, he stares into the distance, but the camouflage netting surrounding them won't allow it, bringing him straight back to the shocking reality and loss of his friend. "We have to retrieve the general's body," he says, moving off, but Hanna grabs his arm to pull him back.

"We didn't have the time to get him out," she said solemnly. "The plane was an inferno."

He sits on the parapet and looks down into the valley. "Maybe cremation is what he would have wanted," he mutters to console himself, but it doesn't help his wretchedness.

"I think he would have chosen life," she adds realistically, making the hardened fighting man shuffle his discomfort.

"I suppose he would," he mutters, embarrassed.

***

TUESDAY, MAY 1ST 1945

***

Littered with burnt-out German planes, tanks and all manner of militaria, Rosenheim airbase had long since seen better days, having served the Luftwaffe right up to its surrender to the American army in March 1945. Having occupied large swathes of Bavaria, the United States 3rd Infantry Division was well into preparing the runways and adjacent fields for use by the United States Army air force. Tents take the place of ruined buildings raised to the ground through Hitler's scorched earth policy during the German retreat.

***

The United States 3rd Infantry Division, nicknamed the Marne Division, landed at St Tropez in the South of France in 1944 and advanced up the Rhone valley through the Vosges Mountains to Strasbourg. They crossed the Rhine on March 26th 1945, before advancing into Bavaria to take Nuremberg, the home of National Socialism, Augsburg, and then Salzburg.

***

Believing the Third Reich was on its knees and they would soon be on their way home back to the lives they'd left behind before the madness of war, American GIs work at a leisurely pace as they clear the area. Robertson drives his American badged Willys jeep through the airbase past the burnt-out militaria and GIs, who glare curious at the British officer in their neighbourhood. He stops outside an oversized command tent and alights to look in to find it lavishly furnished with all manner of luxuries set aside for their vain glorious commanding officer. A small amount of paper covers the desk, with a six-inch silver-plated Star of David taking centre stage. Unaware he is under scrutiny, General Williams stands with his back to the tent flap as he studies maps covering a wallboard.
Conscious of Williams' Prima Donna status and religious values, Robertson moves inside and stands silently as he takes in the garish decor. "Excuse me, sir," he mutters, but Williams ignores the English accent. "Major Robertson, sir. I was ordered to report here."

***

Lieutenant General Michael Williams was born into a deeply religious Jewish family in Sacramento, California, in 1897. He had never truly believed in God or understood the Tanakh and had allowed his religious beliefs to waver into extinction until after the

Allies had stumbled across the concentration camps and what the Germans had done to the Jewish race, and he found himself turning back to his god and asking forgiveness for his abstention. Joining the American army in 1912 as a private soldier to escape his home life and have the opportunity to travel, he gained a field commission in the bloody trenches of Europe in 1918 to reach the rank of captain when he resigned his commission in 1932. Before World War Two, he worked as an accountant for a large oil company in Texas, but on December 7th 1941 (the day of Japan's infamous attack on Pearl Harbor), he was carried away with an overzealous sense of patriotic duty and, like many hundreds of thousands of his fellow citizens he re-enlisted at the first opportunity where he regained the pre-war rank of captain. Operation Torch (the American invasion of Morocco) saw him land in North Africa to fight through Sicily and Italy, where he excelled as a commander in the field to rise rapidly through the ranks. He returned to the United Kingdom in 1943 to assist in training troops for Operation Dragoon (the invasion of Southern France) and was given his command and rose in rank to that of major general.

***

Williams looks Robertson up and down before returning a half-hearted salute that shows his disdain of all things British, which has nothing to do with the war but because of British policy during the mandatory Palestine period of the middle east where the Jews desire to set up the state of Israel had been blocked since 1920. "So, you are Major Robertson?"

"Yes, sir."

"General Waverley didn't inform me you were British."

"That, sir, is irrelevant to why I am here."

Always pleased to keep a junior officer standing, Williams moves to his desk and sits. "I would offer you a chair, Major, but as you can see, I ain't got another."

"Standing isn't a problem for me, sir."

"Good. I understand General Waverley wants you to accompany my men to find the Berghof?"

"Yes, sir."

"Any reasons why?"

Robertson picks the Star of David off the general's desk.

"Put that down, Major!" Williams barks, showing his religious sensibilities work on emotions, not intelligent thinking.

"My apologies, sir," Robertson said, uncaring of the general's emotionality as he replaced the religious relic, but Williams snatches it off the desk and takes a handkerchief out of his pocket to wipe off the fingerprints.

"What I don't understand, Major. Why use a British officer?" Williams enquires, showing his vehement opposition to the thought. "Surely we have enough capable men of our own."

"I put that to General Waverley, sir, but he still insisted I come." Williams obsessively replaces the Star of David in the dead centre of his desk. "And here you are."

"And here I am, sir!"

"But that doesn't answer my initial question."

Robertson can see Williams has been left out of the loop and is after acquiring intelligence, and even though it is irrelevant to his mission, he has no intention of giving him any. "I won't know until I get there, sir. All I know is General Waverley wants me to gather intelligence on whatever I find and report it directly to him."

"Gather intelligence!" Williams presses, showing his increasing hunger for information. "On what?"

"I won't know until I get there, sir," Robertson mutters to Williams' displeasure.

"I know General Waverley of old, Major. He must be up to something."

Robertson wants to laugh but withholds the urge.

"Well, I hope he knows everything up there is fair game."

"I don't know what you mean, sir."

"Whoever gets it keeps it," Williams adds with mercenary arrogance.

"I'm sure General Waverley's not after the spoils of war, sir."

***

Soldiers of all ranks were briefed that looting was forbidden, but trophies of war had been taken since conflicts began, and this war had been no different for soldiers wanting to go home with something of value and make their lives more comfortable than the ones they had left behind.

***

"I'm not looking for anything in particular, sir, especially not looted goods."

"Not what you would expect from a British officer, what," Williams mumbles in a lousy attempt to mimic the typecast public schooled British officer class, but Robertson stays calm, adding to the general's ever-increasing annoyance. "Well, I'm sure my boys will find a seat for you. If you go now, you should have enough time to get some chow on Uncle Sam."

Pleased with the thought of sustenance, Robertson grins. "Thank you, sir."

With dismissive arrogance, Williams moves to the map wall and turns his back on Robertson. "That will be all, Major."

Aware a salute will be a waste of time, Robertson exits but stops outside to look back in disbelief at the American general's manner.

***

Ranting and raving, Hitler looks over maps strewn over the table in the great room with disillusionment as Skorzeny stands by his side, his face showing the meeting had gone on too long for his liking. "Move Steiner's army across from the north!" Hitler shouts. "Wenck will then move the 9th and 12th through to Brandenburg!"

Several taps on the door are quickly followed by Radl entering and moving to Skorzeny's side.

"Did you pass on my orders to General Wenck, Major?" Hitler bellows on noticing him.

"Yes, my Führer," Radl answers awkwardly.

"Well?" Hitler insists on an instant reply, and Radl's glance shifts rapidly between him and Skorzeny, unsure how to answer. "Well, Major?" he impresses.

"Sorry, my Führer," Radl answers, twitching uncomfortably at the thought of having to lie. "He hasn't replied yet."

"And General Steiner?" Hitler adds with more refinement but is still determined on an immediate answer.

"No reply, my Führer."

Hitler slams his fist hard on the table as he mumbles angrily and grips the maps between his fingers. "What the hell are they doing?"

Radl moves behind Skorzeny and whispers. "A word, Otto, in private."

No matter how much he wants the obnoxious briefing to end, Skorzeny is annoyed at his second-in-command's impudence and turns his disdain on him.

"It's important, Otto," Radl insists.

Skorzeny moves to Hitler's side. "Excuse me, my Führer. May I be excused?"

Hitler turns angrily on Skorzeny as he scrunches the maps tighter into his fist before pushing them across the table onto the floor. "Yes, Colonel, you may as well be excused!"

Without waiting for Hitler to change his mind, Skorzeny salutes and follows Radl out of the room.

***

Skorzeny and Radl enter the radio room, filled with the most up-to-date communication equipment within the Reich, to allow Hitler to keep abreast of everything within his crumbling empire. Radl nods at the radio operator, who stands, then salutes and exits.

"What's going on, Karl?" Skorzeny questioned impatiently.

Radl moves to the radio and switches it on. "How's the defence of Berlin going?" he jests.

Irked, Skorzeny sits in the radio operator's chair. "It's not a joke, Karl; it's abhorrent to me. General von Stiffel's death has put me in this shit."

"I'm sure he didn't do it on purpose," Radl said solemnly.

Embarrassed by his offhand comment, Skorzeny puts his head tightly into his hands and closes his eyes. "I didn't mean it the way it came out. I mourn the general's loss as I would my father, but he should be here." He opens his eyes and looks up. "He understood the politics of high command I never will or would want to. He should be the one going through the charade, not me."

The radio crackled into life, and Radl fine-tunes it for Radio Luxembourg to come across loud and clear as an announcer reports the death of Hitler with great enthusiasm. He looks to Skorzeny for a reaction, but he shows no emotion. "Didn't you hear that, Otto?"

"Isn't that enemy radio, Karl?" Skorzeny interjects defensively. "Aren't you listening?"

"I thought I ordered a radio blackout," Skorzeny carries on to Radl's bewilderment.

"I need to know what's happening in the outside world, Otto."

"Why? It's just Allied propaganda. Ignore it."

Unable to understand Skorzeny's dismissive attitude, Radl stares his irritation. "Ignore it! This may have been part of General von Stiffel's overall plan."

Skorzeny slouches back into the chair. "I'm afraid he took that to the grave with him."

"So, what do you intend to do?

Skorzeny stands, readjusting his crumpled uniform, and then moves to the door. "I intend to stand intensely bored as the Führer moves his long-defunct armies around a map. Then no doubt, plan the invasion of America." He laughs awkwardly. "Which, as an SS officer, it is my sworn duty to carry out and which I would do to the best of my ability."

"Good luck with that."

Skorzeny grins and then exits, leaving Radl to listen to the Allied news, which could be better hearing.

***

WEDNESDAY, MAY 2^(ND) 1945

***

The afternoon sun breaks through the trees, hampering Robertson's visibility as he drives cautiously through the winding Bavarian country roads.

New to the European theatre, PFC Brady of the US 3rd Infantry Division sits at his side, slouching back with his feet on the bonnet as he chain-smokes, paying no attention to the beautiful scenery they are passing. Having never witnessed the exhilaration of war, just the long lengths of boredom, Brady feels he is on a leisurely drive instead of entering territory still held by an enemy more than capable of taking his life. "We've been looking for hours, Major," he says agitatedly. "Let's go back for some chow."

Sick of Brady's constant whinging, Robertson knows he had been assigned to him by Williams as a form of aggravation. The road comes to an abrupt end with foliage covering the tarmac forcing the jeep into a skidding stalled stop. Sensing a trap, Robertson draws his Browning and cocks it as his eyes rapidly shift around looking for a threat that doesn't instantly come. Seeing the only way out is to go back the way he came, he restarts the engine and shifts into reverse. Only metres into the foliage, German soldiers lie in defensive positions within concealed trenches and fortifications, looking down on the jeep. Believing the Nazi propaganda that the Allies were there to rape and pillage their way to victory, a seventeen-year-old grenadier stares with anger and hatred at his enemy below. Contrary to his standing orders, he decides to carry out an act of personal revenge and kill the invaders of his homeland. He cocks his unfired Sturmgewehr 44 and stands to bring it to eye height. Knowing his colleagues are duty-bound to prevent him, he quickly squeezes the trigger and opens fire for bullets to smash into and around the jeep as Robertson presses hard on the accelerator and lifts his Browning to fire aimlessly as he reverses at speed. Skidding from side to side in an attempt to keep control. Brady pulls his feet from the bonnet and struggles to lift his M1 carbine when a bullet catches him in the chest knocking him back in the seat as the M1 drops onto the road. Robertson fights to keep control but misjudges his speed and smashes into a tree, almost jolting him and Brady onto the ground. He struggles to get the jeep into first gear and speeds off, skidding as he goes but manages to keep control as he heads off with bullets trailing him along the ground. Brady groans in pain and slumps forward, and Robertson grabs his tunic to prevent him from falling out.

***

The Willys Overland Motors four-wheel drive jeep was designed as a general-purpose (GP) vehicle for the United States Army. An extraordinary success, it served in all theatres with all the Allied Armies. The word jeep comes from the GP, an abbreviation of the slang meaning general purpose.

***

Aware he is to be arrested, the young grenadier drops the Sturmgewehr to the ground as several colleagues take hold of him. Having heard the firing, Skorzeny runs through the trees and foliage to the trench to see the youngster with a Kar 98 rifle pointing hard into his neck. He looks down onto the road but can't make anything out. "What happened?" he orders.

A sergeant comes to attention before answering. "An American jeep drove up and stopped, sir. Next thing I knew, this idiot had opened fire."

Skorzeny looks at the young grenadier, mindful that at any other time during the war he would have executed him for disobeying a direct order, but with the war being almost over, he can't allow himself to order the youngster's death. "Put him in the cells. I will deal with him later."

The sergeant flicks his hand, and the young grenadier is marched off under arrest.

"I'm sorry, sir, he'd opened fire before I knew what was happening," the sergeant explains, expecting to be disciplined for not controlling his small section of men.

"Don't worry, Feldwebel," Skorzeny says solemnly. "This was inevitable to happen. I just wish it was later rather than now."

***

A small forward reconnaissance camp on the north side of Berchtesgaden valley, several miles outside of the town, has numerous GIs relaxing in the belief that the war is over.

Noticing Robertson's jeep approaching erratically, Sergeant Harvey stands animatedly amused. "It's that Brit major, sir."

Major Gates stands to look in bemusement that quickly turns to anger. "He's bloody drunk."

Believing Robertson and Brady are inebriated, the GIs laugh and whoop it up.

"Shut the fuck up!" Gates shouts, getting angrier as the GIs carry on, excited by the small amount of action that had broken the boredom of the day.

Robertson's jeep skids to a halt, and he lets go of Brady who slumps over and he flexes out his cramped aching hands. "He's been shot!" he shouts but gets little reaction from the amused Americans.

Seeing Brady slumped over, bleeding, Gates races over in shocked horror at what is unfolding in front of him. "Medic!" he shouts several times as he grits his teeth in anger.

Harvey takes hold of Brady and lowers him to the ground as Robertson alights. Gates turns his ire on the Scotsman, who speaks before the American has a chance to.

"We came under fire."

Harvey turns his forlorn look of confirmation on Gates, who walks off several paces before turning his ire back on Robertson.

"Bastards!" Gates shouts. "What the fuck happened?"

"We came under fire."

"Under fire!" Gates shouts in disbelief.

"We were at a dead end; then, as I reversed, bullets came out of nowhere."

"Maybe they haven't heard of the surrender, sir!" Harvey interrupts, to Gates' annoyance.

"Bull-shit! Hitler's fucking dead! Get the men ready to move. I'm going to kill those Kraut bastards!"

Harvey runs off at speed, gathering together the GIs who grab their weapons.

"That's not a good idea," Robertson pleads in a tone he believes may help him reason with the American major.

"You think not?"

"I know not!" Robertson argues. "You need to wait for further orders."

Playing to his men's riotousness, Gates laughs. "That isn't my style, Major. I'm not the sort of man who sits on his ass waiting for orders. I don't know how you limeys act, but when shit happens, we in the US Army kick ass."

Unable to agree with Gates' bullish posturing, Robertson shakes his head aggressively. "You're making a mistake, Major."

"It's the Krauts who have made the mistake. Where are they?" Gates demands.

Robertson debates whether to answer when Gates places his hand over his open-holstered Colt sidearm and takes the stance of a cowboy waiting for the fast draw.

"I'd rather not shoot a British officer, but when it comes to my men's safety, you're just above a Kraut in the pecking order. Where the fuck are they?"

Robertson's brow furrows and Gates draws his Colt model 1905 Marine Corps revolver, a gift from his late father, who was a career officer in the United States Marine Corps.

"I won't ask again!"

"The road south of Berchtesgaden," Robertson answers reluctantly. "Take the left fork until the road comes to an end."

"What do you mean comes to an end?"

"When it stops," Robertson answers with sarcasm. "You'll know when it comes to an end because that's where the Germans are."

Gates spins his Colt through his fingers, then drops it into its holster as four jeeps skid to a halt in front. Harvey drives the first, and the others sit in a line full of heavily armed GIs. Harvey throws Gates an M1 carbine to catch and cock before getting in.

"If you want to inform General Williams, fill your boots!" Gates shouts as he stares his condescension directly at Robertson. "But I'm going to kill those kraut bastards."

"Don't be a fool, Major!" Robertson pleads.

Gates lifts his M1 to point. "The bastards that killed Private Brady are the fools. He's only been in theatre three weeks."

"Maybe if you'd assigned me a more experienced soldier, he may have been able to read the situation and would still be alive."

"Well, maybe that reasoning was beyond me," Gates explains, aware he had been set up to take the fall but unable to explain in greater detail as it hadn't been explained to him.

"This is idiocy, Major. Take the time and reason what you have in mind."

Gates gives Robertson a scowling look of mistrust. "Maybe you led my man to his death."

"You can't lay your idiocy on me," Robertson argues with venom, which annoys Gates, but the American knows precisely what he means, having been ordered by Williams to lumber the Scotsman with the division's rookie. "You don't know what you are going up against. Think about it!"

"They don't know what's going against them. The Marne division isn't exactly new to the game," Gates said as he banged on the bonnet, and they drove off, churning up the ground.

Robertson laughs at Gates' bravado, saying the Marne Division, which has only been active since 1917, and the Coldstream Guards; he represents were founded in 1650 and had two hundred and sixty-seven years more active service and many more battle honours than their American counterparts. He moves to the radio tent and enters for the radio operator to look nonchalantly to see him but doesn't get up or salute. "Get me SHAEF, Lieutenant General Waverley's office."

The radio operator lifts the radio mike as Robertson moves to the tent flap and stares at the jeeps driving off into the distance and contemplates what he believes is to come.

***

Unaware of the dangers that await them, the jeeps make their way through the Obersalzberg Mountains. They skid to a halt where the road ends, and Gates alights, his concentration firmly fixed on the surrounding area. Harvey and the other GIs remain in the jeeps talking and making too much noise, to their commander's annoyance.

"Quiet!" Gates shouts, but his order isn't instantly obeyed.

"What is it, sir?"

"Shut the fuck up!" Gates adds angrily.

Amused as to what the problem is for their officer, the GIs quieten but don't take the situation they are in with seriousness.

"The bastards have run," Harvey calls out, making Gates give him a look of disdain.

"I don't think so, Sergeant."

Having contemplated their arrival, Skorzeny and Radl lie concealed in a camouflaged trench within a cluster of trees overlooking their enemy.

"Are the men aware of my orders?" Skorzeny whispers to Radl, who answers with a hearty nod. "Then fire," he adds, still annoyed that his original order hadn't been obeyed.

The Germans open fire, forcing Gates, Harvey and the GIs to dive for cover at the side of the jeeps, where they only manage to fire off a few shots to no avail as bullets smash all around them.

"Can you see anything, sir?" Harvey shouts.

Gates sits against the jeep as the firing slows to the odd crack before ceasing. "I haven't looked, you idiot."

Believing the fire fight is over, Harvey takes the opportunity to stand and fire off a few shots, but Gates pulls him frantically back into cover as several bullets whistle overhead.

"Keep your fucking head down, idiot."

"We're sitting ducks. I'm going for those trees," Harvey shouts as he attempts to stand, but Gates grabs his tunic to prevent him from moving.

"Move, and I will fucking shoot you myself, Sergeant."

"American commander!" Skorzeny bellows in a tone that his enemy won't mistake. "You are surrounded!"

Unable to cope with the threat of capture, Harvey breaks free and runs for the trees as he fires his M1 from the hip as a hail of bullets trails and hits him in the leg knocking him face forward onto the ground screaming in agony.

"Cease firing!" Skorzeny shouts several times until it stops.

Knowing their only way out is surrender, Gates sits uneasily. His search for vengeance waned in futility with each passing second.

Aware he may require terms for himself and his men in the future, Skorzeny shouts. "American commander! The safety of your men is your responsibility! Surrender now, and I promise you fair treatment!"

Gates agonises over his no-win situation as his glance shifts to Harvey lying vulnerably in the open and urgently needing medical attention. He stands, throws his M1 to one side, and then lifts his hands high.

"Alright, men. This is a battle we can win another day," he said, defeated.

The GIs stand and drop their weapons before raising their hands in surrender. Keeping them covered, Skorzeny, Radl and several German soldiers exit the concealed trenches onto the road.

Mystified by the sight of clean, well-dressed, disciplined German soldiers in front of him and not the dirty renegades he had expected, Gates can instantly see the SS colonel is in command. "Can I see to my injured man?"

"Take them away!" Skorzeny orders and his men push and cajole the GIs into captivity. He moves to Gates and looks down at his Colt to recognise the style of revolver and holster. "I see you are a cowboy, Major."

Several medics exit the tree line and tend to Harvey's injury. Gates looks down on the prized revolver his father had given him on the day of his commission in 1942, and Skorzeny holds out his hand to take it from him.

Aware he has surrendered, Gates unbuckles his gun belt and hands it to the Austrian, who walks off. "Excuse me, Colonel. I know this is an unusual request, but would I be able to retain my father's revolver?" Without answering, Skorzeny laughs as he carries on into the distance, with Gates rushing to catch up.

"Don't you know the war is over, Colonel?" Gates explains with a quiver in his voice.

"Lucky for you, Major, yours is," Skorzeny assures as he signals for a German soldier who moves to Gates, prods him in the side with his rifle, and forces him to move reluctantly into the tree line.

Wondering whether his war will ever be over, Skorzeny looks around at the mayhem. "Clear this area. I want nothing to say this ever happened."

***

Looking over maps of Berchtesgaden and the surrounding Obersalzberg Mountains, Williams stands with his back to the tent flap when Captain Benjamin enters and salutes.

"You wanted to see me, sir?" Benjamin said subserviently to his general, who moved his finger slowly across the map without taking his eyes off it.

"Do you know Major Gates, Captain?

"Yes, sir."

"Well, he went to confront some German renegades like the bloody gung-ho idiot he is and hasn't reported back."

"Where, sir?"

"The home of Adolf Hitler," Williams said, turning to face Benjamin with a broad smile covering his face. "I want you to go down there and take command until I arrive."

"Where, sir?" Benjamin repeats his query.

"Weren't you bloody listening?" Williams shouts as he smashes his hand off the map board. "Berchtesgaden! The Berghof! Adolf Hitler's bloody mountain retreat! What sort of dope are you?"

Benjamin straightens himself out and takes a deep breath. "What are my orders, sir?"

Oblivious that Benjamin's questioning is due to his command structure which doesn't allow his officers to take the initiative and think for themselves, Williams shakes his head angrily as he stares his contempt that one of them would need instruction.

"I don't want to go in gung-ho like Major Gates, sir," Benjamin adds to the general's narcissistic enjoyment of the subservient answer of a junior officer.

"Just quell any resistance you come across. You can do that, can't you, Captain?"

"That I can, sir," Benjamin adds confidently, then gives the perfect salute before exiting.

Williams pulls a cigar out of his jacket pocket, places it in his mouth and chews on the end with delight that the continuation of the war will give him another chance to kill more of the guilty in the genocide of his people.

***

THURSDAY, MAY 3RD 1945

***

A Third infantry division convoy, consisting of numerous M36 tank destroyers, M4 Shermans, M18 tank destroyers, trucks and all kinds of military vehicles, moves slowly through the main street of Berchtesgaden shaking the old Bavarian buildings and disturbing the town's perfect idyll as the inquisitive civilians exit their homes to see what is making the commotion. Driving in an open-topped jeep, Benjamin stops outside the Berchtesgadener Hof hotel and alights, looking around, impressed at the military might and honour bestowed on him in being placed in command.

***

The M36, referred to as the Jackson after the American Confederate civil war general, Stonewall Jackson, carries a 90mm gun which proved most effective as a tank destroyer and artillery piece. The prototype was completed in March 1943 and began to appear in the European theatre in September 1944.

***

The M4 Sherman medium tank, named after William Tecumseh Sherman, evolved from the M3 Grant, named after Ulysses S Grant and M3 Lee, named after Robert E Lee, the former the British name and the latter the American, but all were named after American civil war generals. It carries a 75mm gun with a gyrostabiliser that allows it to be fired while in motion. It entered service in 1942 and proved itself throughout the war. However, it would later fall foul of larger, heavily armoured German tanks like the Tiger and King Tiger. Still, the manufacturing might of the United States kept the numbers far more significant than anything the Germans could produce.

***

The M18 tank destroyer gun motor carriage, nicknamed the Hellcat, is a formidable armoured vehicle. Initially designed to combat the threat of tanks, the open-topped turret concealed a 76mm gun that was just as adaptable to be used in an artillery role.

***

Enjoying the morning sunshine and tranquillity, Skorzeny sits on a rocky outcrop overlooking Berchtesgaden Valley as he watches the American military build-up far below with an overriding sense of doom. He reaches into his jacket, pulls out the cigar given by von Stiffel, and places it in his mouth before unsuccessfully searching for a means of lighting it. Reluctantly, he puts it back in his pocket as he hears Hanna approaching from a distance, but wanting time to himself, he doesn't answer her frequent calls of his name. Two P51 fighters of the United States Army Air Force circle high above, but he pays them scant attention, not seeing them as a threat to his solitary figure.

***

The North American P51 Mustang single-seat fighter flew with several Allied Air Forces throughout the European theatre. Due to its long-range capabilities, it was tasked with escorting bombers of the United States Army Air Force to targets and back. After the bombing of German cities had ended, the P51 pilots were given the freedom to hunt out and destroy enemy targets, which they did to significant effect.

***

Noticing Skorzeny as a viable target, the first Mustang zeroes in on a strafing run as its engine screams into a dive. Hearing the increase in revs, Skorzeny stands looking into the bright sunlight as he attempts to hide the glare with his hands, but he cannot determine where the threat is coming from. Also hearing the engine scream, Hanna shouts in despair, making him turn to see her exit a cluster of trees to his rear and stop vulnerably in the open.
"Hanna, get back!" he screams, alarmed, as the first Mustang opens fire with machine guns and fires two T64 HVAR rockets that force him into cover as the ground around is torn up by the 50 calibre bullets as the rockets explode further up, covering him in dirt and debris. Unable to see through the smoke and dust, she shouts frantically, unaware that the second Mustang is bearing down on them. He runs toward her as it opens fire, kicking up the ground and forcing him into the cover of the treeline to land next to her as two rockets explode further up as the fighter screams overhead. Laughing uproariously, he turns onto his back to see her staring with anger and dismay in her eyes.
"You're a bloody idiot, Otto!" she shouts frantically, unable to find any humour in his actions.
"Come on, Hanna!" he mutters with a giggle.
"This isn't a game," she shouts, walking off as he tries grabbing her legs, but she kicks his hand away and carries on as he watches in his innocence.

***

Standing behind his bar, the landlord of the Berchtesgadener Hof hotel shifts awkwardly when Robertson enters on the lookout for a stiff drink. Noticing the giant bust of Hitler, he stops to slap it playfully on the top before carrying on.

"Love the décor, Herr Landlord."

The landlord smiles until the realisation the room is bedecked in National Socialist regalia and straightens his face into a pained scowl.

Robertson slaps the counter of the bar. "Whisky, make it large."

The landlord reaches under the counter and grabs a bottle of Scotch whisky and a glass.

"What can you tell me of the men in the hills, Herr Landlord?"

Unsure where the question is leading, the landlord nervously pours the whisky but spills a little on the counter. "This has nothing to do with me."

"What has nothing to do with you?" Robertson questions, making the landlord pause in thought at having pleaded his innocence without being accused.

"I'm not a Nazi. What they have done has nothing to do with me."

Looking over the landlord's traditional Bavarian lederhosen, Robertson laughs as he draws his Browning 1911 sidearm to tap on the National Socialist party badge that still sits proudly on his lapel. "I won't toy with you, Herr Landlord." He lifts the whisky in salute, downs it in one, and then places the glass on the counter for the landlord to refill. "If you don't give me the information I require, I will have this place flattened to the ground. As lovely as it is."

Believing Robertson is bluffing, the landlord grins weakly but sees the determination in the Scotsman's face making him twitch nervously.

"Normally, we have SS men who guard the Führer here," he explains, deciding not to leave out any detail. "But lately, we have had many different regiments, even Gestapo."

As the landlord continues, Robertson lifts the whisky, ready to take a drink.

"But they left after having a confrontation with an SS colonel. A large menacing scar-faced man."

Recognising Skorzeny's description, Robertson stops as the whisky touches his lips and then lowers it to the bar for the landlord to refill, only to see the glass still full.

"Do you have a telephone, Herr Landlord?" Robertson questioned impatiently.

"I do, but I'm afraid the lines have been down for some time."

Robertson's glance shifts rapidly between the phone and the landlord before holstering the Browning and leaving the whisky untouched; he exits at speed.

Conscious his National Socialist meal ticket is at an end and won't give him the benefits of the past and protect him any longer, the landlord unpins his party badge to place on the counter and lifts the whisky in salute. "To the birth of a new Germany. A stronger Germany. To the Fourth Reich," he said, then swallowed it in one and slammed the glass hard on the counter.

***

General Eisenhower, the Supreme Allied Commander in the European theatre, sits in his office with Waverley, Ingram and Lieutenant General Bedell-Smith, his chief of staff, discussing the peace to come.

***

General Dwight David Eisenhower, fondly nicknamed Ike, was born on October 14th 1890. He entered West Point military academy in June 1911 and graduated in 1915. Missing the fighting of World War One, he moved around within military circles before reaching the rank of brigadier general on October 3rd 1941. Mainly due to his administrative and organisational skills that had been recognised early in his career; when Japan attacked Pearl Harbor, he was assigned to the general staff in Washington until 1942. In December 1943, President Roosevelt promoted him to Allied Supreme Commander in Europe, which he continued to be throughout the war. He wasn't a great field commander but his facilitating between the Allied powers prevented their petty bickering and infighting.

***

Lieutenant General Walter Bedell-Smith, nicknamed the beetle, was born on October 5th 1895. He enlisted as a private soldier in the United States Army in 1911 and was commissioned as an officer while serving in France in 1917. Wounded at the Aisne-Marne offensive of 1918, he stayed in the military after the war becoming General Eisenhower's chief of staff in 1942.

***

Showing impatience for the meeting to end, Eisenhower glances at his watch. "How are things going regarding the Berghof, General Waverley?"

"General Williams reported some resistance, sir," Waverley answers, but Eisenhower interrupts impatiently.

"And is this the redoubt you worried about?"

Annoyed by his commander's attitude toward viable intelligence, Waverley recomposes himself. "With Adolf Hitler dead, I can't see how, sir."

"But there is still fighting in the area?"

"I'm afraid so, sir."

"I'm not happy with this," Eisenhower adds, turning his full attention to his most trusted advisor. "What men do we have down there, Walter?"

"General Patton's Third Army have men not far off, sir."

"No," Eisenhower mutters several times as he shakes his head. "I think we can leave Georgie out of this one."

"The hundred and first were due to jump, but it was cancelled due to the surrender. We could use them," Bedell-Smith interjects.

Eisenhower grins excitedly. "Can you see to that for me, Walter?"

Bedell-Smith nods then stands and exits.

"Keep me informed!" Eisenhower shouts as he picks up a report and begins to read.

Informed their meeting was over, Waverley and Ingram stand, salute and then exit into the busy corridor filled with military personnel from numerous Allied countries.

"What was that all about?" Ingram enquires bemused.

"What?" Waverley said, unperturbed by what had transpired.

"Ike's attitude. What was his problem?"

"He's always like that with me."

Curious about why Eisenhower wouldn't like Waverley, Ingram stops as the general carries on several paces before turning back.

"Come on, General; you can't leave it like that."

"What's to say?" Waverley explains nonplussed. "He doesn't like special operations or intelligence operatives. Still believes wars are won by advancing in lines."

Ingram laughs with disbelief as a sergeant walks over, salutes and hands Waverley a message.

"Thank you, Sergeant," Waverley said as he opened the message and reads as his face changed to one of concern.

"What is it, sir?"

Waverley's mind strays until his face breaks into a long lingering smile.

"Sir!" Ingram said, his tone insistent on an answer.

"It's from Major Robertson. We have to get to Berchtesgaden."

"Why's that, sir?"

"We'll see when we get there."

***

      His eyes closed in an enforced state of relaxation, Skorzeny lies on his bunk enjoying the moment. Footsteps repeat down the corridor with confirmation that his rest is over, and he opens his tired eyes when there is a rap on the door, then the handle rattles impatiently.

Puzzled as to why the door is locked, Radl shouts. "Otto, what the hell are you doing in there? You'd better come to see this!"

Skorzeny sits and lights a cigarette to smoke, enjoying every draw's solitude.

Radl impatiently kicks the door several times and shouts out. "Otto!" With reluctance, Skorzeny stands and opens the door to see a smiling Radl impatiently waiting.

"You need to come and see this."

***

      Leaning on the terrace parapet, Hanna looks up through the camouflaged netting into the sky as 30 Douglas C47s of the United States Army Air Force fly over to drop hundreds of paratroopers of the US 101st Airborne Division into the valley below.

***

      Activated as an infantry division on August 15th 1942, at Camp Claiborne, Louisiana, the 101st Airborne Division was specially trained for air assault. Their first commander, General William C Lee gave them their motto, the screaming eagles when he informed recruits; they had no history but had a rendezvous with destiny.

***

      Commercially named the DC3, the Douglas C47 sky train is an American fixed-wing propeller-driven cargo aircraft. Designed in 1935, its speed and range were well used within the 1930s and World War Two air transport industries by all Allied Armies and Air Forces in every theatre of operation.

***

      Radl moves across the terrace to the parapet, followed closely by Skorzeny, who flicks his spent cigarette over the side. Their glances follow Hanna's into the sky, and they are instantly taken by the magnificent sight of the paratroopers gracefully floating back to Earth. "Should we open fire?" Radl enquired.

Not wanting to waste their limited supply of 88-inch shells that he knows will be required at a later date, Skorzeny plays down the sight of the Americans. "You disturbed me for this?"

Radl taps on his collar's left side, pointing to his rank. "I don't make the decisions, Otto."

Noticing Skorzeny's demeanour, Hanna enquires about his well-being, but he ignores her concern and adjusts his stare to the valley below as the last of the paratroopers disappear out of sight.

"It's just a show of strength. Lightly armed paratroopers sent to intimidate us."

"And are you intimidated, Otto?" Hanna adds playfully.

"A little, but don't tell the Americans. They'll just get big-headed."

Hanna turns to walk off, but Skorzeny takes her hand and pulls her back to face him.

"Is everything alright, Hanna?"

"Of course. Why would there be a problem?"

Noticing the tension, Radl moves to one side but stays on the terrace.

"You seem annoyed with me," Skorzeny said as he tightened his grip, but Hanna brushed his hand away and moved off a few paces.

"Annoyed? Why would I be annoyed? I'm just tired and need a lie-down," she said as she walked off, leaving Skorzeny staring solemnly at her back, and Radl laughed, amused at having witnessed his awkwardness.

"As if I don't have enough shit to contend with," Skorzeny mutters as he walks off.

"Yes, and I'm stuck in the middle," Radl adds as his irritated stare shifts between them as they move in opposite directions.

***

Walking around the burnt-out remains of von Stiffel's Junkers, Benjamin trawls through the ashes looking for souvenirs and picks up several blackened mementoes, unaware of their historical importance. His glance shifts from the Junkers to the paratroopers gathering their parachutes when a C47 flying overhead takes his attention as it rounds the surrounding Obersalzberg Mountains. He keeps his eye on it as it comes down to land, bumping across the uneven ground and coming to a halt just short of him. He adjusts his uniform as the doors open, and Williams jumps out without allowing the aircrew to put the step out.

Well aware of his general's demand to be greeted like a conquering hero, he salutes and comes to attention. "Welcome to Berchtesgaden, sir."

Without returning the salute, Williams looks at the men under his command with great pride. "How's everything going, Captain?"

Benjamin lowers his arm awkwardly but remains rigidly attentive. "We have the area surrounded, sir."

Williams walks off a few paces and looks up into the surrounding mountains and hills. "I won't be happy until we own it."

"That won't take long, sir," Benjamin said to complement the vain glorious general. "You have everything required for an assault."

Williams glares at his subordinate. "How would you know, Captain?" he said, making Benjamin shuffle uncomfortably. "This Berghof must be small." His glance fixes on the burnt-out Junkers. "I couldn't see it from the air."

"It was a JU 52, sir."

"I can see that, Captain. I'm not a bloody idiot," Williams snarls, forcing Benjamin to step back in intimidation. "I won't be happy until the entire Third Reich is burnt to the ground and all the bastards responsible for its genocide are hanging from gallows."

***

Williams and Benjamin enter the Berchtesgadener Hof hotel looking around at its quaintness.

"I've requisitioned this hotel for your headquarters, sir." Benjamin grovels.

The curious landlord turns to see them. "Gentlemen, how can I help you?"

Noticing the Nazi regalia, Williams instantly turns angry. "Get all this shit down immediately!"

Benjamin exits at speed and re-enters seconds later with several GIs who tear down and throw the Nazi regalia unceremoniously to the floor.

"What you don't want, burn!" Williams shouts even though he is aware the GIs are only after souvenirs that have a monetary value, not historic.

With a hefty shove, a GI pushes Hitler's bust over to chip the highly-polished floorboards bringing a large howl of approval from the general as it rocks from side to side. Desperate to place the bust of his idol back on its pedestal, the landlord refrains, aware it wouldn't be in his best interest as he watches his reception decimated of the past twelve years of his life.

"If I were Ike, I would lay waste to this crap hole and leave it where only cattle could graze and the country incapable of committing war or genocide again. Now, what can you tell me of the situation, Captain?" Williams said, turning his full attention to Benjamin, expecting just as quick a reply.

"Well, sir," Benjamin stutters, not having expected the enquiry. "All I know at this time is we have some Germans holed up in the hills that won't surrender."

"So, we could have a full-scale operation going down, and there may be only a dozen fucking renegades hiding in the bushes with catapults." Even though it was he who had ordered Benjamin to the Obersalzberg, Williams always deflects any wrongdoing onto others to keep his self-importance.

"We've received intelligence, sir," Benjamin blusters with trivial information as it comes to mind.

"Intelligence," Williams interrupts incredulously. "And where did this so-called intelligence come from?"

"From the Bürgermeister and other locals we questioned, sir."

"Bürgermeister! Locals!" General Williams snarls in disbelief. "Are you pulling my fucking chain? Most were fully paid-up Nazis until we came to town. What artillery do we have?"

"M36s, Shermans, Hellcats."

"That will do the job," Williams says with a sizeable malicious grin. "Line them up in the valley and put some fucking heat down on that goddam mountain. Kill anything that moves."

"The hundred and first did get another jump in, sir," Benjamin adds with light-heartedness, which only adds to Williams' annoyance.

"Then it's all been worth it!" he snipes. "Get that hardware set up now. I want everything alive on that mountain dead before nightfall."

***

Six M36 tank destroyers, supported by eight Shermans and three Hellcats, drive through Berchtesgaden with shuddering violence, but this time, the locals remain indoors, nervously aware that a battle is about to commence.

***

On a rocky outcrop overlooking Berchtesgaden valley, Robertson glares through his binoculars as the American hardware takes up positions. They begin firing, sending shells to explode on the mountain, with each volley moving through the tree line toward the estimated part of the Berghof, but within seconds, a hail of shells emanates from the hill as the German artillery opens up. He turns his binoculars back into the valley as the shells explode in front of the Americans, forcing the overconfident commanders into their turret, slamming their lids closed, and firing aimlessly. Aware they are in the open and an easy target, they reverse into a fighting retreat.

***

Unaware that the explosions they are listening to are from enemy fire, Williams and Benjamin stand outside the Berchtesgadener Hof hotel and watch in shock as the American hardware trundles past with several of their commanders exiting their turrets relieved to have escaped unscathed.

Benjamin's head swings from side to side as he counts the tanks through with bewilderment. "The Krauts must be well dug in, sir." Believing all battles, no matter how big or small, will have their casualties, Williams enquires nonchalantly. "How many did we lose?"

"They all made it, sir," Benjamin answered astounded.

Stunned, Williams steps away before turning his inquisitiveness back onto the captain. "We lost none?"

"I counted them all back, sir."

"What the hell is going on?"

"We've been lucky, sir."

Williams steps onto the road and watches the American Military vehicles head into the distance, disappointed that his plan hadn't worked. "Do you think so, Captain? Ike wants this concluded fast, and that's what I intend to deliver."

***

Robertson lowers his binoculars and looks at his watch as the sound of a jeep approaching catches his attention. He turns as it pulls up behind for Waverley to alight, leaving Captain Ingram and Captain Jacobs inside.

"I'll get a ride back with the Brit," Waverley said, moving toward Robertson, and the jeep drives off slowly with Jacobs' stare shifting with bewilderment between the Scotsman and his general.

"What's his story?" Robertson asked, turning his intrigued glare on Jacobs.

Waverley looks around to see his officer still staring, engrossed.

"Captain Jacobs, I don't believe he's got one."

"He's got the look of a man who wants one, though."

"He's probably curious as to why I'm talking to a limey," Waverley laughed. "Everyone who enters the slimy world of intelligence wants to gain some sort of notoriety, especially junior officers with no history." Unconvinced, Robertson turns his stunned attention to the American general. "Did you see the advance, sir? Not one of your tanks was hit." Having expected to see the burning hulks of military vehicles, Waverley walks to the edge of the rocky outcrop to look into Berchtesgaden valley.

"I've seen the German army in action from both sides, General, and believe me when I say this, they were holding back."

"They may not have the fighting capability!"

"Their firing was direct and precise."

"Why would they hold back?" Waverley questioned with an awkward laugh.

"You tell me?"

Waverley turns to Robertson with a sardonic smile. "Could Colonel Skorzeny recognise you, Will?"

Taken back by words that seem to have come out of nowhere, Robertson's face grimaces as he debates why the question had been asked in the first place. "I never met him. His time in the limelight was well after mine had diminished."

Waverley moves to Robertson's jeep and climbs inside to bang hard on the bonnet. "Come on, Will, let's get the hell out of here."

"Why do you want to know if I know Skorzeny, sir?" Robertson enquires, moving to the jeep but pauses, his stare fixed rigidly on the American.

"Get in; I need a drink," Waverley said, ignoring his concern.

Keeping his irate eyes on the general, Robertson gets into the driver's seat and turns the engine on. "I've got a feeling I will need one too."

"Just drive, Will; I need that drink now."

Without taking his stare off the American, Robertson puts the jeep into gear and then drives off, leaving a dusty storm in their path.

***

Agitated at having escaped one siege only to end up in another, Dr Bergman's large glass of schnapps shakes as he stares out of the great room's panoramic window into the night's darkness. There is a light tap on the door, and Skorzeny enters expecting to see Hitler.

"The Führer wants to see me, Doctor."

"He's asleep, Colonel," Dr Bergman mutters without taking his stare off the window. "I'm afraid I had to sedate him."

Annoyed his time had been wasted, Skorzeny turns to exit, but Dr Bergman calls out stopping him in the doorway.

"Pardon me, Colonel, but I sent for you."

Angrily, Skorzeny goes to react to being summoned when he notices the man of medicine taking a large nervous drink of the schnapps.

"What's going on, Doctor?"

"I have bad news, Colonel. The Führer needs to be hospitalised at the earliest."

"That may prove awkward," Skorzeny mutters in disbelief of a statement he could well do without.

"He won't live without it, Colonel."

Skorzeny ponders why he was being informed of overwhelming news at such an inappropriate time. "Isn't that why General von Stiffel brought you, Doctor?"

"I'm not the Führer's physician," Dr Bergman answers solemnly with an awkward laugh as he turns from the window to face the ever-increasingly aggravated colonel. "I'm so far down the pecking order I'd be surprised if he truly knows who I am. I know nothing about the medications Dr Morell has him taking. Most are of his own making and very dubious as such, but I dare not cease their experimentation in case it has an even worse detriment on his health."

***

Dr Theodore Morell was born in July 1886 and was notorious for his many unconventional medical treatments. He treated the German Führer as early as 1936 and cured him of several ailments. Nicknamed Der Reichsspritzenmeister (Reichmaster of Injections), he mixed his concoctions, including psychoactive drugs such as heroin and methamphetamine, which he administered to Hitler, who believed had cured him of his many problems but only masked the deeper-rooted complications.

***

Conscious von Stiffel had picked Dr Bergman to accompany Hitler as he is a man who would not be missed; Skorzeny decides to compliment him instead of adding to his inner turmoil. "I have faith in you, Doctor, but you must have faith in yourself and keep the Führer alive." He moves for the door.

"I'm afraid his many malaises go further than my humble capabilities, Colonel," Dr Bergman said, stopping Skorzeny to look back.

"This goes further than all our capabilities, Doctor, but you are the one with the medical certification, so inevitably, the responsibility lies with you. I needn't remind you what is at stake if the Führer dies."

"Before you go, Colonel, I have something for you," Dr Bergman said, reaching into his pocket and taking out the envelope he had guarded since taking it from von Stiffel's body.

"What's this, Doctor?"

"The Führer's last will and testament. I took it off General von Stiffel after his death. I thought it was important enough to require protection."

Skorzeny stares at the envelope, desperate to read the contents but refrains. "You did well, Doctor. Thank you."

Dr Bergman takes a deep breath of anxiousness as Skorzeny exits, leaving him more nervous and agitated than when the conversation had begun as he drains the Schnapps and then hunts out a refill.

***

Pleased they are not out in the cold with the men who surround the Berghof, Williams and Benjamin drink fine single malt Scotch whisky in the lounge of the Berchtesgadener Hof hotel. Waverley and Robertson enter to notice the relaxed feel within the room, and Williams stands showing signs of inebriation to greet his bitter rival.

"Lieutenant General Waverley."

"Lieutenant General Williams."

Weighing each other up, the generals shake hands with mutual mistrust.

"What brings you down here?" Williams questions, making Waverley grin, aware his presence isn't desired. "I knew there must be an alternate reason for sending in your man."

Robertson laughs at the thought of being Waverley's man, and Williams turns his irritability on him.

"Did you get the intelligence you wanted, Major?"

"No, sir!"

"I thought as much with the big guns coming in," Williams said, turning his displeasure onto Waverley.

"So, what is the situation, General?" Waverley enquires. "As you see it," he adds, giving Benjamin a fleeting glance being aware Williams relies heavily on his subordinates for everything.

Williams' glance shifts rapidly between Benjamin and Waverley.

"Extreme at best but hardly past my military capabilities... I intend to have the entire area carpet bombed," he adds in a vainglorious attempt to increase his importance even though Eisenhower had given that order. "Just to make sure none of them survives," he adds with a wink. "That's hardly military capable, General," Robertson interrupts, flabbergasted. "Carpet bombing is indiscriminate and will inevitably result in the deaths of the innocent."

"I didn't know our British friend here was a bleeding heart," Williams replies with bile. "If the result is the deaths of German civilians, then it all works for me. I don't see any of them as innocent."

Angered by such a narcissistic statement, Robertson interrupts as he turns to see Waverley's reaction. "Don't you see a problem in that, sir?"

"Should I, Major," Williams interjects. "Aerial reports of the Obersalzberg show nothing. Then I sent in my armour, and within seconds, they came under heavy sustained fire."

"Then they are hiding something," Robertson explains with what he sees as the obvious.

"Themselves," Benjamin interjects flippantly with a teasing laugh that pleases his general.

"I flew over this so-called Berghof several times and couldn't make out Hitler's Mountain retreat."

Irked to agree with Williams, Waverley grins. "I couldn't see anything when I flew over myself."

"Doesn't that validate what I've just said?" Robertson adds positively to Waverley's nodding agreement.

"Listen, Major, when I want the advice of a British officer, never mind that of a subordinate, I will make sure he knows well in advance," Williams snipes.

"You don't seem to like the Germans or the British, General," Robertson said, then added without allowing him to reply. "If you carpet bomb and obliterate the area as you so desperately want, we will never know what they are hiding."

"I don't care, Major."

"Well, maybe you should put your drink down and take a moment to think about it."

"I don't need to," Williams said with pride his adversary is unaware of. "Ike's already sanctioned my operation."

Curious about why something as important had already been decided without his guidance, Waverley glares at Williams. "Why would that be, General?"

"He wants his war over. What else can I say?"

"How long do we have?" Waverley questions irately.

"He wants it done now."

"How long if you stall, General?" Robertson interrupts with determination.

"Do I need to stall, General?" Williams adds, turning his glare on Waverley as he ignores Robertson's ill-disciplined questioning tone.

"I believe we do," Waverley answered on his British friend's behalf.

"If I knew what was happening and decided to stall," Williams whimpers playing he is in command to his audience. "Say seventy-two hours."

Waverley knows the only way Williams would agree to his request would only be because that is how long it would take to get archived aerial footage of the Obersalzberg and compare them to recently taken photographs and get the Air Force involved to plan a bombing raid.

"Then make that decision, General," he adds in an ordering tone.

Agitated but well aware that Waverley has the authority to overrule him, Williams decides to play along and nods his understanding. "I will see what I can do, General."

"What do you hope to find out, sir?" Benjamin interrupts.

"Just plain and simple intelligence," Robertson adds, making Williams turn curiously to face him.

"I've heard that one before, Major, on many occasions, but as always, the intelligence is far from the truth."

"What else can I say, General?"

"Exactly what you intelligence types always say, absolutely nothing."

"Well, then, don't ask!"

Robertson's apparent insubordination against a superior officer irks Waverley as his irritated stare is directed at him.

"We need the time to send an operative in."

"Have you got anyone in mind, General?" Williams enquires, and Waverley laughs, nodding at the shocked Robertson.

"I take it I've just volunteered?"

"You could say that, Will, but you only have yourself to blame for arguing the stupidity of the task at hand. You are the one who seems to need the question answered."

Waverley and Williams shake hands then Robertson and Waverley walk off.

"What a pompous bastard," Robertson said, turning his irate stare onto Williams, who was staring his contempt at him for not having given a salute.

"That's enough of that, Will, even if you are right."

"So much for being off the active register," Robertson said with a deep nervous sigh.

"How could you be off the active register when King and Country require you to step up again?"

"Fuck King and country," Robertson snipes. "And fuck this war. And fuck the Germans."

Waverley laughs as he slaps the Scotsman on the back. "That's it, Will; keep up the positive attitude, and this will all be over soon."

"Yeah… No doubt when I've got six feet of cold earth over my head."

***

FRIDAY, MAY 4th 1945

***

To prevent anyone from entering or leaving Berchtesgaden Valley, the Americans positioned men and set up hastily made barbed wire barriers across all roads and tracks. A Soviet Gaz Jeep drives toward one of the roadblocks to put the GIs on alert. A vague, shadowy figure sits in the driver's seat, staring forward without moving as the GIs cock their weapons and take up defensive positions. The jeep door opens slowly, and Captain Vasteroff steps onto the road feigning intrigue as to why his journey was being stopped.

***

A robust, dark, devious man. Kapitan Alexei Vasteroff was born in 1894 in the Tsarist state of Georgia, like his beloved ruler, Joseph Vissarionovich Dzhugashvili, lovingly known to some of the Russian people as the man of steel (Stalin). He joined the Tsarist secret police (Okhrana) before the October Revolution of 1917 but soon changed sides to fight against the White Russians in the civil war. He became a member of the Peoples Militsiya in 1925, and in 1934, he was transferred to the Soviet secret police (NKVD). Then, in June 1944, he was assigned to the 3rd Ukrainian Front as an intelligence officer.

***

The secret police of the Bolshevik Russians, the Narodnyi Komissariat Vnutrennikh Del (Peoples Commissariat for Internal Affairs) (NKVD), was set up in 1934 and was responsible for military counter-intelligence and the protection of state security of the Soviet Union through political and state sanctioned oppression. This policy resulted in the murder and torture of millions of Russian citizens and foreign nationals purported to be enemies of the Bolshevik cause.

***

The 3rd Ukrainian Front was founded on October 20th 1943. In their fight against the fascists, they liberated Bulgaria, Romania, Hungary and the eastern part of Austria, capturing the Austrian capital Vienna.

***

Vasteroff had been charged under the direct orders of Stalin, who had been made aware of the possibility of the Wagnerian Assignment via his agents in both the British and American intelligence services to go directly to the Obersalzberg. Stalin had always received such intelligence from his security services with the disinclination of never truly trusting the source or understanding how a man could betray his birth country for an ideal, even though his communist ideals required such actions from many of his followers.

"What is going on?" Vasteroff said in an over-friendly, well-read English accent.

Left in command, a US sergeant moves forward, looking his first Red Army officer up and down with mistrust. "That's not for me to say, sir."

"Not that it matters," Vasteroff adds with an amused confident smile that had been well rehearsed and designed to reassure trust. "I'm on my way to Vienna. I need to get through."

"I can't let you, sir."

Feigning shock and bewilderment, Vasteroff steps back slightly. "Can't let me, but we are Allies in the fight against fascism," he adds, looking around. "So, what's going on?"

"Sorry, sir, I can't say."

"But I need to get to Vienna, Sergeant."

"Sorry, sir, but I am acting under orders not to allow anyone in or out."

"I see. Then I will have to make other arrangements."

Using his highly trained, devious mind, Vasteroff backs off to his jeep, keeping the terrain and the GIs in his sights as he gathers as much intelligence as possible. He gets into the jeep and drives off, watched by the mystified GIs.

"What do you make of that, sarge?" one of the GIs enquires.

The sergeant moves to his jeep, picks up the radio mike, and switches the set on. "That's above my pay grade, but I will inform the decision-makers of what has happened. They can decide what to make of it."

***

Waverley, Ingram, and Jacobs sit drinking fine whisky and smoking large cigars within the dining room of the Berchtesgadener Hof hotel when a lieutenant enters, salutes and then hands Waverley a note to read.

"What's going on, sir?" Ingram enquires, bemused by the change in his general's facial expressions.

"This is going to get out of control," Waverley mutters. "A Russian officer has requested passage through the valley to Vienna."

"Not the best route, sir," Ingram utters with intense interest.

"When refused, he just left."

"Sounds a little suspect to me, sir."

Jacobs interjects naively, believing the Russians should have a part to play in destroying the Germans hiding in the mountains. "Won't that just fuel their suspicions, sir?"

"If he were allowed through, his suspicions wouldn't need fuelling, Captain!" Waverley snipes.

"But we are Allies, sir," Jacobs adds, and Waverley laughs at the thought.

"If I know the Russians, they already know what's going on."

"Surely that's not true," Jacobs adds nervously.

"Captain Jacobs, I need a word with Captain Ingram in private."

Reluctantly, Jacobs moves off a few paces but stops to loiter within earshot.

"What's going on, sir?" Ingram enquires, aware Waverley must have something in mind.

"I'm going to send Major Robertson in."

"The Brit? He'll love you for that."

"He keeps saying he's bored with a sore ass. It will give him something to do."

"What do you think he can do, sir?" Ingram adds, curious to hear his general's answer.

"Find out what they are hiding."

"And do you think they are hiding something, sir?"

"Past events tell me yes," Waverley said, then added. "Major Robertson believes so too. We don't have the time to piss about, and with Ike wanting his war concluded, we will have to act fast."

"Robertson may know what is going on."

Waverley moves to the window taking in the surrounding Obersalzberg Mountains. "I'm afraid not. He's been out of the game too long."

Keeping his eyes in the distance, he is concerned that Robertson may not be up to the task but knows he is their best chance of discovering the truth and hopes his Scottish friend will understand. "I just hope he hasn't lost the edge he had before his capture and imprisonment."

***

Robertson relaxes on a rocky outcrop as he admires the beauty of the Obersalzberg, with the sun slowly dropping through the clouds behind him. Lifting his binoculars, he frustratingly scans the area as Waverley drives up in his jeep and pulls over a short distance off.

"I'm pleased someone has the time to enjoy the view," Waverley quips as he alights.

"I spent many days in the Berghof looking over this beautiful countryside, General," Robertson replied with nostalgic seriousness. "You talk as though you miss it."

"I do," Robertson answers honestly without a moment's thought. "The tranquillity, the peace. You forgot the world was tearing itself apart."

"That must have been nice for you while the rest of us were at war." Amused by the general's scathing remark, Robertson lowers the binoculars as he slowly turns to face Waverley, who laughs. "I haven't heard of anyone telling me about you in a trench up to your balls in shit and mud, General."

"That's why I thought of you," Waverley said as he sat and placed his arm around Robertson's shoulders. "You don't chase a stick if you've got a dog to do it for you."

"And aren't I pleased you did?"

"Because of recent events, I believe I have made the right choice in you."

"Why would you think of me in the first place?" Robertson said, anxiously to hear the general's explanation.

"I've read your file."

Robertson grins in bewilderment that the Americans have a file on such a low figure as him. "Everything that happened to me is common knowledge, sir."

"Not all."

"I'm not sure you need a file on me, General. I'm sure American Intelligence has enough on their plate without wasting their time."

"We have a file on everyone. Enemy and ally alike," Waverley adds with a mischievous wink. "We need to know who is on our side."

"I should be honoured that you still thought of me after reading it."

"You should."

"You must have been mightily bored, sir."

Waverley laughs. "Any guesses about what may be going on?"

Robertson stands, brushing Waverley's arm aside as he moves closer to the edge. "No, sir, but they are definitely hiding something."

"What makes you come to that conclusion?"

"From most places around here you could see the Berghof. It didn't stand out from every angle, but it was visible if you knew where to look. Now no matter how hard I try I can't make it out."

"Maybe you've forgotten."

"No, like I said, it was visible, and I know it was from this very spot. Now, I think it has been deliberately hidden."

Waverley moves to Robertson and looks over the mountains. "Maybe we should get some aerial photos down here to help locate its exact whereabouts."

"There's no need, General. I know how to get there walking. This was my spot to get away from all the National Socialist shit of the Berghof and breathe some fresh air. I walked it on many occasions. Now because I can't visibly locate it doesn't mean it isn't there. It just means it has been well concealed."

Curious, Waverley stares directly into Robertson's eyes while waiting for him to finish.

"Sounds like the Wagnerian Assignment is going ahead without Hitler," Robertson mutters ironically.

Waverley laughs awkwardly, suspicious at the mention of what was supposed to be a secret, and Waverley rubs his chin as he keeps his irate stare on Robertson.

"We also have files, General. Even ones our closest Allies wouldn't expect or want us to have."

***

The Allied intelligence communities had picked up vague reports, and rumours had been past amongst the soldiers of all armies that fanatical Nazis intended to put up a defence and create a national redoubt within the Obersalzberg region around Berchtesgaden and the Berghof where Hitler was to be protected. These reports had been exaggerated beyond recognition of the first telling to finish with thousands of SS men and the Werewolves who had sworn to die rather than allow their Führer to fall into enemy hands being posted there. American military intelligence had known for some time that there was a plan code-named the Wagnerian Assignment but had taken the reports as rumours with little substance or intelligence to back up the claim even though they had classified it as top secret.

***

In believing the knowledge of the Wagnerian Assignment must have been shared, Waverley laughs louder but holds his anger that it was without his knowledge. "There's more to this than we think, and we only have a short window of opportunity before the administrators flatten the place," he adds. "Do you want to pull out, Will?"

Apprehensive about a mission he believes he cannot carry out, Robertson grins his discomfort as he fidgets nervously. "Is it still on?"

"You're not under orders," Waverley adds, sensing the tension in his voice. "No one will think badly of you if you decide not to go."

Unable to take the dishonour of not doing his duty would cause him and British intelligence, Robertson laughs fearfully.

"This is between me and you, Will; no one else has to know. Not even your boss."

"We all have a job to do, General. I just thought I would enquire if it's still going ahead," Robertson adds uneasily. "You know how quickly things change."

Having sent many men and women on missions they had little chance of returning from, Waverley doesn't take the thought lightly of sending his friend into the devil's lair and grins, disturbed by Robertson's resolute stand to do his duty.

***

SATURDAY, MAY 5TH 1945

***

Morning mist and dew settle over the Obersalzberg as the sun rises in the distance making a chilly but beautiful start to the day. Dressed in the soiled, bullet-ridden, blood-stained uniform of a long-dead SS scharführer, Robertson nervously reminisces about his mistreatment at the hands of the Gestapo after his capture and whether he is doing the right thing. Aware of the danger, Waverley and Ingram sit inside an open-top jeep staring at the twitchy Scotsman with little intent of offering an observation on what he is about to do.

"You'd better be on your way, Will," Waverley said, looking at his watch. "The covering artillery begins in ten minutes."

Not being made aware of the barrage, Robertson looks away to hide his anxiety at avoiding the indiscriminate destructive shells and stoically concealed German soldiers on the lookout for potential infiltrators.

"We've set up several artillery pieces in the valley to keep the German's heads down long enough for you to make your way in."

"That will also keep my head down, General. Those shells can't distinguish between friend and foe."

Waverley keeps his amusement to himself as he outstretches his hand for Robertson to shake. "You've got those nine minutes. Good luck, Will; I will catch you later."

"I'm going to give this volunteering thing a bit more thought in the future, sir," Robertson said in awkward amusement.

"What future?" Waverley adds jovially with a wink as their hands come apart.

As he heads down the road, Robertson nervously taps the jeep's bonnet with his knuckles. Several hundred feet later, he stops looking around to get his bearings and sees Waverley's concerned eyes haven't him before moving into the tree line and disappearing. Making his way up through the forested area, he takes cover within view of the German trenches, concealed by camouflage netting, sandbags and broken foliage, and can only make the movement of the defenders. His adrenalin takes hold, and he looks at his watch, then takes several deep anguished breaths as he attempts to calm but nothing can ease his trepidation. Artillery roaring in the distance informs him the barrage has begun making him grimace into cover as the shells fly over to explode in and around the German trench line in front, far too close for comfort. As the area is covered with thick smoke designed to conceal his approach, after several more breaths, he moves forward, keeping his head well down, but one of the German soldiers notices him nearing and stands to aim his rifle, ready to fire.

"Don't shoot!" Robertson shouts, lifting his hands high into the air, feigning he isn't a threat, but the trench takes a direct hit killing the occupants and knocking him back onto the ground as the concussion smashes into his body. After several seconds, he comes around bleeding from a head wound and wipes his eyes to smear blood across his face as he looks around, dazed and confused, until he focuses on the smouldering trench in front as several more shells land close by, forcing him to crawl across the ground and drop into the trench next to the bodies of the recently deceased Germans which shocks him at their mutilation as he cowers for the next shell to hit but falls unconscious. Ready for an expected assault, German soldiers make their way through a support trench and take up defensive positions, followed by a medic who looks around the devastation of the dead, then makes his way to Robertson, who is groaning in pain as he comes around dazed and confused. The artillery ceases bringing an uneasy calm as the cool morning breeze clears the smoke. Robertson attempts to stand, but his legs buckle and he falls to the ground.

"Just take it easy, Sergeant, you're not in danger anymore," the medic explains as he attentively tends to his wounds.

Saddened at the sight of the dead soldiers, Robertson lies back, sensitive that they had been killed when the war was all but over.

***

Waverley and Ingram sit in the dining room of the Berchtesgadener Hof hotel when Jacobs bursts in excited with the news he is desperate to convey.

"I take it you have something for me," Waverley said as he took a large mouthful of cold Bockwurst sausage.

"The eastern checkpoints have reported large numbers of Russian soldiers, sir."

Ingram slams his knife and fork hard onto the table. "What now, sir?"

Having expected their arrival, Waverley carries on eating unperturbed. "Now we finish our food with the thought that we must contend with the bloody Bolsheviks."

"What about General Williams, sir?"

"I think we can leave him out of this, Captain. I've dealt with the Reds before. I speak their language."

"I didn't know you spoke Russian, sir?" Jacobs questioned naively.

"Yeah, Captain!" Waverley snarls. "I'm fluent in Russian diplomacy," he adds with a sardonic laugh as he pushes his food aside, having lost his appetite. "All the words you wouldn't want to hear at a tea party."

***

Enjoying the beauty of the mountains and valleys, Skorzeny and Radl stand on the terrace. Hanna walks up behind, noticed by Radl, who walks off, not wanting to know or be a part of what is sure to be a private moment.

"Now, to add to the fun, we have the bloody Red Army to contend with," Skorzeny said, turning to Radl only to be confronted by Hanna's beauty.

"Karl's gone, Otto."

"I'm pleased you are here," Skorzeny adds sentimentally as he looks around to ensure they are alone. "I've been waiting for the opportune moment as I need a private word." He takes her hand and pulls her to one side. "I've given this a lot of thought."

"Sounds ominous," she said with a giggle.

"I want you to get out of here before it all comes in around us."

"I'd rather stay," she adds with an amused grin that hides her horror at such a statement.

"But it's not safe."

"Safe!" she argues. "You didn't think it would be safe when you volunteered?"

"Volunteered!" he said with an awkward laugh. "I didn't know you would be here."

"That shouldn't make a difference. I'm not averse to danger."

He attempts to play to her sensibilities. "You're not a combatant. You shouldn't be here."

Angered by his sexist insensibilities, she pulls her hand away and walks off several paces before looking back. "I'm going nowhere unless you come with me," she said, aware his sense of duty would never allow him to desert his post.

"You know I can't do that."

"Then change the subject. I don't want to discuss this any further."

Skorzeny turns his stare into the distance. "We all need to get out of here, but General von Stiffel's last orders to me were to protect the Führer."

"But he's dead, Otto."

"That changes nothing. I have never disobeyed an order; you know that."

"And I thought you were a soldier with the courage to disobey when the reasoning was right," she interrupts, unnerving him with her honesty.

"I don't intend to start now."

"Maybe your best option is to get the Führer out," she said, adding rationality to their heated conversation.

"If only it was that simple."

"Make it simple! You're in command. Whatever you order will go." Skorzeny knows she is correct, but aware they are surrounded, he doesn't see it as a viable option. "I'm not in command; the Führer is."

"The Führer isn't fit enough for command; you know that! You need to take over, make the decisions on his behalf and make them as soon as possible. Every second that passes makes it harder for him to get away from here."

Skorzeny knows Göring and Himmler had been stripped of office after they attempted to take over and moves to her side, but she walks off a few paces before turning back.

"I'll leave you to your thoughts. You have a lot to think about."

***

Within sight of the Obersalzberg Mountains, Red Army soldiers of the 3rd Ukrainian front dance and make merry in one of the large open fields on the eastern side of Berchtesgaden Valley. Several large fires burn brightly, adding to the sense that the Russians believe the war is over. A Willys jeep carrying Waverley and Jacobs drives along the country lanes and slows as it passes the masses of soldiers who pay them no consideration. Jacobs observes the men of the Red Army for the first time with great admiration and awe as he sees them as the true conquerors of Nazi Germany, but Waverley's intelligence forward, thinking mind only sees them as significant a threat to world peace as the Nazis had been.

"A grand sight, sir!"

"A what?" Waverley calls out, angered at his subordinates' absurdity. Several T34 and KV1 tanks turn in front of the jeep, forcing Jacobs to break hard and skid to a halt on the grass verge, only just missing a tree. Waverley stands and swears at the tank commanders, who grin back, amused by the American general's exaggerated animation. Embarrassed for not watching the road, Jacobs turns to Waverley.

"Sorry, sir."

"It's not your fault, Captain," Waverley mutters before adding a shout. "It's the bloody Russians!" He looks around with disdain at a people he abhors and believes, through personal experience cannot be trusted. His eyes fix on the shadowy outline of Vasteroff standing just out of view to one side. "Do you speak Russian, Captain?" he asks Jacobs, who answers in a nervous asinine attempt to conceal his fluency.

"A little, sir, but not very good."

"Is that so, Captain? Well, maybe we know the same profanities."

After a moment's contemplation, Jacobs worries that his fluency would be known to his commander and could put him in danger in the future. "I thought you could speak Russian, sir?"

Waverley laughs at the thought of spending any of his valuable time learning a foreign language. "Diplomatic Russian, Captain," he shouts. "I picked up a few swear words in Yalta. That's all you need to know when you speak to the treacherous bastards." He stares at Jacobs, aware he has lied but oblivious to why.

"I don't think that will help, sir," Jacobs adds agitatedly as he attempts to make light of their situation.

Waverley's glare shifts around, showing his dislike of everything Russian. "You think not. Any of you Reds speak English?" he shouts, but the Red Army soldiers ignore him, which adds to his anger as he impatiently looks for any sign of awareness. "Ignorant fucking Bolsheviks!"

"They won't understand English, sir. They're just common soldiers," Jacobs pleads, but Waverley doesn't like his terminology, which comes out in anger.

"Hey, Captain, I come from humble stock."

"Sorry, sir, I didn't mean to imply anything."

Waverley's eyes again fix on Vasteroff as he steps into full view, annoyed by the American general's Western arrogance.

"We are not all ignorant of the English language, General Waverley." Amused by the officer's familiarity and off-hand comment, Waverley grins. "Is that so, Captain? Then why don't you take me to whoever's pulling your strings?"

Not understanding, Vasteroff's glance shifts to Jacobs.

"Who's your commander, Captain?" Jacobs said with coy diplomacy.

Vasteroff comes to attention and answers with an overwhelming sense of pride. "Colonel General Georgi Lischinsky. Commander of the 2nd Battalion 3rd Ukrainian front." He walks toward a command wagon situated twenty yards off. "I will see if he will see you, General."

"See if he'll see me!" Waverley shouts as he jumps from the jeep. "I'll kick the fucking door in!"

Jacobs races to cut Waverley off and grabs his arm to stop him. "Sir, remember we are Allies."

"Allies, my ass!" Waverley shouts aggressively as he angrily pulls his arm away. "They don't know who the fuck they are dealing with."

***

Taking frequent sips from a glass of cognac, General Lischinsky stands within his command wagon two drinks shy of total inebriation as he stares out the window, amused by Waverley's antics.

***

Bombastic and arrogant, General-Polkovnik Georgi Lischinsky is the cliché of the Western world's interpretation of a Red Army Staff officer. He shows little concern for the men he commands who have, in their thousands, been mown down and killed so that ground may be taken and the enemy beaten. Hated by his men who see him as a monster and butcher, his rapid rise through the rankings is due to the courage and spilling of the blood of the brave men of the Red Army who had no choice but to follow his every order as it is better to take their chance against the Germans than the execution squads of the NKVD who follow their advance and would kill them without trial or concern for desertion and cowardice in the face of the enemy to make an example to any other would-be deserters.

***

Vasteroff enters the command wagon and brings his body into tight attention with a sharp, swift salute. Still, Lischinsky keeps his stare on Waverley and Jacobs having a heated discussion outside.

"So, that is the American Lieutenant General Waverley?"

"Yes, Comrade General and Captain Jacobs," Vasteroff answers, holding his salute.

"I see."

"They have requested a word with you, Comrade General."

***

Waverley and Jacobs near the command wagon as Vasteroff exits, stopping them.

"The general may enter, but I am afraid the captain will have to keep me company."

Waverley gives Jacobs a curious glance, then storms towards the command wagon past Vasteroff, who moves to Jacobs' side to unnerve him with his presence.

***

Lischinsky pours a large cognac and takes an equally large mouthful as Waverley barges through the door without waiting to be announced.

"Don't they knock in the land of the free, General?" Lischinsky said with dry humour.

Waverley looks around the command wagon's garish decoration. "Only on social visits, General."

Lischinsky drains his glass and then opens the drinks cabinet to show an extensive array of alcoholic brands looted from all over Europe.

"And this isn't one, of course?" he said, believing Waverley would change his mind on seeing what was on offer.

"You could say that."

"No matter how your political aspirations are, you will respect my command and should join me in a drink to the downfall of the fascists."

"I don't think so, General!"

"I know you Americans like beer, so if you prefer," Lischinsky adds, reaching to open another door in the drink's cabinet, but Waverley stops him dead.

"I find plunder has a sour taste, Comrade."

"How different we are," Lischinsky said with a laugh as he refilled his glass. "We have gathered that you are not here on a social visit and have refused my hospitality. So, what can I do for you, General?"

"Leave," Waverley said with straight-faced determination.

Lischinsky's laugh becomes more heartily as his amusement increases, but this quickly turns to annoyance at the American's dismissive attitude toward the Red Army, whom he believes commands a great deal more respect, having fought and died fighting the brunt of the Axis forces. "Why would I do that? I'm here to defeat the last remnants of fascism."

"That won't be necessary, Comrade. We have everything in hand."

"You say you have everything in hand," Lischinsky repeats calmly, mimicking Waverley's Southern American drawl. "You won't defeat the Germans sitting on your fat Yankee asses."

Angered, Waverley takes several deep breaths to calm himself, "Just leave, Comrade, and leave the Germans to us," he said, exiting.

"Before you go, General!" Lischinsky calls out to stop the Texan at the door. "Allow me to enlighten you as to how this is going to go. My men are a bayonet waiting to gut the fascists."

Waverley laughs at the pomposity of the Russian's boasts.

"I will attack and annihilate them all, General."

"Very animated, Comrade, and might I add a little overconfident."

"Have you witnessed the Red Army at war?" Lischinsky adds with personal conviction. "Maybe you should take the time to. You may learn something about modern warfare." He lifts his glass in salute before taking a large drink and laughing uproariously as Waverley exits.

***

Seeing Waverley's face is red with rage, Jacobs nervously moves away from Vasteroff, and they get into the jeep and drive off at speed.

***

Vasteroff enters the command wagon to find Lischinsky staring with amazement out of the window.

"The Impertinence of the Americans," Lischinsky explains. "The fool wants the Germans for himself."

"What do you intend to do, Comrade General?"

"I don't intend to wait for intelligence before attacking," Lischinsky snarls as he pours another large drink and showing no intent to offer his subordinate one, he downs it in one. "I don't believe my luck. Another chance to kill Germans."

"I've been reliably informed they have sent a man in to infiltrate the Berghof, sir."

"What do you mean, Captain?" Lischinsky enquired, amused by the notion.

"A Major Robertson, Comrade General. A British officer has been sent to find out what the Germans are hiding."

Feeling the effects of too much alcohol, Lischinsky stumbles to his desk and sits. "Hiding! I don't care what they are hiding!"

"No, sir!"

"Then he will die with the rest of them when we attack. Who cares if they are hiding something?"

***

SUNDAY, MAY 6TH 1945

***

Dazed, bloodied and bandaged, Robertson limps through the corridors of the Berghofs underground bunker complex. Unnerved by the passing soldiers who pay him no attention, he frequently stops to rub his aching legs and exits the reinforced steel blast doors into the bright morning sunlight, temporarily blinding him. Feeling the cold, he buttons up his coat and moves to the wall at the foot of the stairs to the terrace that overlooks the valley below and sits to catch his breath. Skorzeny stands on the terrace above, looking through his binoculars into the valley before lowering them to notice Robertson rubbing his legs. Concerned by the injured man's appearance, he walks down the stairs and comes up behind to offer him his help. Robertson turns slowly to face the antagonist he would rather not have met, and taking advantage of his appearance, he acts confused.

"You're still concussed, Sergeant."

Hitler exits the Berghof above and moves across the terrace as his glance shifts annoyingly to the camouflaged netting as he attempts to pull it down; angered, it obscures his view. Ready to complain, he turns to see Skorzeny below, but his stare fixes on Robertson and his face lights up in recognition. "Colonel!" he bellows in a pained voice. "I would like a word!"

Skorzeny turns to see his Führer, and Robertson follows his stare but has to hide his disbelief.

"Yes, my Führer!" Skorzeny shouts obediently.

With great agitation, Hitler walks across the terrace to the parapet out of sight, and Skorzeny turns to Robertson.

"Get to a medic, Sergeant, at the earliest."

Robertson brings his heels together and salutes awkwardly.

"We need all our men fit and able to fight."

"Yes, sir."

Skorzeny heads off up the stairs, three at a time and onto the terrace. Conscious the Wagnerian Assignment is going ahead and that the Allied intelligence services had been caught unawares, Robertson backs off slowly. He looks at the terrace to see Hitler pulling at the camouflaged net before increasing his pace and heading down the mountain. Skorzeny moves to Hitler's side to give the Nazi salute and clicks his heels to echo across the terrace.

"This monstrosity obscures my view, Colonel!" Hitler shouts agitatedly.

Skorzeny glances up at the netting, aware that if the Allies could position the Berghof, they could easily destroy it. "Yes, my Führer. You wanted to see me?"

Hitler has another tug at the netting as he turns his twisted face to look over Skorzeny's shoulder. "Where is Colonel Rumanigger?"

"Colonel Rumanigger, my Führer?" Skorzeny questioned.

"Yes, Colonel Rumanigger!" Hitler shouts angrily. "Inform my old friend I want to see him in the great room immediately."

"Yes, my Führer," Skorzeny mutters, bewildered.

"I won't have my orders ignored, Colonel!" Hitler shouts as he shuffles off across the terrace and enters the Berghof.

"Sorry, my Führer," Skorzeny apologised as he stared into the distance, shocked and isolated. "What the hell is going on?" he mumbles.

Frequently looking back, Robertson's quick-thinking mind clicks into action as he moves off as fast as his injured legs will carry him. He can see Skorzeny standing alone on the terrace and wants to get as much distance between them as possible. Artillery booms in the distance with shells coming down and exploding to send dirt and debris everywhere. He runs and dives into the relative cover of the tree line and scurries across the ground to take refuge under some camouflage netting where the four American jeeps he recognises as the ones taken at Major Gates' surrender sit. Looking out through the smoke and chaos, he knows the attack is an opportunity to make good his escape and vaults to his feet to head through the treeline keeping his body as low to the ground as possible to help prevent further injury from the exploding ordnance.

***

Making good progress and confident of an early victory, thousands of Red Army infantry following in support of T34, KV1 and KV2 tanks advance across the eastern approach to Berchtesgaden valley. German artillery return fire, scattering the Russian soldiers as they are murdered in a hail of fire and death that hasn't been spared for a future negotiating strategy. Having picked a safe advantage point, Lischinsky stares through his binoculars with narcissistic pride at his men's courage.

Fidgeting in desperation to intervene at the unnecessary waste of the brave Red Army soldiers' lives, Vasteroff stands at his side. "Comrade General," he nervously mutters several times before adding. "Our men are being massacred."

"The battle has just begun!" Lischinsky shouts dismissively, then smiles confidently as victory is paramount to him saving face.

The Red Army infantry take a heavy mauling which forces them to retreat disorderly and ignore the orders of their desperate commander. Lischinsky's hands tighten on the grip of the binoculars, enraged at the sight of the battle unfolding in front of him. "Those cowards are making me look foolish in front of the Americans," he screams as his pride quickly wanes and shows the compassion that is missing amongst the generals of the Red Army.

Vasteroff goes to speak, but Lischinsky unclips his holster and draws his Tokarev semi-automatic pistol to point into his face.

"Interrupt me again, Captain, and I will shoot you down where you stand."

Having witnessed Lischinsky's wrath in the past, Vasteroff backs off hastily. "I apologise, Comrade General."

Lischinsky holsters the Tokarev and then drops the binoculars to smash off the ground before kicking them into a broken heap. Self-interestedly humiliated by his soldiers' inability to put up a fight against well-placed artillery and insurmountable odds, he turns his stare into the distance showing no sign of remorse or guilt for the dead, dying and burning tanks that litter Berchtesgaden valley below.

***

Relieved the Russian advance had been thwarted with no casualties to his side, Skorzeny shouts for a cease-fire which is echoed several times into the distance until the firing stops.

"They won't forget that in a hurry," Radl said jubilantly.

Calm descends, but Skorzeny knows their supplies cannot be sustained through many more gruelling attacks.

"Is everything alright, Otto?" Radl adds on seeing Skorzeny's perturbed look.

"Have you heard of a Colonel Rumanigger, Karl?"

"Can't say I have. Why do you ask?"

"The Führer asked for him," Skorzeny answers warily. "He was most persistent." He pauses as his mind races back to where the enquiry happened, then smiles half-heartedly. "Never mind."

***

Looking over maps within the great room as he orders make-believe long defunct armies moved all around Europe and Russia, Hitler stands with an uncomfortable and bored Hanna at his side. Noticing his Führer's agitation, Dr Bergman moves to his medical bag and takes out a syringe pre-emptively filled with a sedative. Skorzeny enters and moves next to Hanna.

"Is there much damage, Otto?" she enquired with concern.

Noticing Hitler's mood and not wanting to add to it, Skorzeny shakes his head vigorously but doesn't answer.

Dr Bergman is genuinely concerned about the fate of the fighting men sitting cold and dirty in the trenches as they put their lives at risk to protect them and interjects to Hitler's annoyance. "It must be hard on the men."

"Every man, a devout National Socialist, prepared to sacrifice his life for Führer and fatherland!" Hitler rants without taking his eyes off the maps.

"Yes, my Führer," Dr Bergman answered subserviently as he backed into the corner.

Skorzeny moves to Hitler's side and patiently waits for his moment to speak. "My Führer, may I have a word?"

Hitler turns with madness in his eyes and pulls off the glasses he had never dared be photographed wearing. "Did you inform Colonel Rumanigger I want to see him?"

Skorzeny's uneasy glance shifts around the room, hoping someone would recognise the name, but he sees nothing that will help him. "Not yet, my Führer."

Annoyed he had been disobeyed again, Hitler slams his fist hard on the map table. "I want to speak to Colonel Rumanigger, now!" he screams.

Dr Bergman hastily moves to his medical bag and puts the syringe away. Knowing Hitler's mood will not allow an injection, he takes out several sedatives instead, but noticing what he has in mind, Hanna grabs the medical man's arm, having seen her Führer sedated one too many times for her liking.

"Is that necessary, Doctor?"

Angered that his medical experience is being questioned in such a manner, Dr Bergman moves off, breaking Hanna's grip, then pours a glass of water and makes his way to Hitler's side. "Your medication, my Führer."

"I don't have time to take your treatments, Doctor."

"They will help your concentration," Dr Bergman mutters as his glance shifts rapidly to Hanna, who shows deep resentment in her eyes.

Sighing loudly, Hitler snatches the tablets and swallows them with a mouthful of water.

"Führer, I need to ask you about Colonel Rumanigger?" Skorzeny interrupts as Hitler waves his hand dismissively as the medication takes immediate effect.

Dr Bergman helps Hitler stumble to a chair to sink deep into its comfort.

"Inform Jodl I want," Hitler mumbles as he falls into a deep, sedated sleep.

"What makes you ask of Colonel Rumanigger?" Hanna enquires, amused by Skorzeny's frustration.

Not having heard her question or received the answer he requires, Skorzeny paces, agitated, until she shouts out to catch his attention.

"Otto! What makes you ask of Colonel Rumanigger?" she insists, her tone decidedly higher.

"I don't know!"

"You must know!" she adds with a giggle.

"The Führer asked for him," he explains.

"The Führer asked for him?" she questions. "I knew of a Colonel Rumanigger."

"You said knew," he interrupts, bemused by the use of the past tense.

"He was a traitor who worked for the British," she adds, shocking him.

"He was caught and, I would assume, shot many years ago."

Skorzeny's mind races back to him conversing with the injured sergeant as he wonders if his Führer is relapsing in memory. However, with the realisation he may have been duped, he turns, knocking Hanna to one side as he races onto the terrace, but nothing moves.

Continually scanning the area, he takes the stairs three at a time and continues down the mountain briskly.

Further down, Robertson moves through the trees before looking towards the trenches below. German soldiers keep the terrain under surveillance in the nearest trench, unaware that their greatest threat is coming from the rear. Seeing Robertson, a soldier walks up behind them and taps him on the shoulder to startle him as he comes to face him.

"Are you alright, Sergeant?"

Robertson's concentration is quickly taken by a stick grenade in the soldier's belt, and taking advantage of his concern, he points off, and as the soldier turns to look, he takes the opportunity to grab the side of his head and smash it off a tree. Only slightly concussed, the soldier turns to be smashed in the face with his forearm to knock him out cold as he crumples to the ground with a loud thud. Looking around to see if he had been noticed, he crouches next to the unconscious soldier and takes the grenade from his belt, primes it and then turns to the nearest trench to under arm throw it in before diving for cover as it lands to panic the soldiers inside as it explodes tearing the life from them. The exploding grenade catches Skorzeny's attention, and he draws his Luger, running toward the sound, increasing his speed with every bounding step. Robertson jumps to his feet and runs toward the smouldering trench and through the trees at a brisk pace with several rifle shots directed at him smashing into the surrounding trees that make him grimace in terror as he tumbles over several times before getting back to his feet and carrying on down the mountain at an ever-increasing speed. The firing ceases as he disappears into the deep foliage that dips him out of their sight and range. Skorzeny reaches the smouldering trench to tower above and for a second his face clouds over at the sight of the dead soldiers. He holsters the Luger, lifts a badly shredded rifle and storms off with determination to kill the traitor. Robertson slides down an embankment onto the main road, breaking from a limping run to a rushed walk. Frequently looking back, ensuring he hadn't been followed, he nears the American checkpoint, slows to a hobbling walk, and lifts his hands, showing he isn't a threat. Under instruction to await his arrival, the GIs move to greet him. One of the GI's climbs onto a jeep covering the road and cocks the Browning M2 heavy machine gun as he turns it toward him with a loud crack stopping him in his tracks.

"Stand down, McGuire; it's our man," the sergeant hollers as he moves to Robertson. "Welcome back, sir," he adds with a salute.

Skorzeny leaps onto the road, cocks and takes careful aim as Robertson turns, seeing his enemy and giving him enough time to dive for cover as the 7.92 bullet grazes his shoulder before he lands in the muddy grass verge with a heavy thud. Skorzeny re-cocks the rifle, annoyed that he didn't have a machine pistol, and fires again to miss the Scotsman as he crawls frantically across the ground into the undergrowth. The M2 opens up, forcing Skorzeny into cover behind the tree line as the hail of .50 bullets tears up the foliage and ground around, sending dirt and tree splinters all over him. Drawing his Browning sidearm, the sergeant moves forward, firing toward Skorzeny and helps Robertson to his feet before backing up to the checkpoint, still firing.

"I need a ride!" Robertson shouts impatiently as he takes hold of his injured shoulder.

***

German soldiers take up defensive positions as the dead get carried away. Having heard the gunfire, Radl stands above the trench as Skorzeny walks up and angrily smashes the rifle off a tree and throws the shattered pieces into the distance.

"What's going on, Otto?" Radl asked, unsure of his commanding officer's actions.

"We've been betrayed," Skorzeny said sharply as he carried on, leaving his second-in-command perplexed by an answer that gave nothing away.

***

Covered in blood, Robertson limps into the Berchtesgadener Hof hotel catching Jacobs' attention. "Where's General Waverley?" he shouts out.

Jacobs vaults to his feet and races over. "I'm not sure, sir," he said excitedly. "Did you find anything out?"

Robertson stops and stares at the young American officer. "How long have you been in this game, Captain?"

Unsure what the question means, Jacobs grimaces for several seconds before answering. "Why do you want to know that, sir?"

"Because there are some questions you just don't ask," Robertson said as he headed up the stairs, two at a time, taking the pain and discomfort as Jacobs desperately attempted to keep up.

***

Dictating a letter to Ingram, Waverley sits on his bed drinking a large Jack Daniels when, without knocking, Robertson barges in followed closely by Jacobs.

Waverley turns concerned to see his British friend holding his bleeding shoulder with determination in his eyes. "Are you alright, Will?"

"It's just a flesh wound, General. Pour me a large one of those, sir."

Waverley moves to the sideboard and picks up the bottle of Jack Daniels to pour a hearty measure into a glass as he keeps his curious eye on a man who shows all the hallmarks of holding information he desperately wants to offload. He hands over the drink, and Robertson downs it in one to enjoy the smooth taste, then hands the glass back, expecting another.

"What's that?" Robertson enquires with a pleasant grin.

"Tennessee gold," Waverley answers with a comical smile. "From my stash."

"I'm honoured, sir."

"You should be," Ingram interjects. "He's never offered one to me."

"I take it you found something?" General Waverley carries on impatiently.

"Pour me another, and I will tell you," Robertson teases and Waverley pours another Jack Daniels and hands the glass over. "Thank you, sir," he said, then drained the glass.

"So, what happened?"

Robertson jerked his head toward the two captains, who stared eagerly to hear what he had discovered.

"Clear the room!" Waverley barks. "I need a private word with the major."

Well aware there are secrets he will never be privy to, Ingram moves to the door and exits, leaving Jacobs standing in the middle of the room, not showing any sign of moving.

"Out, Jacobs," Waverley shouts, grabbing his arm and bundling him to the door. "We haven't got all day."

Leaving the door ajar, Jacobs reluctantly exits but stays outside within curious earshot.

Noticing the door, Robertson opens it slightly to see the captain loitering. "What the fuck's going on?" he snarls.

"Sorry, I thought I may be needed," Jacobs pleads, and Ingram grabs his shirt to pull him away.

Infuriated, Robertson kicks the door closed and then turns back to Waverley. "How long has that arse been in intelligence, sir?"

"Who are you talking about?"

"The man with something to prove."

Waverley pours another Jack Daniels as he speaks. "Captain Jacobs. He's not long been on my staff. You don't seem to like him, Will?"

"I don't know him, but there is something about him. Something I don't like."

"He's harmless."

"He's your man, General, which makes him your problem but I wouldn't be happy if I were you."

"I've very recently become aware of certain suspicions on his posting, but they are for another day," Waverley said as he impatiently handed over the Jack Daniels. "Obviously, you found something out?"

Robertson's fingers touch the glass as he speaks. "Adolf Hitler."

Waverley pauses in bewilderment at a statement he had never envisaged hearing. "Adolf Hitler!" he repeats as he pulls the glass back, then downs the Jack Daniels himself. "You must be mistaken."

"I wish I was, sir."

"Intelligence has reported him dead."

"Well, intelligence has it wrong again, sir."

"Hitler's body has been found and identified on the grounds of the Reich Chancellery."

"By the Russians!" Robertson interjects in a mistrusting tone that Waverley understands. "You've seen them first-hand, sir. The deceit, the lies. I wouldn't believe what a Russian was saying even if I witnessed what he was talking about."

"Deceit and lies," Waverley said, reflecting on his many years in intelligence. "The title of my autobiography if I ever get around to writing one," he adds with a laugh.

"And we don't trust the Russians, do we, General?" Robertson said as he moved to the sideboard to pour a Jack Daniels. "Do you want one, sir?"

Waverley moves up behind and slaps Robertson playfully on the back, "I think I need a large one," he adds as he places his glass down. Robertson pours another Jack Daniels, filling the glass to the top and handing it to Waverley, who struggles not to spill the contents. "The body said to be Hitler's was badly burnt and found with a woman's body."

"Eva Braun!"

"That's what we were meant to believe, sir, but why would she be dead? German radio reported that the Führer had been killed in action fighting the Red Army, but would she? The bodies are fake."

"What makes you think the man you saw wasn't fake?"

Robertson takes a large mouthful of Jack Daniels and recomposes himself with the straightest expression. "He recognised me."

Waverley puts his untouched glass on the sideboard. "What do you mean recognised you?"

"He looked directly at me. I believe he thought I was Colonel Rumanigger."

"The alias you used in Germany," Waverley said, exasperated. "We thought the national redoubt was a myth, but it looks like we need to go back and find out what is going on." He moves to the window and looks out to witness the dusk changing to-night. "You'll have to wait until the morning. Have you heard of a General von Stiffel?"

"I told you I read the report, sir."

"Did you see him at the Berghof?"

Amused at the thought he would be able to recognise one German general from another, Robertson shakes his head.

"We've been caught on the hop. If news gets out that Hitler is making a last stand at his mountain retreat, we'll have every fanatical Nazi taking up arms and heading down here to resume the fight.
"More of our men would be killed needlessly, sir."
"It may give the Russians the excuse they are looking for to carry on and turn their guns on us."
"It could also give us the excuse to turn our guns on them and push them back to their motherland."
Waverley gives out a wry, mischievous smile. "I'd love the chance, but the petty politicians back in Washington don't see it as a viable option. The possibility of pushing the Red Army back to Russia has been discussed at the highest level." He looks Robertson up and down curiously. "How's your shoulder, Will?"
"Alright, but I have been shot, sir," Robertson answers cynically.
"Good," Waverley adds, unconcerned. "What about Colonel Skorzeny? Was he there?"
"He spoke to me."
"That must have given you a fright."
"He's an imposing man, sir," Robertson answers curiously, aware Waverley is up to something.
"You've got to go back in."
The thought of re-entering the Berghof now that Skorzeny knows who he is sends a shiver through the Scotsman. "I don't think so, sir." He touches his aching shoulder with a wince. "I believe he's just tried to kill me. I don't think he would miss the second time around."
"You said you are alright," Waverley said as his face and voice turned serious. "Listen, Will. We need to know what their intentions are."
"Go up there and find out yourself, sir."
"But you've already been introduced to the notorious colonel," Waverley said with mirth.
"Surely what their intentions are is the continuation of the war."
"I thought you read the file on the Wagnerian Assignment?"
"Why would I read that, General? I have better things to do with my time than read every intelligence report that crosses my desk."
"Of course, I could just as easily send Captain Ingram up there and leave British intelligence out."
Robertson laughs at the veiled threat. "And I could just as easily have gone straight to London and left American intelligence out."
"Touché, Major. So, you are going back?"

Robertson rubs his face and head apprehensively. "What do I have to negotiate with?"

"You're clever. Improvise."

"Great, but this time I'm going in my uniform."

"That's all well and good, Will, but we are still on the clock. Ike still wants his scalp at the earliest. We were given seventy-two hours, but I know that has been extended."

"Why would that be, sir?"

"Politics," Waverley answered with a wry, mischievous smile to hide his poor attempt at misdirection. "You know how it is?"

"He'll have to wait until I have eaten, had a bath and a little medical attention."

"You do that, Will. In the meantime, I need to make some calls," Waverley said, looking at Robertson sternly. "You won't get anything done hanging around here aimlessly. You'd better be on your way."

"Well, if we aren't going to keep it within our little family, I also need to use the telephone," Robertson said as he limped to the door and looked back at Waverley, who had his telephone to his ear.

"You need to tell your boss to speak to mine otherwise, this won't work, General."

"Leave the politics to me, Major."

"Politics, of course, sir," Robertson mutters, amused, as he exits.

***

MONDAY, MAY 7TH 1945

***

Smart and pristine in the uniform of a Coldstream Guards officer, Robertson drives in an open-top Willys jeep flying the largest white flag he could find from the radio antenna in the hope the Germans would see it and not fire on him. He pulls over where the road stops and pauses for several tense seconds, hardly daring to look at the threat; he knows it is bearing down on him. He brings his legs slowly onto the tarmac lifting his hands to show he isn't a threat as he walks hesitantly toward the tree line. "I need to speak with Colonel Skorzeny!" he shouts several times.

Having been made aware of Robertson's approach, Skorzeny and Radl walk to the trench line and stand above the soldiers whose itchy fingers cover their triggers as they look coyly up at their commanding officer for orders.

"What about?" Skorzeny shouts in reply.

Robertson turns to where the voice had come from. "I will only speak with Colonel Skorzeny."

Radl turns with curiosity to face his commander. "How does he know you are here, Otto?"

Skorzeny grins as he steps over the trench and moves through the treeline. "That's Rumanigger," he calls out, to Radl's amazement. "Of course it is."

Robertson watches nervously as Skorzeny and Radl step out of the treeline and move toward him.

"Colonel Rumanigger," Skorzeny said maliciously as he drew his Luger to point. "I had hoped you were dead."

Amused at being called a name he hadn't been referred to for such a long time, Robertson taps his injured shoulder. "I take it this was your bullet, Colonel?"

Skorzeny's face remains emotionless. "And now you come in the uniform of the enemy."

"I'm Scottish born and bred," Robertson explains impatiently. "My name is Major William Robertson. I work for British military intelligence."

"You work in intelligence?" Skorzeny said with a smirking laugh. "Something you haven't shown in coming back here."

"Under the terms of the Geneva Convention," Robertson starts, but Skorzeny moves closer, still aiming his Luger. "I'm here under a flag of truce," he pleads.

Skorzeny's glance shifts to the white flag and rounds the Luger to fire once to snap the antenna for the flag to fall to the ground. Robertson looks at the flag fluttering away, then turns back to face the grinning Austrian who is enjoying the tormenting of a man he doesn't know but desperately despises.

"I need a word in private, Colonel."

"What makes you think I would want to speak with you?"

"I can help."

Desperate to pull the trigger, Skorzeny turns the Luger back onto Robertson.

"What I have to say maybe your only option," Robertson says off the cuff.

Skorzeny looks at Radl for inspiration but has yet to receive any. "Then you had better come through."

"Is that a good idea, Otto?" Radl questions.

"Why not, Karl? I'd like to hear what he has to say, wouldn't you?"

Skorzeny stands aside, allowing Robertson to pass and walk off through the foliage. They move up the road to the Berghof as Robertson, hoping for another sight of Hitler, looks up to the terrace only to see Hanna staring disapprovingly down at him.

***

Entering the bunker complex, they move through a long, dimly lit corridor with numerous sinister doors on either side before stopping in front of one that Skorzeny opens for Robertson to stare into its darkness.

Skorzeny flicks the light switch for a dull bulb to come on after several flashes. "If you don't mind." He gestures for Robertson to enter, but the Scotsman hesitates, forcing the Austrian to push him inside. "I will take it from here, Karl."

Radl pauses in the doorway, unsure of what to do.

"It will be alright, Karl. Go get yourself some breakfast."

Uncertain, Radl grins, walking off with the door closing behind him.

"I remember being in a room like this courtesy of the Gestapo," Robertson said with nervous jest. "I take it I am supposed to be intimidated by your prowess, Colonel."

Skorzeny grabs Robertson violently by the shoulders, forces him into a chair in the centre of the room, and then circles slowly. "So, you believe you can help? What makes you think I need any?"

"You're surrounded, Colonel."

Skorzeny pauses, deep in thought, as he keeps his angry stare on his adversary. "Then tell me how?"

"Maybe I should be speaking with your Führer, Adolf Hitler."

Having hoped Robertson hadn't seen his beloved leader, Skorzeny stops staring at the back of his enemy's head. "I can see you have a very high opinion of your prowess and standing, but you can speak to me."

"Like I have already informed you, I am here to help."

Skorzeny laughs. "So, you have said, so why don't you enlighten me on how you believe you could help?"

Not having given the improvisation side of his visit any thought, Robertson pauses as his mind races over what to say. "You are surrounded," he blusters to the Austrian's irritation.

Taking a tighter grip on his Luger, Skorzeny replies with angst in his voice. "You've already harangued the point, and I am more than aware of the situation I find myself in."

Sensing Skorzeny's agitation, Robertson attempts to calm the situation. "Nobody knows the Führer is here. The world believes him dead."

Skorzeny fails to understand the meaning of Robertson's words and how he could benefit from the situation being laid at his door.

"I only informed my immediate superior, General Waverley, of what I saw. Like me, he's anti-communist and already at blows with the Russian commander, General Lischinsky."

"Colonel General Georgi Lischinsky," Skorzeny said with an amused grin.

"You know him?"

"Of him... I blew up his command wagon in forty-four, but sadly he wasn't in it," Skorzeny muses, but his frivolity quickly changes back to seriousness. "You were about to explain how you intend to help?"

Robertson attempts to stand, but the Austrian pushes him violently back into the chair, infuriating him. "The Russians have staked a claim to half of Europe."

"And the Americans and British, the other half, no doubt?" Skorzeny snipes.

"I can't speak for the Yanks, but the British are an army of occupation and will leave in time."

Skorzeny laughs. "As history proves of all empire builders, that statement is far from the truth."

Robertson is mindful that the British Empire is on its last legs and believes they couldn't sustain a long occupation. "What you need to worry about is the Russian intention to separate Germany."

Shocked and saddened by the revelation that his beloved fatherland is to be forcibly separated, Skorzeny turns to hide the shock this has caused his shaken temperament.

"So that the German people won't be able to wage another aggressive war."

Skorzeny grumbles. "The Führer won't stand for it."

"He has no choice in the matter!" Robertson said, his voice elevated. "In case you haven't noticed, you have been soundly defeated."

Angered, Skorzeny pushes Robertson over the chair to knock his hat off as he lands on the floor, then pounces to push the Luger hard into his face until the realisation his enemy is speaking the truth dawns on him, and he relaxes slightly.

"I take it your predicament is beginning to dawn on you? You are totally surrounded, and the opportunity to get the Führer out is lessoning with every second you hesitate."

"To what end?" Skorzeny said as he moved aside, and Robertson sat brushing himself down.

"Then we can rally our men together and push the Russians back to their motherland."

"I don't think so," Skorzeny mutters, unconvinced.

Having heard the idea of fighting the Russians being debated by officers through drunken bouts of excited keenness, Robertson had believed them foolhardy words, but if it helped in his negotiations with the Austrian, he would carry on the pretence. "We have the support of numerous high-profile people and high-ranking officers and politicians."

"And you can count on this support?" Skorzeny questioned his disbelief.

"Yes."

Skorzeny laughs with hilarity. "Nobody wants the continuation of war, especially not the German people. Don't you think they have suffered enough?"

"Then what is all this about if not prolonging the war?"

"You wouldn't understand."

"You didn't think this area would go untouched?" Robertson adds, belittling the proud SS officer who rounds angrily but pauses to calm down quickly. "You couldn't have picked a more recognisable area to hide in. It was sure to be searched and conquered."

Recognising the Obersalzberg as a perfect area for defence but not a place to hide if you want to remain undetected, Skorzeny grins his uncomfortable agreement. "I didn't pick it. I inherited it."

"Firstly, we need to get the Führer out of here, then we will be in a better position to gather our soldiers to go up against the Reds," Robertson said as he stood, but Skorzeny lunged to push him hard against the wall as he prods the Luger into his face. "You seem to want to prove yourself against an unarmed man, Colonel."

"I don't need a gun."

"Yet here you are threatening me with one."

Skorzeny prods the Luger into Robertson's face with deep desperation to end his life.

"Remember, Colonel, I came under a flag of truce."

"And why should I care?"

"If you don't understand the meaning of a flag of truce, why don't you pull the fucking trigger and get this fucking shit over? Then you can sit here until the Americans and Russians annihilate you and your beloved Führer."

Calming with reason, Skorzeny lowers the Luger to his side and backs off, embarrassed by his over-zealous behaviour.

Robertson straightens himself out and picks up his hat to dust down before putting it back on and adjusting it to fit. "I'm here to help, but you don't seem to want to help yourself."

"Why should I trust you?"

"Why would I be here if it wasn't to help? This area has already been targeted for destruction."

"Destruction," Skorzeny mutters uneasily. "In what way?"

"They intend to carpet bomb the area and wipe out the last remnants of National Socialism."

Skorzeny knows his options are limited and running out faster than he could ever have anticipated. "I need to hear this from your superior."

"You can take my word for it."

"I can't take the word of a traitor."

Robertson doesn't take kindly to this, and it shows on his weary face. "I'm not a fucking traitor."

"I don't know who you are. Major Robertson, Colonel Rumanigger. Either one I don't trust or like."

"I'm not here to make friends," Robertson retorts. "You don't need to go along with this. You can stay here and die."

Skorzeny holsters his Luger, then opens the door and stands aside. "After you."

Robertson goes to exit but pauses, believing he may be walking forward to be struck from behind.

"No need to worry," Skorzeny adds, amused by his enemy's hesitancy. "You're safe for now."

Robertson nods, then exits, followed closely by Skorzeny. They make their way through the bunker complex, passing numerous inquisitive soldiers who are amazed to see a British officer walking freely with their commander. They exit outside and move off down the road, noticed by Radl, standing on the terrace watching.

"What's going on, Otto?" Radl shouts, running down the stairs two at a time to catch them up, then looks at Robertson curiously as to why he is free.

"I'm going out," Skorzeny answers blasé.

"Out!" Radl said fearfully. "Is that a good idea, Otto?"

"I'll explain when I get back," Skorzeny adds, determined.

Aware he is wasting time arguing with his commander, Radl stops leaving Skorzeny and Robertson to walk into the distance and disappear into the tree line. They exit the camouflage net next to Robertson's jeep as Skorzeny scans the area for a threat.

Robertson reaches into the rear of the jeep and pulls out an American army jacket to throw at Skorzeny. "Put that on, Colonel."

Not wanting to wear the uniform of his enemy, Skorzeny throws it back.

"You can wash yourself later," Robertson said, handing the jacket back. "But you need to come with me incognito. We can't have you being identified."

Finding amusement in Robertson's words, Skorzeny takes the jacket and puts it on over the top of his uniform before getting into the rear of the jeep.

Robertson looks at Skorzeny's Knights Cross flowing over the top. "You might want to conceal your honours or take them off, Colonel."

Having just received the oak leaves to his Knights Cross from his Führer, Skorzeny looks at his greatest pride, then tucks it under the American jacket and buttons it over. Believing he is getting some rapport going, Robertson smiles, only for that to be shrouded in mistrust as the Austrian draws his Luger to point.

"You won't need that, Colonel."

"I'll be the judge of that. If this is all a rouse to capture me, you will be the first to die."

"Now, who's got a high opinion of his own importance?" Robertson said, driving off.

***

Waverley sits on the edge of his bed within the Berchtesgadener Hof hotel discussing through coded words the circumstances of the Wagnerian Assignment as he listens to a voice on the other end of the phone when he's disturbed by a light tap on the door. Robertson enters, and Waverley stares in amusement at the unexpected ignorance of the interruption until Skorzeny follows changing his demeanour sourly.

"I'm afraid we have got some new developments, sir," Waverley said over the phone to stop the voice on the other side. "I will have to get back to you," he adds, replacing the receiver. "This isn't what I had in mind, Will."

Believing introductions were required, Robertson goes to speak only to be interrupted abruptly by Skorzeny with haste in his voice.

"Forget the formalities. I'm not here to make friends. I believe you are aware of the situation, General. I am here to find out what your intentions are?"

Not privy to Robertson's improvisation, Waverley keeps his curious stare on the Scotsman before turning it onto the Austrian.

"Your plan has flaws," Skorzeny adds to Waverley's relief. "The German people have had enough of war."

"Haven't we all," Waverley adds. "I take it you have a plan of your own, Colonel?" he adds, turning his stare on Robertson for inspiration on what had been discussed, but the Scotsman's face shows he can't inform him without giving the game away.

"My last order was to oversee the fortification and protection of the Berghof pending the arrival of the Führer."

Robertson checks the corridor as if expecting someone to be listening on the other side. "I informed the colonel we need to get the Führer out of the Berghof."

"Not an easy task with the Red Army breathing down our necks," Waverley adds as he moves to the window, taking several moments before speaking. "Go back to the Berghof, Colonel." He turns to face the Austrian. "And prepare for a move." He outstretches his hand for Skorzeny to shake, but the tension is evident as the Austrian backs off with his glance shifting between the general's face and hand.

"I can't take the hand of my enemy, General."

Waverley can understand Skorzeny's feelings and sentiments toward his old enemy, having only offered it as a pretence to cooperation, and pulls it back. "There'll have to be trust, Colonel."

"Trust has to be earned, General."

"Yes, it does," Robertson replies, and Skorzeny turns slowly with scorn. "That works both ways, Colonel."

Skorzeny exits, followed closely by Robertson, who smiles awkwardly at Waverley.

"You said improvise, sir."

Contemplating Robertson's words, Waverley shakes his head, distressed, as he closes the door and picks up the phone. "Get me Washington, six, five, zero, zero, zero." He moves to the window and watches as Robertson and Skorzeny exit the building and get into the jeep. "Those developments, sir," he adds over the phone. "They are worse than we originally thought. We will have to meet in person."

***

Skorzeny enters the Berghofs opulently decorated great room, moving to the panoramic window to gaze through the camouflaged netting and appreciate the tranquil beauty of the view. The weight of the task at hand shows on his weary face as he realises he is still wearing the American uniform, which is hastily launched across the massive room into a heap. The door opens slowly for Hanna to enter stealthily and move up behind to whisper his name several times until he turns, delighted by her presence, and affectionately takes her warm hands into his.

"How do you do it?" he whispers. "I look into your eyes, and all I see is peace."

She smiles, pleased but slightly embarrassed by words she can't comprehend as the truth. "I don't think so, Otto. You can't go through what we have without being affected in some way."

Wanting to reassure her, he believes a kiss and embrace will show her his feelings and moves forward, but as their lips touch the door opens and Radl enters, preventing their coupling.

"Sorry, I didn't mean to interrupt," Radl said, embarrassed as he backed off, but the door bursts open for Dr Bergman to enter.

"Colonel, I need an urgent word with you."

Aware he had interrupted what was sure to be an intimate moment, Radl adds. "We can leave this for another day, Doctor."

Dr Bergman believes what he has to say is far too important to wait. "I can't stay long, Colonel; the Führer needs me."

"Of course, Doctor. Please come in and explain what is on your mind." Skorzeny and Hanna's hands come apart slowly, and she backs off to the door and exits unnoticed.

"Sorry, Otto," Radl interjects for Skorzeny to nod his understanding.

"We need to get the Führer to hospital," Dr Bergman adds, determined to catch Skorzeny's undivided attention.

"I agree, Doctor, but how can we escape a siege?"

"Not being a military man, I wouldn't begin to hazard a guess, but I suggest you find one at the earliest," Dr Bergman insists. "The stresses he has been under these past years are insurmountable."

"Aren't we all under stress, Doctor," Radl adds.

"That may be, Major, but the Führer has been ailing for many years. I know this isn't what you want to hear, but I'm just telling you how it is."

"As always, far too late to be of benefit," Radl snipes to Dr Bergman's ire.

Feeling the pressure closing in on him, Skorzeny looks for Hanna to find her gone. "You'll have to excuse me," he said as he exited, leaving the door wide open.

Feeling dismissed but not understanding why, Dr Bergman looks at Radl. "What's going on, Major?"

Radl moves to the door and looks out to see Skorzeny disappearing into the distance. "Just prepare to leave, Doctor. The colonel will think of a way to get us out. He always does."

***

Hanna enters her bedroom and goes to close the door, but Skorzeny pushes from the opposite side, preventing her as he enters. "What's going on, Otto?"

Skorzeny closes the door then takes her tightly by the hands. "You're the only part of this insanity that makes any sense to me," he said, making her blush with satisfaction, and without another word, he seized the moment to take her into his arms and kiss her passionately before they fall to the floor and make love.

***

Robertson and Waverley sit in the general's hotel room, looking at each other through drunken eyes as two empty bottles of

123

Jack Daniels sit on the sideboard. Waverley leans back and selects two fine cigars, one of which he gives to Robertson, who places it gently into his mouth as the general strikes a match and lights both for them to take deep draws and enjoy their Cuban heritage. Waverley picks up the first bottle of Jack Daniels to find it empty before dropping it to the floor and picking the second to find it equally depleted. Unsteadily, he moves to the sideboard only to find no more bottles of his favourite, but a large bottle of Napoleon brandy stands untouched.

"I'm afraid we are out of Jack," Waverley says wretchedly as he lifts the brandy to show Robertson. "But when needs must."

Robertson eyed him keenly through the thick smoke. "I can fall onto any alcohol as a substitute," he mutters earnestly.

Understanding, Waverley's eyes narrow as he pours, then hands Robertson a glass of the brandy to take a drink to twist his face in dislike.

"What's wrong with you?"

"That is fucking awful, General."

"I thought you could drink anything?"

"Obviously not," Robertson said with a schoolboy giggle.

"It's best Napoleon brandy, you heathen."

Robertson downs the brandy and then hands the glass back. "It tastes like shit next to Jack, but I'll force myself to have another before I get on my way."

"What a hero," Waverley said sarcastically as he poured another couple of brandy's, spilling a small amount on the floor. "That's the ticket, Major. We'll make you an honorary American if we finish this bottle."

Robertson laughs at the thought. "Don't put me off, General. It tastes bad enough to start with."

***

Like sweethearts having made love for the first time, Skorzeny and Hanna enjoy the tranquillity and calmness of the moment as they dress.

"I'm not sure about this, Otto," she said, overly concerned for her lover's safety.

"We don't have a choice, Hanna."

"You can't think," she states, but he grips her hands tightly to stop her from finishing the sentence.

"It may be our only chance."

"It's not like you to be taken in."

He takes in a long anxious breath. "I haven't," he mutters solemnly before laughing. "Yet!" He lets go of her hands and leaves her saddened and frightened for his life as he exits.

"Be safe, Otto," she said, tears welling in her eyes to run slowly down her cheeks.

***

Feeling the effects of too much alcohol, Robertson stumbles along the hotel corridor, using the wall to steady himself. Stopping outside the room set aside for him, he pulls the half-smoked cigar from his mouth and drops it to the floor to smoulder into the plush carpet. Fumbling for the door handle, he topples inside to land on the floor in a crumpled heap and lies for several minutes before regaining his composure to stand. As his eyes became accustomed to the dull light coming through a break in the slightly parted French window curtains, he failed to see the figure of Skorzeny standing in the corner. Sensing someone in the room and acting confused, he lowers his arms slowly and reaches for his Browning, but Skorzeny pre-empts his actions and moves with haste to point his Luger into the back of his head.

"Close the door, Major, and keep your hands where I can see them." Robertson lifts his arms into the air and kicks the door shut for the room to fall into darkness. Without taking his eyes off his quarry, the Austrian disarms the Scotsman and backs into the French window to throw the Browning outside and open the curtains fully to allow the moonlight to illuminate the room enough for Robertson to recognise him.

"Once more, we meet, and once more, you have a gun threatening me, Colonel."

Skorzeny lowers then holsters the Luger.

"That's better. There's no need for the farce. You are welcome to visit when it suits you. Now, what can I do for you?"

"I believe I have devised a way of getting the Führer out of the Berghof," Skorzeny adds, pleased with himself.

"You know how to get the Führer out?" Robertson said, walking to his bedside cabinet where a bottle of whisky and a glass sit. "Please join me."

"I don't think so."

"I didn't think you would, but you will have to excuse me. I've got a feeling I will need a stiff one."

"I think you have had enough."

"Alright, Mrs Robertson," the Scotsman said sarcastically with a laugh to suit, but Skorzeny didn't understand his bad attempt at humour. "There's never enough when there is shit to contend with. Anyway, I find the days go better with several stiff drinks whooshing through my veins."

Although saddened, Skorzeny understands why men who have witnessed war first-hand need some form of stimulant to allow the days to pass without the horrific memories overshadowing their thoughts. Robertson takes a large drink and stumbles back onto his bed. "That's good stuff, Colonel. Are you sure you don't want one?"

"Listen, I don't have the fortitude to watch you in your stupor."

"Is that so? Well, it's your shilling, so why don't you enlighten me about your plan?"

"I'm afraid the Führer requires hospital treatment," Skorzeny explains solemnly as he stares, embarrassed by the request for help from his enemy.

Disappointed but not shocked, Robertson puts his glass down. "You need to organise a cease-fire."

"That, Colonel, may be harder than you would think."

"Surely your general has the authority to organise such an act?"

Unaware of where General Waverley's authority extends, Robertson shakes his head slowly.

"Then we will be able to take advantage to get the Führer out to safety," Skorzeny adds, influencing the conversation in his favour.

"What would make you think there was the possibility of a cease-fire when all the generals want to do is destroy you."

"You informed me that we had those generals on our side," Skorzeny snipes.

"Not camped out in the valley."

"Well, with or without their help, we need to get the Führer out."

"What's your plan?"

"We captured several Americans. Surely you will need to get them back before you annihilate us."

His attention accentuated, Robertson nods. "No doubt."

"And while you carry out such an act, we can get the Führer out under cover of the cease-fire."

"I can't see the Russians being happy with that."

"You said you were here to help!" Skorzeny interrupts angrily. "How do you hope to do that with all the negativity surrounding your every word?"

"You call it negativity. I call it the realisation of the facts at hand."
Skorzeny moves to the French window to stare out into the darkness.
"Leave that for the generals you have on your side. Surely, they can
come to some arrangement."

"Are you sure you don't want a drink, Colonel? I get the feeling you
need one. You look a little tense."

"I'd love one," Skorzeny said, and Robertson grinned as he opened the
draw to reach for another glass. "But I'm particular about who I drink
with."

Irritated by words he knows are designed to insult, Robertson pushes
the draw closed and then laughed. "As you can see, I am not," he
retorts, making Skorzeny grin at the irony. "I need to take this to
General Waverley. He has more clout than me. Go back to the
Berghof, and I will see to things from this end." He stands, switches
the light to illuminate the room, and turns to find Skorzeny has slipped
through the French window. Pleased the Austrian had gone, he slumps
on his bed, falling into a deep alcohol fuelled sleep.

***

TUESDAY, MAY 8TH 1945

***

Relaxing in his office, Eisenhower reads German Field Marshal Erwin Rommel's book, Infanterie greift an (Infantry Attacks), with amusement until several light taps on the door take his attention, but he ignores it for several seconds until a fourth louder rap reverberates. "Come!" he bellows, his voice showing he hasn't the time or patience for a visitor.

Waverley enters then closes the door before giving a futile salute.

"What can I do for you now, General?" Eisenhower snaps, unhappy with the interruption to his evening's relaxation. "I'm trying to have some time to myself here?"

"Sorry, sir, but we have more developments."

"Developments?" Eisenhower said as he looked disinterested at his watch. "My understanding is the area has been obliterated."

"We've had to put that on hold, sir."

Enraged that his order has been countermanded, Eisenhower holds his composure as he listens to Waverley's dogged explanation.

"We need to negotiate a cease-fire, sir."

Eisenhower slams the book hard onto his desk. "I won't negotiate with the Nazis, General. The surrender of Germany is unconditional."

"I understand that, sir, but we need to get our men who have been captured out first."

Politically aware the release of prisoners is paramount, Eisenhower pauses, saddened he hadn't thought of it himself in the first place. "I believe I can give you grace for that, but I want that monolith of Nazism flattened and taken off the face of this earth. I don't intend to stand by and watch this Berghof become a pilgrimage site for disgruntled Nazis craving past glories."

"I agree, sir," Waverley said as he saluted.

"Keep me abreast of all happenings, General."

Waverley exits with haste as disinterested in meeting Eisenhower as much as he was in meeting him.

***

Waverley enters his office, followed seconds later by Ingram, who excitedly wants to know what the commander-in-chief had to say about Hitler still being alive. Waverley rounds his desk and sits before angrily pushing some papers onto the floor.

"What's going on, sir?" Ingram enquires, concerned.

"I didn't inform him," Waverley answers flippantly.

Showing what he believes is a monumental mistake, Ingram sighs heavily.

"He's won his war. It's all politics with him now."

"That aside, sir, why wouldn't you inform him?"

"He's not interested in the trivialities of war. Never has been. His eyes are on higher things."

"Not interested in the news of Hitler being alive in Berchtesgaden?" Ingram mumbles, unable to understand his general's decision. "We'll get twenty-years hard labour, sir."

"The cease-fire has already been arranged," Waverley said and then added with a hint of sarcasm. "Oh, and they shoot people for treason. Jail is too good for them."

Pondering how to react, Ingram stares out the window into the distance before turning back. "Do you think this is the right course of action, sir?" he said nervously about the possible ramifications to his military career. "Because I can't see how it could be."

"I wouldn't have done it if I didn't. You know we play to higher powers in this game."

"I suppose we do, sir, but I hope they have more power than our commanding general."

"Our commanding general, as you put it, is just like us. A puppet in the overall running of things. You just can't see the strings or who is pulling them."

Ingram laughs nervously about what the future holds for him.

"He has his part as we have ours, albeit he is higher up the food chain than us mere mortals."

"I'd hardly class you as a mere mortal, sir."

"Wouldn't you? If you ever reach the rank of general, you will realise you are not as high up as you would think, and there is a great deal more hindrance ahead."

***

Believing the problems and politics of their command are over for the day, Eisenhower and Bedell-Smith sit lounging in Eisenhower's office, but their relaxation is disturbed by a knock on the door. Believing his orders have been disobeyed again, Eisenhower glares angrily at Bedell-Smith, who stands to confront when a captain on his staff enters and salutes.

"Apologies for the interruption, sir, but there is a Captain Ingram here to see you."

Aware he works for Waverley, Eisenhower recognises the name. "I informed you we didn't want to be interrupted."

"Yes, sir, but Captain Ingram insists it is imperative you hear what he has to say."

"More cloak and dagger rubbish," Bedell-Smith utters pessimistically as he retakes his seat. "Give me conventional war any day."

Eisenhower's curiosity is aroused to discover what is so urgent as to ruin his evening. "Send him in, Captain."

The captain moves into the corridor, and Ingram enters some seconds later and stands to attention just inside the doorway as he waits for Eisenhower to look up, then salutes.

"Relax, Captain," Eisenhower said, recognising Ingram's twitchy state of mind. "You're amongst friends here."

Ingram comes to ease.

"You work for General Waverley?" Bedell-Smith enquires, already aware of the answer.

"Yes, sir."

"I've just spoken to your boss," Eisenhower interrupts. "So, what can I do for you?"

"I'm uncomfortable with what I have to say, sir."

Eisenhower's gaze shifts curiously between Bedell-Smith and Ingram.

"General Waverley has negotiated a cease-fire with the Germans, sir."

"I've just spoken to him about this," Eisenhower grumbles. "Why would you come to me with information when you must know I already know?"

Still considering his best course of action, Ingram recomposes himself and takes a deep breath. "The cease-fire is a fabrication to get a person they believe to be Adolf Hitler out to safety."

Eisenhower and Bedell-Smith look at each other before laughing at the ridiculous statement.

"Adolf Hitler!" Bedell-Smith mutters as his laugh turns into a nervous cough with the realisation of the political ramifications of such a rumour doing the rounds hits home.

Showing increasing interest, Eisenhower stares stone-faced at Ingram. "You must be misinformed, Captain."

"I'm afraid not, sir. Major Robertson infiltrated the Berghof and reported him alive and well."

"I don't," Eisenhower stutters with a slight giggle. "I can't believe it."

"Who the hell is Major Robertson?" Bedell-Smith enquires.

"He works for General Waverley, sir."

"And he works for me!" Eisenhower shouts angrily.

"Does he?" Bedell-Smith mumbles sceptically to Eisenhower's exasperation.

"He's a British intelligence officer," Ingram carries on to Eisenhower's increasing ire. "I believe he's SIS, sir."

"Why is a British intelligence officer working for General Waverley?" Unaware of the answer, Ingram shrugs his shoulders

Annoyed, Eisenhower slams his fist hard on his desk. "And we are to take this identification as reliable?" he shouts, standing and forcing his chair back across the floor.

"I believe he worked intelligence for the British in Berlin before the war," Ingram explains. "That's all I know about him. They say he knew Hitler personally."

"So, that would make it a positive identification?" Bedell-Smith said with a stern grin.

Eisenhower paces as he flexes out his aching hand to disperse the pain. "This just keeps getting better. I find it hard to believe that an officer in the United States Army would treacherously disobey his standing orders and carry out such an unprincipled deed."

"Not a risk you can take," Bedell-Smith interrupts stopping Eisenhower dead.

Conscious that any scandal, no matter how large or small, could scupper his political expectations of election into the White House and becoming a future President of the United States, Eisenhower's glare turns on Ingram. "Where is General Waverley now?"

"He's on his way to Augsburg to set up everything required for Hitler," Ingram adds, intensely intimidated by Eisenhower's look. "He left his office a few hours ago, sir."

"You will have to show your commander-in-chief loyalty from now on, Captain."

Unaware he had just become an important pawn in the world of politics and military intelligence, Ingram nods. "Yes, sir."

"I want General Waverley and this Major Robertson arrested immediately," Eisenhower orders. "I want the head of British intelligence in this office within the hour. They will all pay for defying me."

"I will see to it," Bedell-Smith said as he moved for the door.

"If this is true about Hitler!" Eisenhower adds with a shrill. "I want them all in irons at the earliest. I don't want to deny the hangman his spoils."

Bedell-Smith turns to Ingram. "Follow me, Captain," he said, and Ingram saluted, exiting and leaving Eisenhower rubbing his throbbing hand before picking up the phone and dialling.

***

Lischinsky sits behind his desk in his command wagon with Vasteroff standing patiently awaiting his next command when there is a knock on the door for a lieutenant to enter and stand rigidly to attention as he awaits the general to look up and inform him to speak.

"Message from Moscow, Comrade General," the lieutenant says as he hands Lischinsky an envelope, then salutes and makes a hasty exit. Lischinsky opens the envelope and takes out the telex to read, and his face changes to one of enraged shock as the written words echo through his mind. "Moscow has agreed to a cease-fire," he grumbles as he angrily scrunches the telex tightly into his fist. "So, the foolish Americans can get back their men that the Germans captured."

"Uncharacteristically humanitarian of them, Comrade General," Vasteroff remarks making Lischinsky vault out of his chair in anger. Believing he had spoken out of turn and that his general's ire was aimed at him, he backs off, straightening himself out and comes to attention to await the onslaught. "Apologies, Comrade General, I didn't mean to imply."

Lischinsky moves to the window to stare over the surrounding Obersalzberg Mountains and ponders why his high command would agree to a cease-fire. "I think we should offer some assistance of our own, don't you, Captain?"

"I can't see them wanting our help, Comrade General."

Lischinsky turns angrily to face Vasteroff, who forces his body more rigidly into attention. "That's why I am a general, and you are a captain, fool."

"Sorry, Comrade General," Vasteroff apologised in terror of recrimination.

"But they will be getting it anyway, and you, Captain, will be giving them that assistance on my behalf."

"What do you intend to do, sir?"

Not having a positive idea in mind, Lischinsky grins, amused but doesn't answer.

***

The high command of the Red Army military (Stavka) dates from the Imperial armed forces of the Tsarist era to that of the

Soviet Union. They meet regularly in the Kremlin in Moscow to discuss military strategy, and although many high-ranking military figures sit at these meetings, Stalin's voice is the only one taken seriously.

***

WEDNESDAY, MAY 9TH 1945

***

Dew glistens over the grass covering the Obersalzberg Mountains as Skorzeny stares apprehensively down the road from the Berghof. Radl, Hanna and Shint stand further back, not feeling their commander's responsibilities but still apprehensive about what his plan entails. His face covered by a blanket and heavily sedated, Hitler lies on a stretcher as Eva and Dr Bergman stand next to him, wearing doctor's coats to stand out as civilians. Further down and guarded by German soldiers, Gates and the GIs sit dejectedly, paying no attention to their surroundings, unaware of the history unfolding before them. Carrying the Colt model 1905 Marine Corps revolver, Skorzeny moves to Gates and takes it out of its holster to empty the barrel of bullets onto the ground, then hands it and the empty holster to the major before moving off. Pleased to have his family heirloom back, Gates smiles and shouts his gratitude which Skorzeny ignores. An American Dodge WC54 ambulance and a General Motors Company CCKW truck, flying white flags, approach from the distance and a German soldier calls out their sighting.

"Are you ready, Doctor?" Skorzeny shouts.

Nervously aware of the job at hand, Dr Bergman nods as he adjusts his white coat and constantly checks the vitals of his Führer. Four hundred yards behind the American ambulance, a Russian Zil 5 truck follows, not flying a flag of truce.

"We have more visitors, Otto," Radl said, pointing.

Skorzeny walks to the edge of the road with a good view of the approaching ambulance and trucks to instantly recognise the Russian following. "We'll have to do this fast."

Robertson drives up in the ambulance and stops in front of Skorzeny, leaning out of the window, smiling broadly.

"I see you have brought friends," Skorzeny said, pointing behind for Robertson to look.

"I didn't invite them," Robertson replies frantically. "We need to get the Führer into the ambulance quickly." He alights with the American truck stopping behind.

Shint and Radl lift Hitler's stretcher into the rear of the ambulance and fix it securely in place as Dr Bergman and Eva follow, and Skorzeny slams the door tight behind them to conceal their presence. The Russian truck drives up as fast as its 5.6-litre engine will allow and skids hard to a halt behind the American truck. Vasteroff alights and pushes arrogantly through Gates and the American soldiers to their annoyance as they attempt to climb onto their truck. Vasteroff tries to look into the rear window of the ambulance, but Robertson moves in front, preventing him.

"I wasn't informed there were casualties, Major," Vasteroff enquires curiously as he watches Harvey limp over to the American truck and clamber on board.

"And you are?" Robertson snarls.

Vasteroff salutes, coming to rigid attention. "Kapitan Alexei Vasteroff. I am here at the compliments of Colonel General Lischinsky to offer the assistance of the 3rd Ukrainian front."

"That won't be necessary, Captain; we have everything under control," Robertson snipes as he pushes Vasteroff toward his truck.

"I have a vehicle to help convey the Americans to safety," Vasteroff said as he turned with his arm outstretched as if introducing the Russian truck to all around.

Allowing his hatred for the Red Army to overtake the moment and increase the underestimated tension, Skorzeny snarls with venom. "We don't need the help of sub-humans!"

Annoyed that the enemy he believes had been defeated by the Red Army is addressing him on personal terms when he should be more subservient, Vasteroff turns to Skorzeny as he reaches for his Tokarev TT semi-automatic pistol, which forces Robertson to grab his arm and pull him around to face him as the sound of several German soldiers cocking their guns echoes across the mountains. Vasteroff looks around nervously, aware he is amongst people who despise him and all he stands for.

"That's enough, Colonel!" Robertson shouts, holding Vasteroff's arm tight as he struggles to get free.

Skorzeny lifts his hand for his men to lower their weapons and stand down.

"What are you doing?" Robertson adds angrily as he pushes Vasteroff closer toward his truck. "This is a tense enough situation without you adding to it."

"Russian medicine for the injured!" Skorzeny shouts to Robertson's irritation.

"I think you should leave, Captain," Robertson said in an ordering tone which Vasteroff didn't take kindly to as he angrily pulled his arm away.

"General Lischinsky will be angered you refused his offer of assistance, Major Robertson."

"Inform the general of our thanks, but we have everything under control. If we knew you were coming, we might have come to some understanding."

Vasteroff turns to Skorzeny and glowers in recognition as he moves back to his truck and drives off.

"He recognised you, Colonel," Robertson said.

Skorzeny smiles, then laughs. "The scar is always a giveaway, but he also knew your name and rank. How could that be?" he adds mistrustingly as he walks to Shint and Hanna. "You know what to do." he whispers, keeping his curious eye on Robertson.

Shint steps back salutes, and then walks off, having been given his orders.

Skorzeny takes Hanna's hands and kisses them affectionately as Robertson looks on. "We'll meet again soon?" he says lovingly, bringing a smile to her troubled face, but this quickly wanes as she notices the Scotsman's smiling interest.

Their hands come apart, and Skorzeny walks off, leaving her deeply sad as he gets into the ambulance. Once again, the war parts them, and she worries about his future. She turns to walk off and sees Robertson smiling curiously as he gets into the ambulance before it drives off down the road. As the ambulance moves along, Robertson frequently looks at Skorzeny with a childish grin.

"You got something on your mind?" Skorzeny snipes.

"That's one lovely lady, Colonel," Robertson answers, but Skorzeny ignores him and doesn't reply.

"Where are we heading, Otto?" Radl enquires.

"Augsburg," Robertson interrupts.

Skorzeny turns his mistrust onto the Scotsman. "Augsburg! Why Augsburg?"

"We have a hospital set aside for the Führer where he will be safe and well looked after."

***

Set in a small quiet, inoffensive part of the city, Augsburg sanatorium had been built in 1859 and had changed its purpose several times over the years from a sanatorium to an asylum and then back to a sanatorium due to the high casualties of the war. Before hostilities it had seen heinous criminal activities as the Nazis had used it to murder disabled and mentally impaired people during their brutal Aktion T4 euthanasia programme to rid the Germanic gene of affliction and withhold the master races theories.

***

Requisitioned by the American Military in January 1945, the sanatorium had been used for why it had been built initially and had tended to the injured and ailing during the Allied advance through Germany. Although cleaned and disinfected, the buildings still emanate an overwhelming feeling of immortality and bereavement, not the health-giving comfort a hospital should impart. Waverley had ordered a special ward set aside for Hitler and his party to be kept secure and for him to be nursed back to health. Located at the unused rear, he believes he will be able to hide the dictator from the prying eyes of the outside world that want him to stand trial on the heinous charges of bringing the World to War and the deaths of over fifty million people. The ambulance drives through the large wrought iron gates supported on both sides by heavily carved stone columns that show the sanatorium at one time was of the finest repute. Noticing a Dodge light truck exiting with Waverley sitting in the rear, Robertson glances at the general, who he believed would be awaiting their arrival and watches through the side view mirrors as he disappears into the distance. Ingram and numerous Military police officers exit the sanatorium rear and stand, adding to Robertson's belief that they are his welcoming party and Hitler's security detail. Robertson alights and opens the ambulance's rear doors for Dr Bergman and Eva to exit and an MP to quickly bundle them inside out of sight. Bemused about the heavy presence of military police that seems to be coming from all angles, Robertson assumes Waverley had overestimated Hitler's protection and moves toward Ingram. Skorzeny and Radl alight, both unnerved by the number of MPs surrounding them.

"I didn't expect to see you here, Captain," Robertson said curiously of the Americans as he rounds on him.

"There are some new developments, Major," Ingram said, lifting his hand in a pre-arranged order for the MPs to cock their weapons in a show of strength. "You are all under arrest!"

"What's going on?" Robertson enquires with haste, but Ingram ignores him.

Showing elation at his minor role in Hitler's capture, Ingram arrogantly surveys the scene as the MPs disarm everyone.

Skorzeny's glance shifts around as the realisation of his predicament sets in. "We've been betrayed, Karl," he said, turning his irate stare onto Robertson, who hadn't taken his betrayed eyes off Ingram. "Ike didn't like your plan, Major."

"Who the fuck informed him?" Robertson shouts, mortified by the thought.

Believing he had carried out his duty and that, for whatever reason, his commanding general was acting without honour, Ingram answers with pride. "I did."

Enraged at his stupidity in walking Hitler into a trap, Robertson pushes the American against the ambulance and punches him several times. However, an MP using his M1 carbine strikes him hard on the top of his head, knocking him to the ground. In great pain, Robertson kneels, rubbing his head with blood flowing through his fingers. Ingram straightens himself out, wipes the blood off his face with his sleeve, and then spits onto the ground next to his attacker.

Having watched the arrest from the safety of an upstairs window, Colonel Fraser exits the building enjoying the role of the victor over the vanquished. "What do we have here?" he said, scanning the scene until his stare fixed on Robertson. "So, this is the British traitor."

***

Colonel Howard Fraser entered West Point military academy at the age of eighteen and graduated in 1924 into the artillery. He served worldwide, training recruits in the use of the artillery role on the battlefield. When in 1937, his leadership qualities were recognised, he was transferred to Military Intelligence in Washington to serve on Eisenhower's staff for Operation Torch (the invasion of Morocco) in November 1942. Power hungry and self-centred, he used influential connections in the military and senate to get him a role within the Office of Strategic Services (OSS) under the direct orders of his old West Point friend, General Eisenhower, making him a man the European commander-in-chief trusts enough to carry out a clandestine investigation in the hope of dispelling or confirming what Ingram had informed him of.

***

Unhappy at being called a traitor by his own side, Robertson turns his ire on Fraser. "And who the fucking hell are you?"

"And Colonel Skorzeny," Fraser continues, ignoring Robertson's rant as he walks up to an MP to take the Austrian's Luger off him. "A lovely trophy for a trophy hunter like myself."

Skorzeny is desperate to retaliate but knows he is outgunned and may cause harm to his Führer if he tries anything.

Fraser points the Luger between Skorzeny and Radl. "Take these two bastards away," he said with loathing.

Several MPs grab Skorzeny, but the Austrian holds himself straight and proud as numerous blows knock him to his knees.

"Karl, I can only apologise! I have walked you into a trap!" Skorzeny shouts as he stares his contempt at Robertson, who glances back, betrayed but not convincing enough to make the Austrian believe it wasn't a set-up.

An MP rushes Radl, but he lifts his hands in compliance, aware he is outnumbered, and follows, not wanting to endure the same painful embarrassment his commander had endured.

To attack Fraser, Robertson attempts to stand but gets held back by two MPs who pull his arms behind his back and hold him tightly, making him wince in pain.

"You are under arrest," Fraser blusters with self-importance.

"On what charge?" Robertson shouts, confident the American has got his reasoning wrong.

"What other charge could there be for a traitor other than treason."

"Treason my arse!" Robertson shouts before laughing. "You don't know what the fuck you are talking about, Colonel."

"And I think we can add the lighter charge of insubordination toward a superior officer."

"Superior, my arse," Robertson said, adding to his laughter.

Fraser turns to Ingram. "You did a good job, Captain. You will make major for this."

Robertson's laugh becomes exaggeratedly boisterous. "Major! He'll be lucky to keep his fucking job."

"You'll be lucky to keep your life, limey," Ingram retorts. "I've been reliably informed they shoot traitors."

Fraser doesn't take kindly to Robertson's flippant attitude. "Get the traitor back to Rosenheim at the earliest. If you have any problems, shoot, but only injure him. We don't want to spoil the executioner's fun."

Ingram unclips his holster and places his hand over his Browning. "With pleasure, sir."

The MP¬s shove Robertson toward the jeep to be handcuffed and then manhandled into the rear.

***

Stripped of his medals and battle honours by trinket hunting GIs, Skorzeny stares out of the barred cell window of the old Bavarian police station in Augsburg that had been set aside to detain him and Radl. Aware he is less than three miles from the sanatorium where the man he had sworn to protect is being held makes him dejected and helpless.

Not feeling the responsibilities that burden his friend, Radl lies on one of the bunks, only despondent by the thought of being incarcerated. "Sit down, Otto," he said, irritated by his commander's self-loathing shuffling. "Relax, there's nothing we can do about it."

Aggrieved at being disarmed so easily and allowing his Führer, friends and comrades to be handed to the enemy without a fight, Skorzeny shouts, "Relax! General von Stiffel will be looking down, annoyed and frustrated at how easily I handed the Führer to the Americans! Not a single bullet was fired in his defence!"

"You can't blame yourself, Otto."

"Can't I! I was in command!"

"Of another man's plan!"

"Who else can I blame?" Skorzeny shouts, then quickly calms. "I can't be excused from my duty."

"You didn't know the plan in full, Otto. General von Stiffel took that with him to the grave."

Angered at his idiocy, Skorzeny grabs the window bars and pulls at them aggressively, hoping they will come away. "When I meet Rumanigger again, I am going to put a bullet in his fucking head."

"You can't kill him, Otto."

"Can't I?" Skorzeny snipes with bitterness.

"He's doing his duty as you were doing yours," Radl said as he stood to look out through the barred door. "He's an English soldier."

"Who cares. I'm still going to kill the bastard."

"We have visitors," Radl interrupts as he moves to his bunk.

The cell door opens, and Fraser enters smiling, the arrogance of the winner of a game he hadn't played an active part in. Not intending to show respect to his enemy, Skorzeny sits and lifts his feet onto the bunk.

"Hello again, gentlemen. Let me introduce myself. My name is Colonel Howard Fraser. I work for United States military intelligence and would appreciate you answering a few of my questions."

"Ask Rumanigger," Skorzeny retorts with a cackle.

"Rumanigger! Who the hell is Rumanigger?" Fraser said, genuinely unaware.

"As if he doesn't know," Radl adds with a sneering shake of his head.

"I have questions that need to be answered whether today or another. Once I have the required information, I can transfer you to a regular prisoner of war camp."

Skorzeny laughs at the thought. "SS Standartenführer Otto Skorzeny, SS number 295979."

"SS Sturmbannführer Karl Radl, SS number 297438."

"If you are going to adopt that immature attitude, you will be my guests for the foreseeable future."

"You're wasting your time," Skorzeny snarls. "We have nothing to say to you today or any other day."

"Is that so? Maybe I should come back when you've had time to reflect," Fraser says, his tone more menacing. "As SS officers, you will both be aware there are many ways to make men talk, some better than others, but that choice will ultimately have to be yours." He walks to the door and pauses a few seconds before looking back. "If that man is Adolf Hitler, I'm going to hang him from the Brandenburg gate."

Angrily, Skorzeny vaults to his feet, but Radl jumps up just in time to restrain him before he makes contact with the American colonel, who bangs fearfully hard on the cell door for an MP to open.

"I see I touched a nerve."

Concerned for his Führer's life, Skorzeny calms. "How is he doing, Colonel?"

Fraser laughs. "Colonel Howard Fraser 0-15275."

Skorzeny breaks free of Radl's hold and makes his way to the cell door as it is closed in his face, and he kicks it several times as he looks through the bars at the American colonel, still laughing as he walks off into the distance.

"You walked into that one, Otto," Radl said with a laugh.

Skorzeny turns fast and angry to face his friend, showing he isn't in the mood for mirth.

"Sorry, Otto, I'm just trying to calm things down."

"I don't need to calm down!" Skorzeny shouts as he walks back to the window and looks through the bars and the freedom it beholds. "I need to get angrier. I've dishonoured my family."

"You need to get things into perspective. Nothing could be done. If you'd fought back, the Führer could have been injured or killed in the firefight."

Skorzeny smiles with understanding. "We need to get the hell out of here, Karl," he adds with the obvious.

***

Unconsciously sedated and oblivious to his surroundings, Hitler lies in a hospital bed in the secure ward of the Augsburg sanatorium. Dr Bergman and Eva sit to one side, falling in and out of a bored consciousness. The silhouettes of two-armed MPs cast shadows through the glass door showing all inside they are prisoners of the United States Military and not the honoured guests they naively believed they were to be.

The door opens, and Fraser enters smiling with arrogance as he ponders the plaudits and medals; he believes he will be showered with for being the man to arrest and bring Hitler to justice. "How is he, Doctor?" he enquires, not caring about the answer.

Dr Bergman comes around sluggishly to find Fraser towering high above and stands to recompose himself as his eyes become accustomed to the bright light, and Fraser repeats his question. "Not good, I'm afraid."

"Will he live?" Fraser enquires with the only question that truly interests him.

Having heard Fraser's questioning, Eva comes around. "Why would you care," she says as tears of exhaustion and concern stream down her face.

Callously, Fraser turns to stare directly into her bloodshot eyes. "I don't, Fräulein Braun, but my superiors, for some unimaginable reason, do. Is he fit to travel?"

"My name is Frau Hitler!" she shouts, and Fraser holds in his desire to laugh.

"Is that so?"

"He shouldn't be moved, Colonel," Dr Bergman intercedes. "He isn't well enough to travel."

Voices can be heard outside as two shadows appear beside the MPs when the door opens slowly for two doctors under Fraser's command to enter.

"If you don't mind, I will wait for my doctor's diagnosis. I believe they will be more forthcoming with the truth."

Annoyed that his professional opinion and honour had been blatantly overlooked, Dr Bergman stares and shuffles his contempt. "Why do you need your own diagnosis?"

"The patient will get a thorough, unbiased examination," one of the doctors interjects in an overpowering manner that demeans the German doctor more.

"When you are finished, report your findings to my office," Fraser adds.

Eva stands and takes hold of her husband's hand. "Where do you intend to take him, Colonel?"

"You will find out when you get there," Fraser answers dismissively, then exits.

Disheartened, Dr Bergman steps back to allow the doctors through before examining the man they recognise but have been ordered not to question his identity.

***

The jeep, driven by an MP with Ingram in the front and Robertson handcuffed in the rear, travels slowly through the Bavarian countryside, heading toward Rosenheim airbase. Believing he is the victor, Ingram keeps glancing back at Robertson, who initially ignores his interest, then gives a wink and puckering his lips to give a smacking kiss that enrages the American captain.

"Pull over," Ingram orders turning to the MP, who carries on until he repeats the command with more venom.

The MP breaks hard, forcing the jeep into a skidding stop with a loud screech of tyres and a cloud of dust.

Athletically, Ingram leaps out like a boxer entering the ring for a title fight, then turns his irate stare on Robertson. "Get him out."

The MP alights and grabs his M3 grease gun to aim at the Scotsman, who laughs at the animation of the two men attempting to intimidate him.

"What's going on, Major?" Robertson said with sarcasm to the captain's imminent rise in rank.

Ingram rubs his sore face with one hand and beckons Robertson to alight with the other.

Conscious he is being invited to a rematch of their scuffle, Robertson grins with delight. "Did you like that one, Major," he said as he touched his blood-soaked head. "I think you won the first round with the help of your friend here." He glances at the nonplussed MP, who shakes his head in denial. "Well, it was one of you red cap arseholes." The MP doesn't take kindly to being called a red cap which is a term used to identify a British military police officer and cocks his M3.

"Another hero who needs a weapon to threaten an unarmed man," Robertson said to the MP's ire.

Ingram shouts out high in confidence that underestimates Robertson's strength and prowess. "I don't need a weapon! You wanna try that again now I'm ready, limey."

"You seem confident of victory. Have you read my file?" Robertson said as he stepped from the jeep and lifted his handcuffed hands. "You think you could un-cuff me, Major!" he sneers. "Or is that an advantage you need?"

Ingram turns to the MP and snipes. "Keep him covered. He's a sneaky bastard."

"How could you know that?" Robertson said as Ingram un-cuffs him. "You must have read my file."

Confidently, Ingram throws the handcuffs into the rear of the jeep. "I don't need to read the file of a man whose ass I'm going to kick."

Keeping their eyes on each other, Robertson and Ingram start circling as the bored MP relaxes against the jeep and pulls out a carton of cigarettes to set himself up with a smoke.

"I like a man with confidence," Robertson snipes as he passes the MP and swings around to elbow him in the side of the face knocking the cigarette out of his mouth and him sideways. The MP attempts to lift the M3, but Robertson punches him in the face several times, knocking him onto the ground out cold and dropping the M3 to land close to Ingram's feet.

Robertson laughs as Ingram's unnerved glance shifts between the M3 and him. "Do you think you can make it?" he teases as his confidence increases and Ingram's visibly wanes.

"I don't need a gun, you limey bastard," Ingram shouts as he reaches slowly for his holstered Browning sidearm.

Robertson laughs. "So, you don't need a gun?"

Embarrassed by his nervousness, Ingram unclips the holster, allowing Robertson to launch himself forward and kick him hard in the chest with the sole of his right foot, forcing the American to smash against an adjacent tree. Ingram draws his Browning, attempting to take aim, but Robertson grabs his hand to prevent him from bringing it to bear as several bullets are discharged uselessly into the air. Robertson twists Ingram sideways and smashes him off the bonnet knocking the gun out of his hand and onto the ground, but Ingram manages to break free and takes the opportunity to catch his breath as his glance shifts between Robertson and the Browning lying further off.

"You still fancy your chances, Major?" Robertson mocks forcing Ingram to charge forward for them to crash together.

They scuffle vigorously, with Ingram landing several blows to Robertson's abdomen, but the Scotsman takes them with great determination before landing a few of his own, which puts the American onto his knees and then all fours to cough and splutter in pain.

"You've never been in combat, have you, Major?" Robertson sneers as he takes the opportunity to finish the American off and brings his elbow to bear, knocking his adversary flat onto his face leaving him panting and exhausted as he attempts to catch his breath.

Scraping his face across the rough ground with blood pouring from his mouth, Ingram stares at the M3 and, believing he can muster the strength to get it, he lifts himself onto all fours and scurries with all the gusto of a lame dog toward it, but Robertson kicks him with great force to hammer him over the ground and into unconsciousness. Not having wanted to hurt either of the Americans, Robertson checks their vital signs before dragging them off the road and leaving them on the grass verge out of danger. "Enjoy your promotion, Major," he said with a smile and sarcastic salute as he picked up the M3 and Browning.

***

THURSDAY, MAY 10TH 1945

***

Spread out in defensive positions across Berchtesgaden valley, an extensive array of military hardware points up the mountains as paratroopers and GIs wait for any eventuality to come from the Germans. Williams and Benjamin stand out on the road, looking up toward the German defences as they debate their next move. Further up, Shint exits the tree line onto the road carrying a white flag by his side. He pauses, looking down on the Americans for several tense seconds before starting his long demeaning walk toward them as he waves the flag showing it is one of truce and he is no threat to all the guns aiming at his person.

"Sir," Benjamin said on noticing him approaching. "We have a visitor." Williams looks to see the smartly dressed SS officer nearing. "Now, what is going down?" he said as he moved forward. "I hope that's not a flag of truce. Ike's orders are unconditional."

"Stand ready!" Benjamin shouts, and the paratroopers and GIs take up defensive positions expectant of an assault.

Several Shermans and Hellcats break cover as their commanders take hold of their M2s to point toward the solitary, unthreatening figure of Shint approaching.

"That won't be necessary," Williams commands as he moves to meet the SS lieutenant colonel, followed closely by Benjamin, who delights in being at the side of his general.

Shint comes to attention and salutes, but neither Williams nor Benjamin return showing a dishonourable trait of the victorious by not acknowledging a defeated enemy.

"To the victor, the spoils," Benjamin said with arrogance to bring a bigger smile to his general's face.

"What can we do for you, Colonel?"

Dismayed, Shint lowers his arm. "My name is Obersturmbannführer Shint of the first SS Panzer Division. I offer the surrender of the Berghof to the American army as agreed."

Williams grunts with satisfaction as he looks past Shint over the Obersalzberg mountain range. "How do you intend to carry this out, Colonel?"

"On your order, my men will file down toward your position."

Williams pulls a cigar from his jacket and places it in his mouth. "Bring your men down," he adds to his arrogant posture as he chews the end off the cigar and spits it onto the ground.

Shint stands to one side and waves the flag energetically to give the pre-arranged command for the German soldiers to leave their defensive positions and exit the treeline and file down toward their incarceration. He looks at the white flag, saddened as to its veritable meaning, then throws it to the ground unceremoniously to watch it flutter in the wind.

"Get the men ready to process the prisoners," Williams orders adding with a point. "Put them in that field for the meantime. There they will pay for breaking the surrender."

Not having given the victor's revenge a thought, Shint's stare shifts between Williams and the men under his command, believing they would be better treated.

"This will be your fourth star, sir," Benjamin said as he pulled a zippo out of his pocket to fawningly light Williams' cigar, but the general moved off, only interested in the sight of the surrendering Germans.

"We need to get them into a proper prisoner of war camp at the earliest," Williams adds. "That has barbed wire and fences to prevent the bastard's escaping justice."

Benjamin follows and lights Williams' cigar, which he puffs on heartily to blow large columns of smoke into the air as his gaze switches to Shint.

"You made the right decision, Colonel. We were about to annihilate you."

Unaware of Eisenhower's demand to eradicate the entire area through highly intensive bombing, Shint laughs confidently at his men's ability to defend the redoubt.

Long lines of demoralised but undefeated German soldiers, including Hanna and Wilder, walk down the main road past the heavily armed Americans who cover their approach with smugness. Believing they were undefeated, the Germans grudgingly throw their weapons onto the grass verge as they enter the field, where they are herded into groups. As the last of the Germans throw their only means of defence onto the ground, Shint turns to Williams and draws his Luger to present for the general to take as a prize, but as he glances past the defeated German, the sight of acrid black smoke billowing from amongst the trees to reach high into the sky catches his attention.

"What the hell's going on, Colonel?" Williams shouts, purposely betrayed by the sight that beholds him.

"I was ordered to burn the Berghof, General. Nothing is to fall into Allied hands."

Shocked that the building was in the process of being destroyed before he had the chance to collect the valuable spoils, Williams snipes with venom. "What the fuck for, Colonel?"

"That wasn't my decision to make," Shint said with pride at carrying out his orders.

Williams moves to an MP and whispers before walking off, showing his displeasure. "Benjamin put that fucking fire out immediately."

Unsure of how he is going to carry out such an act with no firefighting equipment, Benjamin orders the paratroopers and GIs to run up the mountain towards the Berghof.

"And put that bastard in irons!" Williams adds, pointing at Shint.

The MP rounds on the SS colonel and pushes him onto the jeep's bonnet to be handcuffed and then bundled into the rear.

Concerned at how Shint had been arrested, Hanna moves to the field's boundary and watches as he is driven off. "Something's wrong," she mutters, moving to confront Williams, but Wilder grabs her arm and holds her back.

"Leave this to me, Flight Captain. I will see what I can find out," Wilder said, moving toward the nearest paratrooper, who turned fast and cocked his M1 Garand to stop him in his stride.

"Back off, Kraut!" the paratrooper snarls.

"What's going on?" Wilder enquires innocently as the paratrooper lunges forward to prod him hard in the chest with the Garand's barrel forcing him back.

"Hopefully, now you bastards have surrendered the end of the fucking war."

"Why are we being held?" Wilder questions. "This wasn't part of the plan."

The paratrooper laughs, unnerving the German captain. "What plan is that, Kraut?"

Wilder moves back to Hanna, aware she would have overheard.

"We've been betrayed, Flight Captain." He turns to the paratrooper, who carries on laughing. "Do you know how long we'll be here?"

"You see any stars on my jacket?" the paratrooper growls angrier. "Get the fuck back where you were before I shoot you down."

Wilder can see the determination in the paratrooper's eyes to carry out his threat as he and Hanna back further off. "What did you make of that, Flight Captain?"

Not enjoying the peace that should be the end of her war, Hanna looks around for a means of escape.

"Not that we can do much about it," Wilder adds, looking at the Americans pointing their guns with intent to kill them.

"That isn't my style, Captain," she says with determination as her glance shifts from Williams being driven off in the rear of his command car to Benjamin, who is walking down the road having feigned his attempt to quell the fire for his general's benefit. "I need to speak to your commander," she shouts, moving forward but gets stopped by a paratrooper. "I need to speak to your general."

Curious as to why the common-looking German woman would require time with his commander, Benjamin stares at her, hoping she would have information that may make his sycophantic self-importance look good in front of the self-admiring Williams. He lifts his hand and beckons the paratrooper to allow her through. "The general's gone," he explains calmly. "You can talk to me."

Feigning fright and intimidation, Hanna's glance shifts around before stopping on Wilder for several exaggerated seconds as Benjamin follows her stare. "I'm a maid here in the Berghof," she mumbles timidly. "I know things they don't want me to say. Information, your general, may need."

Benjamin's glance shifts intriguingly between Wilder and Hanna, and he quickly concludes that she is being intimidated by the German officer. "What information could you have that would be relevant to General Williams?"

"I'm not prepared to discuss that with you," she answers, attempting to make the information she doesn't have sound more important. "After I have told you, you will send me back to where I am in danger." She turns her deceitful frightened glare back onto Wilder.

Benjamin attempts to determine if the information will be worthwhile for him to send the petite beautiful vulnerable-looking woman back to see Williams. "Then get back in line," he calls out insensitively.

Hanna makes her way into the field but keeps her distance from Wilder in the pretence of fearing him.

"Take her to the general!" Benjamin shouts for a corporal to walk over and grab her harshly by the arm. "Inform him I sent you."

"Yes, sir."

The corporal aggressively pushes Hanna toward a jeep.

"There's no need to be harsh, Corporal; she's just a maid."

Enjoying his moment of power, the corporal ignores his captain's words and pushes her against the jeep before manhandling her inside. Hanna's glance shifts coyly to Wilder, who nods knowingly as she is driven off.

***

Driving at speed along the beautiful Bavarian country roads, the corporal chews heavily on gum as his glance shifts lecherously between the road and Hanna. Seeing her as an easy target for his depraved mind, he mutters with a self-indulgent grin. "Sorry about that back there. I have to look the part in front of the officers," he adds with a mocking smile which she ignores. "So, babe, where are you from?" he mumbles, clapping and slurping heavily on the gum, which she finds obnoxious as the jeep slows to a steady cruise. "Come on, babe; the war's over. It can't hurt to fraternise a little."

Giving the impression of innocence, she shoots the corporal a momentary look of unsophistication.

"Come on. Where are you from? How many times do I need to ask?"

"Berlin," she mutters in a hushed, gentle tone.

"Not that there's much left of it!" he shouts, followed by a haughty laugh as he breaks hard to force her forward as the jeep skids to stop in a cloud of tyre smoke. Believing he had found another vulnerable destitute German refugee whom he could take advantage of and would sell her virtue for food, he stares excited and lustful at what he hopes is to come. "So, you err, looking for a man," he persists. "I mean, we've got a little time and." He reaches into the rear and takes hold of a bag which he opens to show indulgences such as chocolate, stockings and tinned food. "For friends, if you get what I'm saying. You can take your pick."

Although disgusted at the thought of selling her virtue, feigning excitement and awe, she looks into the bag. "I haven't seen such luxuries in a long time." She looks around, but all that surrounds her are muddy fields with a boundary of bushes to one side. Attentively aware she has the opportunity to make good an escape but could so easily be shot down, she grabs a pair of stockings then hastily alights to walk off.

"Hey, where are you going?" he shouts as he lifts his M1 carbine, ready to stop her by force, but she steps through a gap in the bushes and disappears without a shot being fired.

She rounds the bush to crouch out of sight and throws the stockings into the distance, disgusted by what they stand for. "Give me a minute!" she shouts as her eyes shift around, looking for anything that could be used as a weapon.

Believing he has the advantage over her vulnerability, he takes out a cigarette to light and smokes triumphantly. Looking for a means of escape, she is conscious that her only option is to take the corporal out and steal his jeep. She notices a heavy length of broken branch on the ground just by her side and gathers it up.

Suddenly, his patience snaps, and he flicks his cigarette into the distance and vaults out of the jeep. "Hey, what's taking the time? We're on a schedule here." He moves toward the hole in the bush and sticks his head through as she bounds forward to smash him across the back of the head, knocking him into the mud where a second blow makes sure he isn't getting up for a while.

Coming from a privileged background through her Nazi affiliations, Hanna had never felt the hand of starvation and couldn't truly judge the ordinary women who had no choice but to sell their bodies to feed themselves and their children. Dropping the wood on top of the corporal, she strips him of his Browning and holster, which she tightens around her slim waist, then scoops up the M1, exits the bushes and moves to the jeep, where she leaps on board and drives off at speed.

***

His wrists chafing due to the tightness of the handcuffs, Shint exits a side room of the Berchtesgadener Hof hotel followed by a large mean looking MP corporal and Williams, whose face shows anger at not gaining the intelligence he craved from his prisoner.

"Put him with the others!" Williams commands.

The MP corporal forces Shint toward the door as Lischinsky and Vasteroff bombastically enter in an ambassadorial display of overconfidence. Like long-lost friends, the American and Russian generals shake hands vigorously, and Shint laughs at their fabricated comradeship.

Williams and Lischinsky share a great deal in common, not just as generals of their respective armies but also in their hatred of the German race. The reason Williams despises the German people is also why he should despise despotic Russian generals like Lischinsky, who was also responsible for the deaths of the Jews under the orders of Stalin.

"At last, a general I can deal with," Lischinsky said with a hint of irony. "Good to finally meet you, General Lischinsky," Williams said, unaware of the Russian's mentality and intolerance toward him as a person. He points at Shint. "Have you met Lieutenant Colonel Shint of the Waffen SS, General?"

Showing no recognition of his enemy, Lischinsky doesn't venture a look. "I will see him the day he hangs."

"You first, you Russian bastard!" Shint bellows, forcing the MP corporal to grab him harshly and push him toward the door.

"I can only apologise for that, General. Some people don't know when they have been defeated," Williams said with a laugh, but he didn't get a reaction from the straight-faced Russian.

"Not a problem. Where do you intend to take this Lieutenant Colonel Shint of the Waffen SS, General?"

"We have a police station set aside in Augsburg."

Lischinsky glances at Vasteroff and gives the slightest of nods.

"As far as I am aware, General, all the renegades are now in custody."

"What about your prisoner, Adolf Hitler?" Vasteroff interrupts with the pre-arranged question that corresponds to his general's nod.

Not knowing about the Wagnerian Assignment or what had transpired since, Williams looked around, bemused. "Adolf Hitler!" he mutters with a pained laugh. "Where the hell did that come from?"

"You have him in your custody," Vasteroff adds impatiently.

"I think you have been misinformed," Williams said as his mystified glance shifted around. "My understanding is the Red Army found the charred bodies of Hitler and his mistress in the ruins of the Reich Chancellery in Berlin."

Believing he is interrogating an enemy, Vasteroff's tone becomes more aggressive. "I think not, General; we know you!"

"That's enough, Captain," Lischinsky interrupts with a feigned laugh to break the awkward moment. "I think the general has answered enough of your questions." He reaches to shake Williams' hand again. "Thank you for bringing this to a quick conclusion, General. At last, Germany has surrendered and without the conditions the fascists so desperately wanted."

Lischinsky and Vasteroff exit onto the street and move toward their car as their driver salutes and opens the rear door.

"They are withholding information, Comrade General."

"No doubt," Lischinsky said perceptively.

"Did you find out what you wanted to know, sir?"

"I believe I did. The American idiot knows nothing."

"He may be a good liar," Vasteroff adds to Lischinsky's irritation. "Why didn't you enquire about Colonel Skorzeny, Comrade General?"

"They don't need to know what I know, Captain. Berlin has fallen, and the Germans have surrendered but there is still sporadic fighting which Marshal Stalin wants to end. I will await the intelligence from Operation Myth with anticipation, but until then, I will assume the remains in the Reich Chancellery aren't that of Hitler's. Moscow believes the bodies may be him and his whore, but I am unconvinced and shall await confirmation. With that, I still want the answers to what this General Waverley and Major Robertson are up to and what they are hiding from us. Return to Augsburg. Find out what I want to know."

"Yes, Comrade General," Vasteroff said with a subservient nod. "The people that have the answers are there."

***

Operation Myth was given to Smersh (the counter-intelligence organisation of the Red Army) to capture Hitler or recover his body. In the hunt for the German dictator, they caught and using many forms of torture and humiliation, interrogated Hitler's staff from the Führerbunker at the time of the surrender. The acronym Smersh was taken from the Russian words Smert Shpionam (death to spies). They had many tasks during the Great Patriotic War, but the main one was to secure the Red Army's rear and investigate any individual organisation or criminal element deemed detrimental to the Soviet cause.

***

Driving at speed as she winds through the small Bavarian country lanes without a destination, Hanna has a deep desperation to find Skorzeny and free him, but her luck runs out when an explosion lifts the jeep into the air as a tyre bursts, forcing her into a spin before coming to a halt on the grass verge facing the opposite direction. She sighs heavily and leans on the steering wheel, pleased to have escaped with her life, before alighting and looking down at the blown tyre. The sound of a vehicle catches her attention, and not wanting to be caught in the open, her glance shifts up and down the road to see an approaching jeep in the distance. Looking for cover but finding none, she lifts the bonnet in the hope of feigning a breakdown and conceals herself underneath as she draws the Browning and cocks it with anticipation of having to defend herself. Believing a colleague is in distress, the jeep pulls up behind to help. Unaware of the danger he is in, an MP corporal alights casually and walks toward Hanna as she steps out, pointing the Browning to stop him as he reaches slowly to unclip the holster strap to his sidearm. Gullible in the thought that all he is facing is a frantic German woman who is no threat to him, the MP corporal smiles confidently.

"I wouldn't do that if I was you!" Hanna said, raising her voice. Unthreatened, the MP corporal's glance shifts between Hanna and Shint sitting in the rear of the jeep, and she fires past his head, making him grimace in shock and attentively understand she means business.

"I could just as easily kill you, Corporal."

Realising he is only a prisoner escort; the MP corporal unbuckles his gun belt, drops it to the ground, and then lifts his hands slowly in submission.

Hanna turns curiously to see Shint smiling as he lifts his hands to show he is handcuffed. "Release the colonel," she orders the MP corporal, who reluctantly moves to Shint to carry out her command.

"I don't believe it, Miss Reitsch," Shint said, dropping the handcuffs to the ground as he alighted and rubbed his chafed wrists. "The more I know of you, the more I stand in awe." He lifts the MP corporal's gun belt and fastens it around his waist.

Hanna turns to the American and points the Browning toward his face. "You can drive."

Defiantly believing he had done enough by surrendering, the MP corporal backs off, shaking his head. "I'm going nowhere!" he shouts, and she fires a shot past his ear again, making him grimace in terror at the sound that will deafen him for the foreseeable future.

"I don't have the time to argue. You either drive, or I will be forced to shoot you. I can't leave you behind to inform your superiors. The choice is yours. I will give you five seconds to decide."

The MP corporal stares at the unthreatening woman as she counts down before getting into the driver's seat without waiting for her to finish.

Shint gets into the rear and draws the Browning to point into the American's back. "What a rescue," he said in awe, slapping Hanna on the back as she got into the jeep.

"This isn't a rescue, Colonel; it's the jeep I needed," she says dolefully. "I didn't know you would be in it."

Aware he is just an afterthought, Shint sits back, grinning broadly, with nothing able to take away the elation at having been freed. Hanna reaches into the bag and pulls out a bar of chocolate to hand to him. "Chocolate," he said as his face brightened at such a delicacy. "Where did you get it?"

"Never mind that, just enjoy."

Hanna can see Shint is overcome and smiles with delight as he tears off the wrapper and takes a large bite.

"This is good," he adds. "This is the first chocolate I've had since I swapped the American prisoner's bread for some in the Ardennes."

Hanna prods her gun into the MP corporal's side. "I assume you were taking the major to the same prison you have Colonel Skorzeny in?"

Not having heard the name Skorzeny before, the MP corporal can only shake his head.

"Well, that's as good a place to start," she adds. "We can go now."

***

Augsburg police station had been closed to local law enforcement to be used by the American military and hold the significant conspirators of the national redoubt. Demoralised and worn out, Skorzeny and Radl sit on their bunks within the cell block, bored with playing poker.

The cell door opens, and Colonel Rosen enters before it slams behind him and bolts. "Good morning, gentlemen," he said, but neither Skorzeny nor Radl looked up.

***

Wearing the uniform of the 1st Household Cavalry Regiment as a cover for his main role within British Military intelligence, Colonel Rosen is a highly-educated graduate of Cambridge University and Sandhurst military academy. Being Robertson's superior, he had been brought in at the request of SIS, who was not happy at Eisenhower's accusation that they were involved in concealing what is believed to be Hitler's doppelganger. Now the powers that be want to know what reason such a fabrication could be for.

***

Agitated by the British officer's attempt at friendliness, Skorzeny laughs. "Looks like they've forgotten our numbers, Karl." Unaware of the Austrian's reluctance to give information and not having had a briefing from his American counterparts, Rosen doesn't understand the irony and remains emotionless as his stare shifts between the two prisoners.

"Shut the door on the way out!" Radl adds as he gives Skorzeny a confident wink.

Understanding military humour, Rosen laughs. "My name is Colonel Harold Rosen of British Military Intelligence."

"Like Rumanigger, Karl," Skorzeny interrupts with a laugh. "Another man we can trust with our lives."

"I'm here to ask you some questions." Rosen carries on as he takes a seat in front of his enemy.

"If they are the same ones the American wants to know, don't bother," Skorzeny snarls with bewilderment as if he would answer the same questions because a friendlier British officer asked them. "Ask him, and he will give you our numbers."

"As you can see, I am British. I don't know what you said to my American cousins, who wouldn't inform me if I asked. So here I am required to enquire myself."

Skorzeny laughs. "SS Standartenführer Otto Skorzeny, SS number 295979."

"SS Sturmbannführer Karl Radl, SS number 297438."

"I see," Rosen said, attempting to interrupt. "I get the joke now."

"No joke…You work for the same puppet master," Skorzeny adds, turning his menacing stare on the Englishman. "And as we have already said, we have given our names, ranks and serial numbers, and as you know, Colonel, that is all we are required to give under the Geneva Convention."

The thought of a Waffen SS colonel quoting the Geneva Convention after all the atrocities their regiments had committed throughout the war makes Rosen laugh and shake his head at the hypocrisy. "Let's say the man the Americans have in the hospital is Adolf Hitler," he carries on, making Skorzeny shake his head in bewilderment at what he sees as a ridiculous statement. "Just humour me for a second, Colonel. Who approached you with the plan to get him out of Berlin and while we are on the subject? Who approached you with the plan to get him out of the Berghof?"

Skorzeny takes hold of the cards and pushes them across the table to Radl. "It's your deal, Karl."

"Same stakes, Otto?"

"Haven't you won enough?" Skorzeny said with straight-faced irony.

"These are just simple questions that require simple answers," Rosen interrupts.

Radl deals the cards, and Skorzeny lifts his and smiles, pleased by the hand given.

Rosen can see he won't get any answers that session and stands to push the chair back into the corner. "We'll leave it for now," he said, knocking on the door. "Just to let you know. Germany has surrendered. It was signed at Rheims for the Allies, then repeated in Berlin for the benefit of the Russians."

Skorzeny and Radl carry on playing as if they hadn't heard, but their faces show the news has burnt deeply into their souls.

"The war is over, gentlemen. All hostilities have ceased, and the Berghof has surrendered, so you are going to be here for a long time." Skorzeny laughs, confident in his ability to escape any place of enforced incarceration.

"Who signed the surrender?" Radl enquires, increasing Skorzeny's irritation, and receives a retaliatory kick under the table, making him wince in pain.

"I believe it was General Jodl at Rheims and Field Marshal Keitel in Berlin."

"They don't have the authority to speak for the fatherland," Skorzeny snarls as he turns his angry stare on the British officer.

"They were the most senior German officers present. I believe the new Führer of Germany, Admiral Donitz, couldn't make it."

"Admiral Donitz doesn't speak for the Reich."

"That may be the case, Colonel, but you have been soundly defeated, and the sooner we get this shit over the sooner we can start the peace, and I can go home to my wife and children and hopefully live a long, contented life."

"Peace," Skorzeny sneers, believing there will never be such a thing as long as the Red Army is in Europe.

"Yes, Colonel, peace," Rosen adds as he exits and the cell door is slammed and bolted behind him.

Skorzeny stares his frustration at his cards and throws them over the floor before standing and walking to the door. "What's going on?" he mutters calmly as he stares through the bars at Rosen walking off.

"They have the Führer, yet he's talking as if they don't."

"It sounded that way to me."

"We need to find out why," Skorzeny said as his determined glare shifted from the door to the window with the realisation of his incarceration hitting home. "As a child, my mother told me we all have a guardian angel that looks after us through times of need. I believed this all the way through the war. Now I feel she has deserted me."

"What makes you think your guardian angel is female, Otto?"

Skorzeny smiles awkwardly. "I just know."

"We've got away from tougher scrapes than this."

Skorzeny grins and then looks around the brick walls before turning his glare back out of the barred window unconvinced.

***

FRIDAY, MAY 11TH 1945

***

Behind the reception counter of Augsburg police station, an American MP sergeant reads the latest copy of Stars and Stripes magazine. He continually laughs at the funny stories and pictures as he flicks through the pages of the American classic. Shint enters, followed by the reluctant MP corporal and Hanna, dressed in the uniform of an American paratrooper to conceal her blond hair under a helmet.

The MP sergeant folds the magazine and pushes it to one side as he looks up sternly. "We've been expecting you for some time," he said, unlocking the cell block door and enters, followed by Shint.

Remaining rigid, the MP corporal doesn't want to follow, but Hanna prods him hard in the kidneys with the barrel of an M1, forcing him into the cell block. She closes the door behind and follows them down the passage and around the corner to where several locked cell doors carry on into the distance.

The MP sergeant glances back at Shint and notices his hands flowing freely by his side. "Hey, bud," he said, turning on the MP corporal. "You took a chance not cuffing the Nazi bastard."

Hanna pushes the MP corporal aside to point the M1 into the MP sergeant's face shocking him. "You'll find it was me who took the risks, not cuffing the Yankee bastard, Sergeant."

Shint calmly disarms the American. "Where are the other guards?" he interrogates, and the MP sergeant reluctantly points at a door. "I'll see to them," he adds as he heads for the cell and barges in with a loud, shrilled shout to take the other MPs by surprise, capturing them.

"Where's Colonel Skorzeny?" Hanna questions the MP sergeant, who grudgingly answers.

"End cell on the right."

Sitting at a table in front of the barred window, Skorzeny keeps his eyes on the outside, dejected in his incarceration, as Radl lies further back on his bunk, his head turned away from the door as he falls in and out of a monotonous slumber. The cell door opens for the MP sergeant and MP corporal to enter, but Skorzeny ignores them, unaware Hanna had entered behind.

"We should leave, Otto," she said for Skorzeny and Radl to turn in unison and stare in bewilderment of the beautiful woman dressed as a paratrooper with an M1 in hand.

"You were right, Otto," Radl said with the widest of grins. "Your guardian angel is female."
Skorzeny nods as he keeps his loving stare on her. Three MPs enter with their hands on their heads, followed by Shint, who has them covered by a M1928A1 Thompson machine gun.
Momentarily forgetting his surroundings, Skorzeny turns menacingly on Shint. "Did you carry out my orders, Colonel?"
"Yes, sir," Shint replied with a brisk proud salute as he came to attention. "But we've been betrayed."
Not giving Shint's bravery a second thought, Skorzeny exits followed by an elated Radl at being free, and gives Shint a mocking wink. Disillusioned and underappreciated, Shint moves to exit, but Hanna places her hand tenderly on his shoulder to stop him.
"Don't worry, Colonel," she explains. "He appreciates your efforts more than he lets on. He doesn't have time to single you out and thank you personally."
"The colonel doesn't have to thank me for doing my duty," Shint said with pride in serving. "It's you who made this all possible, not me."
Saddened by the brave man's words, Hanna smiles her warmth and then exits, leaving the SS colonel standing with a deep desperation to prove himself to Germany's foremost soldier. Since his early days in the Hitler Youth, he has craved acceptance and recognition from his superiors and looked around at the MPs who stared their bemusement as he exited, slamming the cell door and incarcerating them. Skorzeny, Radl and Hanna enter the empty reception, followed by Shint, who moves to the window to scan the exterior for any threat.
"What now, Otto?" Hanna enquires.
Skorzeny looks around until his stare fixes on her, amused to see her in an American Screaming Eagle uniform. "Now we go get the Führer," he said with fortitude.

***

Paying no attention to the gothic beauty of the buildings that dominate and carrying the cavalier manner of the victor, Vasteroff drives through the beautiful town of Augsburg. Seeing a lone MP standing guard outside the main entrance to the sanatorium, he pulls over and stops in front of the nonplussed American, who comes to attention on seeing Fraser drive up behind and stop in an open-top jeep. Fraser and Vasteroff alight in unison, and the Russian turns with a smile, already aware of whom the American officer is.
"Colonel Fraser," Vasteroff said as if talking to an old acquaintance.

Unsure how to take the stranger's over-familiarity catches Fraser's attention which turns entirely on the Red Army officer.

"Colonel, my name is Kapitan Alexei Vasteroff."

Aware of Vasteroff's uniform, Fraser interrupts, speaking in perfect Russian. "Narodnyi Komissariat Vnutrennikh Del."

Vasteroff smiles and shakes his head. "Your Russian is good, Colonel, but I am just a liaison officer representing General Lischinsky of the Third Ukrainian Front."

"Your uniform informs me of a different story, Captain, so what exactly can I do for you?" Fraser rudely interrupts.

Vasteroff stares into Fraser's eyes as he looks for a reaction that may give away the desperately required intelligence. "I need to speak with your prisoner, Colonel."

"And what prisoner are you referring to, Captain? We have millions of them, and this is a hospital."

"Adolf Hitler!"

"Adolf Hitler!" Fraser repeats several times, then laughs, giving Vasteroff a mistaken sense of information. "Where did you get that intelligence from? Even this place would be past bringing him back to life."

"General Waverley at your supreme headquarters informed my general that I could ask him a few questions."

Even though Fraser doesn't work under the command of Waverley, he knows him well enough that he would never give intelligence to the Russians. "I don't think so. You need to speak to Marshal Zhukov's command in Berlin. I believe they have Hitler's body. Maybe they will be able to help you with those questions through a medium," he adds, believing his words funny, but the Georgian remains straight-faced.

"I was given permission by General Waverley to speak to him," Vasteroff pleads, irritated, but Fraser cuts him short.

"I can't see how. He's been relieved of his command and is at this moment on his way back to the United States in disgrace."

Conscious all information, no matter how small is intelligence, Fraser's statement catches Vasteroff's attention. "And why would that be, Colonel?"

Having inadvertently given away too much in the first place, Fraser has no intention of indulging in Vasteroff's thirst for knowledge. "Now, if you don't mind, Captain, I have things to do." He pushes past the Georgian and enters the building as the Russian attempts to follow, but the MP prevents him from entering.

Vasteroff backs off toward his car as he keeps the MP and the surrounding area under surveillance and notices all doors are equally guarded by alert, heavily armed MPs.

***

Being the only one dressed in the uniform of their enemy, Hanna positions herself behind the reception counter. Nervously hoping no-one enters, she notices the stars and stripes and flicks through the pages with agitation at what she believes is American propaganda before pushing it onto the floor. The sound of a car stopping outside is followed seconds later by a door slamming, making her nervously draw the Browning under the counter and point it toward the door. She glances at the cell block, aware she is in the open, alone and only able to speak a poor, broken English with a deep Germanic slant that would instantly give her away. The door opens slowly, and she tightens the grip on the Browning as her glance shifts rapidly between the cell block and the door, desperate for Skorzeny or one of the others to come to her rescue. Rosen enters and moves up to the counter. Believing Hanna to be an MP on duty, he is shocked when she lifts the Browning to point and lunges forward, knocking the gun out of her hand onto the floor as he pushes her hard against the back wall. Giving her several blows to the abdomen makes her whimper in pain, but she endeavours to push the more prominent man back, but his greater strength prevents, and he holds her tightly.

"What the hell is going on?" he snarls, but she doesn't answer, and he slams her several times against the wall until her helmet falls to the floor to reveal her long blonde flowing hair. The sight of the beautiful woman embarrasses the career soldier enough to back off in shock at how aggressive he has been toward her. "What the hell is going on?" He draws his Webley revolver but keeps it at his side as his glance shifts around, unaware of the immediate danger he is in.

Ignorant of what had happened, Shint exits the cell block dressed as an MP and sees Hanna distractedly standing against the wall, shaking.

"Where the hell have you been?" Rosen snarls, believing Shint is there to help, but the German lifts the Thompson to point into the back of the Englishman's head.

"Drop it, Colonel."

Rosen keeps a tight hold of the Webley as he turns his glare on Shint, whose eyes show determination that he won't hesitate to kill him, so he drops the revolver to the floor and backs off with his hands held high.

Hanna straightens herself out as Skorzeny and Radl enter with the uniform of their enemy over the top of theirs.

Skorzeny glances at Shint and Rosen, then smiles with delight at his capture. "What brings you here, Colonel? Have you forgotten our numbers?"

Embarrassed at being taken so easily, Rosen looks away as Skorzeny turns to see Hanna's distressed state and takes a concerned hold of her trembling hands to calm her.

"He took me by surprise," she explains, showing her anguish. "I couldn't do anything about it."

Realising Rosen had assaulted his lover, Skorzeny lets go of her and smashes the British officer in the face with the side of his fist, bursting his nose and knocking him against the wall. "You piece of shit," he shouts as he grabs him hard around the throat and punches him several times in the stomach to wind, making it hard for him to breathe.

"I didn't know it was a lady," Rosen pleads as he gasps for air, but Skorzeny tightens his grip.

Upset at the violence unfolding in front of her, Hanna shouts out. "Otto, leave him alone!"

"We don't use women in combat," Rosen explains, making Hanna stare her disgust at a remark she believes makes out she is less capable of waging war than a man.

"Otto, we don't have time for this," she pleads.

The sound of a vehicle stopping outside catches their attention, and Radl moves to the window to look out.

"We have another visitor, Otto. Looks like an American officer."

"What the hell is going on? Is it open day or what?" Skorzeny said as he pushed Rosen brusquely toward Shint, who took him forcibly around the neck. "Lock the bastard up with the others."

Rosen rubs his bleeding nose as he looks Skorzeny up and down, unsure why he is dressed as a GI. "What are you doing, Colonel?"

Skorzeny ignores the Englishman's hunt for intelligence as he turns to Hanna, concerned for her well-being.

"You'll all get the firing squad for this."

"Hanna, get into the back," Skorzeny pleads, and she picks up the Browning and Webley, then moves into the rear with haste.

 Shint prods Rosen hard in the back with the Thompson's barrel, forcing him toward the cell block as Radl positions himself to the side of the door as the sound of a car door slamming echoes into the room.

Skorzeny moves behind the reception counter, draws his Browning and turns his back to the door as he holds the gun tight against his chest out of sight.

Wearing the uniform of an American major general, Robertson enters and walks up to the reception to slap the flat of his hand on the counter. "I'm here to take the prisoners, soldier."

Radl steps out from the door, prods the barrel of his Browning hard into Robertson's temple, and disarms him of his sidearm. Robertson's shocked eyes turn to Radl before flicking to Skorzeny, who turns amused at the sight of him and his uniform.

"Major General Rumanigger, I believe," Skorzeny mocks. "You've been promoted since we last met. So, what do we owe this pleasure to?"

"Colonel Skorzeny, I'm pleased to see you," Robertson pleads, but the Austrian is having none of it.

"Of course you are."

Amused at seeing his SS uniform under the American one, Robertson looks Skorzeny up and down. "What happened to your medals, Colonel?"

"Some bastard took them as a trophy."

"I see you managed to escape."

Skorzeny lifts the Browning to point hard into Robertson's forehead, imprinting his skin. "No thanks to you. I don't need a reason to kill you, Rumanigger, but to come here today once again dressed in the uniform of my enemy."

"I'm here to help!" Robertson shouts.

Skorzeny's finger drops onto the trigger and squeezes it gently before letting go and lowering the gun to his side. "Lock the bastard up before I forget I am an officer and put him down like the rabid dog he is."

Radl prods his Browning into Robertson's neck and pushes him toward the cell door.

"What are you doing, Colonel?" Robertson pleads. "The plan could still work. You'll not make it without my help."

Skorzeny holsters the Browning. "You're not a man I can trust."

"I've done nothing for you to mistrust me."

Laughing cynically, Skorzeny grabs Robertson angrily around the throat and pushes him hard against the wall. "Done nothing to mistrust you? You're the one who got us in this shit!" he shouts, pushing the Scotsman onto the floor. "To my ever-increasing dishonour and humiliation, I believed you and your ridiculous plan, and all I achieved was to hand the Führer over without a single bullet being fired in his defence."

Robertson sits and straightens himself out. "That wasn't me."

"If it wasn't you, which of your alter egos was it? The colonel, the major, the general, which one?"

"Do I need to explain again?" Robertson said mockingly.

"No," Skorzeny utters calmly. "Get him away from me before I dishonour myself further."

"Before you take me to the cells. How long do you think you would have lasted in your redoubt if it wasn't for me? General Eisenhower had the area pencilled in for carpet bombing. All of you would have been annihilated, including the Führer."

Skorzeny stares his angst at his enemy.

"I see desperation in your eyes. Are you counting how long you would have lasted without my help, or do you want me to tell you?"

Aware Robertson speaks the truth, Skorzeny looks away, embarrassed by words he desperately doesn't want to hear.

"I know it goes against the grain, Otto, but he may still prove useful," Radl interjects.

Believing his friends' words to be a preposterous statement and one he wouldn't expect to hear from his second in command, Skorzeny calls out, angered. "I can't see how, Karl! Maybe you should explain."

Amused to find a two-star American general sitting on the floor, Shint and Hanna enter.

"What's going on?" Hanna enquires.

"You can trust me!" Robertson pleads.

Hanna's stare shifts frantically between Robertson and Skorzeny before she identifies the stranger. "What's going on, Otto?" she reiterates with haste. "What is he doing here?"

Skorzeny ignores Hanna's deep concern as he turns to Shint. "Keep a look out, Colonel. We don't want any more unwelcome guests."

Shint walks to the door and exits to keep guard from the outside.

Hanna moves swiftly to Skorzeny's side and grabs his arm impatiently, waiting for the answer to her question, but he pulls away and steps off.

"You can't trust him, Otto!"

"I don't, but Karl thinks he could prove useful."

Hanna turns her disapproving stare onto Radl, but he shrugs his shoulders, uncaring of her irritation.

"How he hasn't said," Skorzeny adds as his glance fixes menacingly on his second in command. "He was about to explain."

"Maybe you should let him explain how his plan can still work?" Radl adds, amused by Skorzeny's irritation.

Skorzeny turns on Robertson. "But say it slowly so this foolish Austrian can understand why he hasn't had you taken outside and shot," he adds sardonically.

Robertson attempts to stand but Skorzeny aggressively kicks him back down.

"What the hell, Otto!" Hanna calls out. "You can't be serious about listening to what this treacherous idiot has to say!"

"Don't worry, Hanna! It won't do any harm to listen."

Taking a deep, thoughtful breath, Robertson recomposes himself and sits with his back pushed tightly against the wall. "First, we need to get the Führer out of the hospital."

"Never!" Hanna shouts derisively at the most obvious of comments.

"We know that," Skorzeny adds, exasperated. "If that's all you bring to the table, then we have nothing else to discuss."

"I'll be no good to you in those cells."

"Is that so," Skorzeny adds calmly. "And the support of the American and British armies you promised?"

"I didn't promise anything."

"You said!" Skorzeny shouts angrily but doesn't finish the sentence.

"That I'm afraid we don't have."

"Never had!" Skorzeny retorts with hatred,

"Why do we need him?" Hanna interrupts with determination to be heard. "He's done nothing but get us out of the safety of the Berghof and into the open where we were captured and the Führer taken."

"She has a point," Skorzeny said, turning to Radl, who nodded. "Then take the bastard outside and shoot him."

"I don't think that's a good idea, Major," Robertson said as his glance shifted nervously between his enemies, staring their contempt on him, expecting a bullet.

"That's exactly what should be done," Hanna interrupts.

"I got you out of the Berghof before it was due to be flattened," Robertson argues. "It was hardly a safe place to be."

"This man can only get in the way, Otto," Hanna continues. "He will see to it we all die or spend the rest of our lives incarcerated."

Still intrigued as to how the Scotsman can help, Skorzeny probes deeper. "You still haven't informed me how useful you believe you can be?"

Robertson knows what he has to say is the only way to save his life. "I'm dressed as a major general of the United States Army and carry an identification to back that up."

Unable to convince himself to the truth, Skorzeny shakes his head disapprovingly.

"I speak like a Yank without an accent. Something none of you can do."

"He has a point," Radl said, turning to Skorzeny, who hadn't taken his stare off Robertson.

"What do you get out of it?" Hanna adds mindful all men have a price or a personal agenda.

"The chance to get at the Russians," Robertson mutters unconvincingly.

"That isn't going to happen," Skorzeny snarls, irritated at the stupidity of his enemy's statement.

"Then get the Führer to safety," Robertson adds to everyone's disapproval which comes with several shakes of heads and loud tuts.

"That's our goal, not yours!" Hanna shouts.

Skorzeny pulls Radl out of Robertson's earshot. "You seem happy to have the traitor come along, Karl."

"If you remember, Otto, I said to shoot the bastard. If he comes, it's because you want him to. I couldn't give a shit."

"I believe there's more to this than is evident to us."

"He may prove useful," Radl adds, gaining Skorzeny's curiosity as he turns his stare on Robertson, who smiles back coyly.

"I still can't see how."

"He's just told you, Otto."

"I can't bring myself to trust him. Everything in my being is urging me to kill him."

"I don't trust him either, but he did come back to help."

"He has another agenda," Skorzeny carries on suspiciously. "We're just bit players in his overall plan."

"Talking about plans. You're in command. Either shoot him or use him; the choice is ultimately yours."

Skorzeny pauses in thought. "No, Karl, but I am curious to see how this plays out."

"Come on, Otto, this isn't a game! We can't wait for him to make his play!" Hanna shouts. "He may even walk us into the hands of the Russians."

"I'm aware of that," Skorzeny snipes, then pauses for several seconds in deep thought. "I will use him for now, but he's your responsibility," he adds, grinning at Radl.

"Great," Radl mutters sarcastically, overjoyed at the thought of being Robertson's keeper.

"If he makes a wrong move, kill him."

"If he makes a wrong move, you can kill him yourself."

***

Reading over a report he had just written for General Eisenhower, Fraser sits at his desk in his office at Augsburg sanatorium as he drinks from a large glass of neat bourbon that had at one time been the property of the SS doctor who had been in command of the euthanasia programme within the sanatorium and was the previous occupant of the office. He leans back to sink into his plush leather chair and relaxes. Skorzeny's Luger sits on the front of the desk, a highly-prized trinket for the conqueror to glare upon and take great pleasure in.

***

Skorzeny, Robertson and Radl move along a brightly lit corridor looking for any clues on the whereabouts of Hitler.

"Do you know where they will be keeping the Führer?" Skorzeny enquires of Robertson, who shakes his head, genuinely unaware of orders given during his enforced absence.

Seeing an MP nearing from the opposite direction, Robertson steps out, and the MP comes to attention with a salute.

"I'm looking for Colonel Fraser's office, soldier?"

"Straight ahead, sir; it's the third door on the right."

Robertson turns his back on the MP, who adds a second salute before walking off. "Sometimes you just have to ask," he said smugly, and Skorzeny pushed him harshly forward. "That's not very clever. If we were seen someone would wonder why a lowly private was pushing a two-star general about."

Taking offence at this, Skorzeny moves to push him again but Radl steps in front to prevent his friend from carrying out his threat.

"He's right, Otto. Check your uniform."

Skorzeny looks down to see no badges of rank. "We don't want to know where Colonel Fraser is. It's the Führer we are here to get."

"Well, I wasn't going to ask where the Führer is, was I?" Robertson explains in disbelief. "Nobody other than Colonel Fraser and a few of

168

his lackeys will have an idea of what is going on, but we can go ask him, can't we?"

Every word that emanates from Robertson's mouth makes Skorzeny despise him more. "Move, General, before I forget I'm just a lowly private and put a bullet in your fucking head," he said, and Robertson laughed at the thought of the exalted colonel having such a lowly rank. "But never forget I'm in command and don't need another reason to shoot you down."

"So, you keep saying, Colonel."

***

Fraser lifts the report to read it over again before placing it back on his desk and scribbling a few words of notation on the side along with his signature. Unknown to him, the door opens slowly as he mutters at what he has written. "Who the hell is Colonel Rumanigger?" Drawing his Browning, Skorzeny enters and points it at Fraser as Robertson and Radl stand to one side as if part players in the act. Becoming aware of their presence, Fraser looks up angrily to realise who is standing before him. "Colonel Skorzeny," he said calmly as he pushed the report off the desk onto the floor in a veiled attempt to hide the contents, unaware the Austrian had no interest in it. His glance shifts between Robertson and Skorzeny's Luger lying in front. "And Major General Robertson. What can I do for you this fine day?"

"We thought you would have forgotten our numbers, Colonel," Skorzeny said, amused but not receiving a response from Fraser's humourless mannerisms. "I heard you mention the name, Rumanigger," he adds, curious about the statement, but the American believes he holds the upper hand and doesn't answer until the Austrian points the Browning hard into his face forcing him to take the threat a great deal more serious as he backs off slightly.

"What do you want to know, Colonel?"

Skorzeny notices his Luger and quickly snaps it up to replace the Browning, which he hands back to Radl. "I want to know what you know of Colonel Rumanigger," he adds, giving Robertson a mistrusting look.

Aware of his predicament, Fraser glares across the room to the hat stand where his gun belt hangs well out of reach. "The first I heard of this Colonel was when you mentioned him." Keeping his eye on Skorzeny, he opens a drawer to his side to reveal a Walther PPK he had taken off a German general as a trophy. "I hadn't heard of him before that, Colonel," he said, attempting to placate the Austrian as he reached slowly for the gun.

Skorzeny lowers the Luger and steps aside as Radl moves around the back of the room, and noticing Fraser's actions, he walks up behind, slamming the drawer on his fingers, making him wince in pain. Radl opens the drawer and lifts the Walther to show Skorzeny, who laughs. "Very naughty, Colonel, and what did you intend to do with that? Shoot us all?"

Not having thought that far ahead, Fraser grins weakly.

"Now it's my turn to ask the questions."

Fraser stands laughing and showing the arrogance he is renowned for. "Colonel Howard Fraser 0-15275."

Skorzeny grins then smashes the American hard across the face with the Luger knocking him back onto the floor and bursting his nose. "Don't mistake me for someone with morals, Colonel. I don't have the time to piss about. Where is the Führer?"

Fraser rubs the blood off his nose, then stands, brushing himself down, and moves to his desk to sit. "Colonel Howard Fraser 0-15275," he arrogantly adds, then spits blood onto the floor. "You see, Colonel, I also know the rules of the Geneva Convention."

Skorzeny grabs the American harshly by the hair and pulls his head back into the chair as he pushes the Luger hard into his face. "I believe the war is over, Colonel. Those rules don't apply here. You could call us terrorists now, and you know what comes with terror."

Fraser turns his eyes onto Robertson. "Do you intend to stand by and watch this Nazi bastard murder me, Major?"

"He's the one with the gun, Colonel," Robertson said nonplussed. "All you have to do is answer his questions. On the other hand, I could go outside and ask one of the MPs who will inform a major general of where your prisoner is, negating your reason to live."

Skorzeny turns fast to face Robertson, believing he had said the MPs wouldn't know, but Robertson shakes his head, attempting to dismiss his concern.

Fraser's glare shifted around the room, aware that no one cared about his life. "Alright, Colonel, you win."

Skorzeny releases his grip, and Fraser slouches back into his chair. "I'm going to enjoy watching you all in front of a firing squad."

"That's the second time I've been threatened with such a death," Skorzeny said as he grabbed Fraser to lift him to his feet and push him out of the door. "Next time, I may take offence."

Moving down the corridor with increased pace, Skorzeny prods his Luger into Fraser's back and forces him to increase his pace.

"Don't forget, Colonel, you; will be the first to die.

Ahead, two MPs stand guard outside the secure ward and come to attention with a salute at the sight of their commanding officer approaching. Radl steps out to point his Browning, and the shocked MPs look around anxiously as they lift their hands in surrender.

Unarming them of their sidearms, Robertson steps aside and places one of the Browning's into his empty holster, and Skorzeny turns his Luger aggressively on him.

"I'll take the guns."

Robertson hands the Browning in his hand over.

"Don't take me for a fool and the one in your holster."

"I need to be armed, Colonel."

"You'll be alright. We will protect you," Skorzeny said sardonically. With great reluctance, Robertson draws the Browning and hands it over.

"I take it all is not well in the world of treason," Fraser said with a laugh. "All of you will be executed for carrying on the war after the capitulation of Germany."

Robertson pushes Fraser against the door of the secure ward, then opens it and shoves him to stumble inside. Heavily sedated and tucked tightly into a bunk, Hitler lies with Eva on an adjacent bed hunched up as she attempts to rest.

Staring out of the barred window into the distance, Dr Bergman turns to see Fraser and the MPs in bewilderment at their entrance. "Colonel, I was hoping you would visit. I need a word with you about." He stops mid-sentence at the sight of Skorzeny and Radl entering behind.

"Colonel Skorzeny. I am pleased to see you again."

Skorzeny moves with haste to Hitler's bed, looking him over with concern. "How is he, Doctor?"

"He's resting but not good overall."

"Get everything you need. We have to get out of here fast."

"But he isn't fit to travel, Colonel, and with this being a hospital, it is the best place for him to stay."

Skorzeny's stare shifts around the room before stopping on Fraser, who laughs. "We have no choice, Doctor, get what you need."

Eva wakes, startled by a room full of visitors, and Dr Bergman takes her hands to reassure her. "What's going on, Doctor?" she mumbles.

"Colonel Skorzeny is here to rescue us."

Eva's eyes focus affectionately on Skorzeny, who smiles reassuringly to give her an overwhelming sense of safety and security she hadn't felt in days. "Where are we going, Colonel?"

"Switzerland," Robertson interrupts to Skorzeny's indignation.

Skorzeny rounds on Robertson and pushes him hard against the wall as he lifts his Luger, ready to kill Fraser and the two MPs, but Robertson grabs his arm to prevent him from bringing the gun to bear, and they scuffle a little until Radl points his Browning at the Scotsman.

"That won't be necessary, Colonel," Robertson explains.

Curious about Robertson's reasoning, Skorzeny lowers the Luger.

"We don't need to commit murder, Colonel," Robertson carries on as Skorzeny's stare shifts to Fraser and the MPs.

"Tie these up and let's get out of here," Skorzeny adds after a moment's thought.

***

Its engine ticking over, an American ambulance sits at the rear entrance to the sanatorium. Shint and Hanna stand at the open back doors, scanning the area for signs of a threat. Skorzeny exits, gripping the Luger tightly in his right-hand expecting trouble. He turns back to the door and nods for Radl and Robertson to exit at speed, carrying Hitler on a covered stretcher to load straight into the ambulance's rear, followed by Eva and Dr Bergman.

Angered, Skorzeny lunges at Robertson to grab him harshly around the neck and pushes him back against the wall in a tight grip making it hard for the Scotsman to breathe. "You stupid bastard," he snarls as he punches him hard in the stomach to drop him to his knees, winded. "We can't go to Switzerland now that they know our destination."

Wincing from the blow, Robertson straightens himself up, and Skorzeny grabs him tighter and turns to Radl.

"Karl, shoot the bastard!" he orders. "I've had enough of his shit."

Radl lifts his Browning to point, but Skorzeny remains in the firing line.

"You'll have to move, Otto."

"Just a second, Karl. I want to know why he shouted out our destination."

"To get him off our trail," Robertson mutters, hardly able to catch his breath, and Skorzeny loosens his grip slightly to allow him to speak. "Who said we were going to Switzerland?"

Intrigued, Skorzeny lets go and steps back, aiming the Luger.

"Switzerland isn't our destination," Robertson explains as his voice croaks. "The best place for the Führer to go is Spain. He has many friends there."

Sceptical, Hanna interrupts. "Spain is far away. How would we get there?"

Robertson points at the ambulance and adds flippantly. "We could always drive."

"Didn't you hear?" Hanna snipes. "Spain is far away. Over the Alps and the Pyrenees."

"If Hannibal can get elephants over the Alps, I'm sure we can get an ambulance to Spain."

Skorzeny looks to a reluctant-looking Radl and nods but doesn't receive a positive look in reply. "Let's get moving. The sooner we are on the road, the better for me."

***

Shint drives aimlessly through the Obersalzberg Mountains with Skorzeny and Robertson at his side. He switches the lights on as darkness falls, but they hardly illuminate the road ahead. "Surely we don't need the blackout covers now that the war is over?"

"We probably need them more," Skorzeny explains, winding the window down to get a better view. "We need cover for the night. These roads are far too dangerous to drive in the dark."

"Wherever we go, the Führer would be instantly recognised."

"Where better to hide than in the lair of your enemy?" Shint quickly interjects to Skorzeny's amusement.

"You got somewhere in mind, Colonel?"

"The Kehlsteinhaus."

Skorzeny contemplates their situation as his eyes switch around the sullen faces looking at him for a decision.

"That's not a bad idea," Robertson interjects, but Skorzeny ignores his unwanted input.

"Do you know how to get there?" Skorzeny enquires of Shint.

"I have an idea, Colonel."

"The Eagles Nest it is."

"You've no doubt been there, Rumanigger," Skorzeny said irritably, making Robertson snigger at what seemed like jealousy.

"Don't worry, Colonel," Robertson retorts. "You're still the Führer's favourite. I was only invited three or four times to have tea with him."

Annoyed that his Führer had a close relationship with a man he believes is a traitor, Skorzeny keeps his angry stare out of the window.

"Of course, I was also a regular at the Berghof," Robertson brags aware it will annoy Skorzeny further, but the SS colonel doesn't rise to the boast, and they settle back for the rest of the journey.

***

With the idea of gaining entry no matter what it takes, Vasteroff drives up to Augsburg sanatorium and stops outside. He unclips his holstered Tokarev with the words of Lischinsky to use any means necessary, even shoot his way in to gain the intelligence ringing through his ears. Aware he would be gunned down, disgracing his general which would instantly be passed onto his family who would suffer mistreatment and torture, he re-clips the holster sensibly, deciding more diplomatic means of entry are required. Surprised that no MPs are standing guard, he enters unchallenged and hastily through the corridors. Expecting to be stopped, he checks the rooms to no avail but on seeing an MP nearing from the opposite direction and anticipating confrontation, he takes a packet of cigarettes out of his jacket and places one in his mouth. "Have you got a light, soldier?" he said in a friendly unthreatening manner that disarms the MP as he took a box of matches out of his pocket and struck one to light his cigarette. "Do you want one?" he adds as he inhales slowly and comfortably. The MP places a cigarette in his mouth and lights it as he gives Vasteroff a curious look of recognition of his Red Army uniform. "You may be able to help," Vasteroff said to give the impression of being invited. "I have a meeting with Colonel Fraser, but he didn't say where he would be."

"He'll be in his office, sir."

"He did say he may be visiting the prisoners."

"He may be on the secure ward then, sir," the MP adds, pointing. "Straight ahead, fifth door on the left."

Vasteroff thanks the MP with a nod, then walks off, puffing heavily on the cigarette as he counts the doors, amazed at how easy his ingress had been.

***

Bound and gagged tightly within the secure ward with ripped-up sheets, Fraser and the two MPs sit as the colonel struggles to escape, but this only exhausts him. The door opens slowly to catch his attention as he awkwardly jerks his neck to see Vasteroff enter, taking a large draw off his cigarette.

Amused at what beholds him, Vasteroff drops the cigarette to the floor and stamps it out. "What do we have here?" he said as he moved in hesitantly. Believing it to be a trap, he closes the door and draws the Tokarev as his stare shifts around the room. Noticing the empty bed and medical equipment, he moves to Fraser and pulls his gag down. "Quick, Captain, untie me," Fraser implores as he frantically shuffles in the chair.

Still believing he is somehow being fooled, Vasteroff moves to the door and opens it to check outside. "Why would I do that, Colonel?"

"They're escaping," Fraser said, heightening the Georgian's attention.

"Who's escaping?"

Knowing he can't give the intelligence away, Fraser recomposes himself. "Untie me, Captain, please. I must get out of here."

"First things first, Colonel. When you said they are escaping, did you mean Adolf Hitler?"

Knowing he cannot answer honestly, Fraser's stare shifts around the room before stopping angrily on Vasteroff, who moves over to point the Tokarev hard into his face.

"I advise you to answer, Colonel."

Fraser believes Vasteroff won't use violence and confidently keeps his stare of contempt on him.

"Then, we have nothing more to discuss," Vasteroff said, defeated, as he pulled Fraser's gag back up as the American unsuccessfully struggled to prevent him. He moves to the door, then stops and turns back. "I will find out what is going on, Colonel. I promise you that."

Angrily unable to speak, Fraser shuffles as Vasteroff holsters his Tokarev and exits.

***

Only illuminated by the moon in the cloudless night sky, the ambulance drives cautiously through the darkness. Climbing higher up Mount Kehlstein as Skorzeny had deemed it astute to switch the lights off to prevent them from being seen from a distance, making Shint's driving task even more dangerous.

"I thought you knew where it is?" Skorzeny shouts to Shint's ire.

"I have a vague idea, sir, but this is from memory," Shint replies without taking his eyes off the road. "And it was in the daytime I drove here," he adds as an argument to defend his actions.

"We need to find cover."

"We can always sleep in the ambulance."

"The Führer commands more security than the back of an ambulance!" Skorzeny shouts at what he believes to be a ridiculous statement.

"Of course, sir," Shint apologised, embarrassed.

Several taps come from behind the bulkhead, followed by the faint voice of a concerned Dr Bergman. "Keep it down, please. The Führer needs to rest."

Aware that all the words he needs to say will be vociferous, Skorzeny takes several shallow breaths to calm down and turns his attention back onto the road. The road to the Kehlsteinhaus is overgrown, showing signs that it had long since been unused. The ambulance drives up and then stops where the road ends.

Shint sighs with relief as he lets go of the nervous tension that has overwhelmed every inch of the drive. "I believe we are here, Colonel." Skorzeny alights, stretching out his aching body, followed by Robertson and Shint, who carry out the same much-needed task. They look around for any signs of the tea house entrance but bushes, trees and camouflage netting conceal the large stone-built doorway.

Skorzeny draws his Luger. "Check the area out. No lights."

Robertson and Shint move to the bushes and start pulling them away as Skorzeny opens the ambulance's rear doors for Hanna to look out, smiling, pleased that the long journey is at last over for the night.

"Are we here, Otto?" she enquires with a yawn.

"We think so, but the way things have been going, who knows?"

She notices the Luger in Skorzeny's hand, and believing there must be a threat, she turns her shock onto him. "What's with the gun, Otto?" Skorzeny lowers the Luger to his side and then holsters it. "It's just a precaution," he said with a confident wink.

Small arms fire opens up in front, forcing them all to scatter into the trees for cover as bullets smash into the ambulance and kick up the ground surrounding them. Hanna backs into the rear of the ambulance and covers her Führer with her body as several bullets come through the thin shell and exit the other side with Radl, Dr Bergman and Eva frantically dropping to the floor in terror. Robertson scurries across the ground and reaches for his holster, but he is quickly reminded that he is unarmed and unable to protect himself. Shint cocks the Thompson and attempts to run into the trees as he opens up with ferocity but only manages a few steps as his cramped, injured leg prevents him from moving fast enough making him an easy target as several bullets smash into his body, and he falls to his knees then over face-first into a crumpled heap and draws a long last gasping breath of life before dying.

Drawing his Luger, Skorzeny moves stealthily through the foliage and sees two men with MP40s crouching in offensive positions ahead and moving from tree to tree toward them. Noticing him, one of the men turns to fire, and he has to take cover as bullets smash all around. He stays deadly still until the firing ceases, and the men turn their aim back towards the ambulance, allowing him to spring to his feet and fire several rounds to drop the two men to the ground rapidly. Keeping his aim, he steps forward as he fires in the men's direction until the magazine clicks empty, and he ejects it onto the ground and replaces it with speed and cocks it to fire a few more rounds until he can confirm they are no longer a threat. He moves slowly forward when a bullet hits him in the shoulder, knocking him back against a tree and onto the ground writhing in pain as several more bullets fly harmlessly overhead. "Hold your fire!" he shouts several times, aware the shot had come from a friendly gun. Taking several deep breaths, he enjoys the calm and then stands awkwardly, grimacing in pain as he holds his shoulder with blood oozing through his fingers. He looks at the bodies of the two men lying covered in blood and dirt, showing signs of having lived rough for a considerable time. Exiting the foliage, he moves with intent toward the ambulance but stops, shocked at Robertson, Radl and Hanna standing over Shint's lifeless body, which had been turned to stare into the star-filled sky, his eyes wide open. The wasted life of a fellow soldier always affects him negatively, but he doesn't show his inner turmoil as he crouches to close the colonel's eyes for the last time.

Hanna notices Skorzeny's injury and moves over with concern for him. "Otto, you've been hit," she said with a shrill in her voice as Robertson and Radl stared.

"Stings a little, doesn't it, Colonel?" Robertson said with mirth as he tapped his shoulder.

Skorzeny shoots Robertson an angry glance until the irony of what he had said brings out a sardonic grin as he moves off.

"Who attacked us?" Radl enquires.

"My guess would be Gestapo," Skorzeny answers with knowledge. Hanna touches Skorzeny's arm, making him wince. "It needs to be seen to, Otto."

"Why would the Gestapo be shooting at us?" Radl enquired, and Skorzeny tugged at his uniform for him to look and be reminded he was still dressed as an American.

"Maybe we should lose the disguise."

With great haste, the American uniforms are discarded to the ground, but Robertson bundles them up into his arms.

"They may be needed," he explains.

"I will never wear that uniform again." Skorzeny declares. "I am a soldier in the Waffen SS, and if I am about to die, I will do so with honour."

Robertson places the jackets into the rear of the ambulance. "Don't allow your pride to overrule common sense, Colonel. You can't walk around looking like a recruiting poster for the Waffen SS."

Skorzeny ignores Robertson's ramblings as he turns to Radl. "We need to get the Führer into cover."

Spreading out in different directions, they search for the entrance leaving Skorzeny, who turns to stare solemnly at Shint's lifeless body in embarrassment for taking an initial negative impression of an officer who had proven his worth at such a young age. Radl moves up behind and slaps him gently on the back, bringing him out of his engrossed saddened state.

"I will see to the Colonel, Otto."

Skorzeny grins weakly then moves off.

***

Built as a present for Hitler's 50th birthday in 1939 and situated eighteen hundred and forty-three metres above sea level, it takes in magnificent commanding views over the Obersalzberg Mountains, Königssee, Salzburg and beautiful panoramic views of the Bavarian Alps. The Kehlsteinhaus, which translates into English as the house on the Kehlstein, was known as the Eagle's nest. Erected on a peak of the Hoher Göll, it was commissioned by Martin Bormann, Hitler's private secretary and the second most powerful man in the Reich and took thirteen months to complete under his demonic watchful eye.

***

Robertson and Hanna rummage through the foliage and tear at the camouflaged netting to reveal the large, ornately carved stone entrance and mahogany door. They stand aside as Skorzeny barges forward to open the double doors and enter a large stone domed lobby as their boots echo on the marble floor. They reach the ornately designed lift, and Skorzeny presses the button for the door to gracefully open and reveal the beautifully crafted polished brass and Venetian mirrors that line the interior.

"This place is still the magnificent overwhelming monstrosity I remember," Robertson said with humour that wasn't echoed by the others.

They enter the lift and with a great judder, it starts on its long journey to rise one hundred and twenty-four metres, creaking and vibrating all the way, which exposes its lack of maintenance before coming to a great shuddering halt that gives them all an impression that the cable will snap and they are about to plummet to their deaths.

Expecting more Gestapo, as the door opens slowly, Skorzeny draws his Luger and steps hesitantly into the semi-darkness. "We are German soldiers. Hold your fire," he shouts, but no reply lets him calm slightly. A large red Italian marble fireplace (presented by the Italian Dictator Benito Mussolini) dominates the extensive main reception, with logs crackling inside to keep it at a pleasant, comfortable temperature. Several covered windows allow only a small amount of moonlight to illuminate, revealing the large decorative wooden beams that run the width of the ceiling and give a sense of age even though the structure is barely six years old. Skorzeny scans for threats as he crosses to the fireplace and takes in the heat from the glowing embers. Two unmade bunks lie amongst numerous boxes, crates and works of art that lean in lines against the walls. He looks back at Robertson and Hanna and nods for them to exit the lift, which they do enthusiastically, pleased to escape its creaking sense of doom.

Skorzeny holsters his Luger and pulls out a box of matches to light several candles that illuminate the room into many more shadowy corners. "Now we know why the Gestapo were here."

"What's all this, Otto?" Hanna questions excitedly as he walks along the line of works of art.

"Spoils of war!" he answers, tapping on one of the boxes.

Well aware of the Nazi desecration of European and Russian culture, Robertson adds with disdain. "Looted from all over Europe."

Skorzeny pulls the lid off a box to show many diamonds which sparkle in the candlelight as he sifts them through his fingers. "Even though it pains me to agree with the traitor, he's right. This is plunder." He debates what to do next as he moves from window to window, looking through the blackout canvas to take in the night-time views of the Bavarian Alps. "We need to get the Führer up here fast," he said as he turned back to Robertson and Hanna, who moved to the lift. "Get Karl to gather some wood for the fire. The Führer needs to be kept warm."

**

In a state of high excitement, Lischinsky sits at his desk within his command wagon when there is a knock on the door, followed by Vasteroff entering and coming to attention with a rigid salute.

Slurring his words due to his excessive alcohol intake, Lischinsky looks up. "What did you find out, Captain?"

"We've been duped, Comrade General."

Already knowing the answer but wanting to know if Vasteroff does, Lischinsky enquires. "What do you mean, duped?"

"To prevent us from discovering what is happening, Comrade General. I have been informed that the American General Waverley has been dismissed and is on his way back to the United States."

"I see... And what do you believe is going on?" Lischinsky questions in a menacing tone the captain is well used to, but all Vasteroff can do is straighten out his awkwardness. "What do I have you around for if you can't give me the answers I need?"

Vasteroff forces his body more erect unable to answer.

***

Amazed at the numerous priceless works of art that litter the Kehlsteinhaus, Skorzeny, Hanna, and Radl flick through the paintings.

"There must be masterpieces from all of the greats," Robertson said, lifting a small Rembrandt to scrutinise its magnificence. "They must be worth millions of pounds."

Skorzeny looks at Hitler lying heavily sedated on a stretcher closest to the fire with Eva at his side holding one of his cold sallow hands. Robertson walks to the other side of the room and sits in the corner to distance himself from the enemies he readily Allied himself to.

"If only we had a convoy of trucks," Radl said to Skorzeny's nodding agreement.

"The rightful owners will want it back!" Robertson shouts, but Skorzeny ignores him as he pulls a bag out of his pocket.

"Gold and diamonds are untraceable. Gold is heavy, but diamonds," he adds as he rattles the bag.

"You surprise me, Otto," Hanna interrupts, never believing he would indulge himself in the spoils of war.

"This isn't for me, Hanna, and it shocks me you would think so. We can use it to help the Führer's future," Skorzeny adds, believing that keeping Hitler from the Allies would be costly and the diamonds would help in the many days to come.

Dazed and confused, Hitler is awoken by the raised voices as his sedation wears off. His hazy eyes focus on Robertson, bringing a wry smile to his haggard face. "Colonel Rumanigger," he mumbles in a pained weak voice that carries around the room.

As all eyes fix on him, Robertson's glance shifts between Hitler and Skorzeny as he stands and moves toward the frail dictator. Radl takes hold of an MP40 and moves stealthily closer.

Hitler lifts his trembling hand, and Robertson takes it gently. "Colonel Rumanigger, I knew it was you. Are we still at the gates of victory?" Looking for inspiration on how to answer, Robertson turns to Skorzeny, whose face only shows mistrust and anxiety at how close his enemy is to his beloved Führer. "Yes, my Führer."

"Adolf, you need to rest," Eva calls out, concerned by him conversing with whom she had been reliably informed by Hanna was a man not to be trusted.

***

Hitler had suffered from numerous illnesses over the years. He was reported to suffer from Irritable Bowel Syndrome, skin lesions, Parkinson's Disease, Asperger Syndrome and an irregular heartbeat due to symptoms of Syphilis Tertiary. It was also alleged that he only had one testicle but this was untrue even though he had been injured in the groin at the battle of the Somme in the Great War. His teeth were rotten and caused him endless pain and problems. He had a non-cancerous polyp removed from his throat and had severe eczema on his legs. All of the symptoms caused him to create addictions to several drugs due to the over prescription and experimentation by his compliant physician, Dr Morell. Most believed he suffered from hypochondria as numerous ailments increased in later years, but this was probably due to the stresses caused by Germany losing the war.

***

Worn out after the least amount of exertion, Hitler lies back and lets go of Robertson's hand for him to back off slightly as he stares straight through him as if he had disappeared and falls back into a deep unconscious sleep. Eva moves in front of the Scotsman to block his view of her husband, showing him the contempt and mistrust that forces him further off. Radl lowers the MP40 and moves aside.

Feeling all eyes on him, Robertson's glances around the room to find he is being ignored. He moves to Skorzeny and grabs his injured arm to make him wince in pain as he is pulled around face-to-face. "I saw the gun, Colonel."

Skorzeny pulls his arm away, giving him more pain, and he moves off with no intention of explaining his second in command's dutiful actions.

"You ordered your goon to kill me if I step out of line?" Robertson shouts making Radl laugh. "You think I'm some sort of sneaky bastard with no honour, but I have never betrayed a thing in my life."

"Can you keep the noise down?" Dr Bergman whispers, concerned the commotion will add to Hitler's stress. "The Führer needs to get his rest."

Ignoring the doctor's words, Skorzeny comes face to face with Robertson, their foreheads almost touching in an aggressive show. "When you swear or show allegiance to a person or cause, then go against that. You tell me another word that covers it?"

"Treason!" Hanna shouts, making Robertson turn angrily to face her. "I'm an officer in His Majesty's Army."

Not liking the tone Robertson had used against Hanna, Skorzeny draws his Lugar and points it hard into the Scotsman's face. "I don't give a shit who you think you are. You are a lying bastard of a traitor, and I should have shot you down the first time I saw you."

Robertson backs away from the Luger, but Skorzeny follows, keeping it prodded hard into his forehead. "We're more alike and have more in common than you think."

"I am nothing like you!" Skorzeny shouts, infuriated by the comparison. "Traitors like you disgust me."

"More than you think, Colonel," Robertson adds condescendingly. "Why don't you do it? Pull the fucking trigger and get all this shit over with. You'll be doing me a fucking favour to stop hearing you whine about traitors and your failings as an officer."

Skorzeny cocks the Luger with determination to end the Scotsman's life and keeps his aim.

"This fucking traitor has got you all the way here. If not for me, you'd be buried under several tonnes of rubble."

With desperation to pull the trigger, Skorzeny clenches the Luger tighter.

"Do it, Colonel. Then see how far you get."

Hanna places her hand over the Luger and pushes it away from Robertson's face. "Come, Otto. This can wait for a time when we are not in the Führer's presence. Let me take a look at that shoulder."

Skorzeny gives Robertson one last look of contempt before walking off with Hanna.

Robertson moves in the opposite direction when his sight fixes on Radl laughing. "You're all fucking mad!" he shouts. "You don't realise when someone is trying to help!"

***

SATURDAY, MAY 12TH 1945

***

Well aware of his Führer's dislike of tobacco, having awoken early, Skorzeny stands some distance from him as he puffs anxiously on his first smoke of the day. Moving from window to window, he pulls the canvas aside to survey the beautiful mountains when he notices the ambulance missing from where it had been concealed the night before. He looks around, stopping his stare on Dr Bergman sitting beside Hitler when it dawns on him that Robertson is missing. Moving with haste, he pushes boxes aside for priceless ornaments to smash to the floor and wake everyone as he frantically searches the room.

"What's going on, Colonel?" Dr Bergman enquires.

"Have you seen Rumanigger?"

"No," Dr Bergman answers as he glances the room over.

"What the fuck."

Radl jumps up with his MP40 cocked and ready to fire. "What is it, Otto?"

"We've been here too long!" Skorzeny shouts. "Get ready to move."

"Where's the traitor?" Hanna yells, looking around desperately.

"He's gone."

Hanna turns shocked to Skorzeny.

"Don't say it," he defends. "I never trusted him either, but I was talked into him staying."

"Not by me," she shouts as he turns his disdain on Radl.

"I said to shoot the bastard," Radl moans in his defence. "Remember?"

"Now isn't the time for recriminations. We need to get out of here fast."

As they gather their belongings together, the lift screeches to a halt and the door opens for Robertson to walk nonchalantly through as Skorzeny lunges forward to send him sprawling across the floor into a crumpled heap.

"You bastard! I knew I shouldn't have trusted you!" Skorzeny shouts, then draws his Luger to point hard into Robertson's face.

Aggravated by the pain of the gun digging harder into his skin, Robertson looks up. "You know, Colonel, someday you will have to start trusting people."

"I trust people, Rumanigger, just not you," Skorzeny said as he moved off, keeping the Luger pointed at his enemy, "Karl, go take a look outside."

Radl moves to the window to see the ambulance parked where it had been the night before.

"Where have you been?" Skorzeny questions as Robertson sits on one of the boxes to recompose himself.

"Into Berchtesgaden to get intelligence. I told you this uniform would come in useful."

"To deceive us into running into a trap."

"Why would I want to trap you when all I needed to do was leave you at the police station?" Robertson shouts, tired of having to explain his actions again. "Why would I come back here when you are already trapped? All I would have needed to do was inform the Yanks you were here and got on a plane home ending my war. So, come on, Colonel, you seem to know all the answers. What the fuck am I doing here?"

Radl looks at Skorzeny and shrugs his shoulders, making Robertson laugh.

"Believe it or not, Colonel, I had an idea that might save us a long drive."

"Oh, yes," Skorzeny said, sceptical of any suggestion from the traitor. "And what would that be?"

"Fly," Robertson adds as if it was the obvious answer.

Skorzeny steps back and then laughs, followed by others who add to Robertson's awkwardness. "I take it you have an aeroplane?"

"As it happens," Robertson answers arrogantly, stopping the laughter as everyone turns their bewilderment on him.

Hanna looks at Radl. "I thought you were ordered to shoot him, Karl?"

Radl lifts his MP40 to point, but Skorzeny beckons him to lower it with several exaggerated flicks of his right hand.

"Stand down, Karl. When I want him dead, I will let you know."

"I wish you'd make up your mind," Radl said, aggravated by the constant changes in his friend's demeanour.

"Where is this plane?" Skorzeny questions attempting to hold in his excitement that is self-evident to all.

Radl lowers the MP40 and stands back as he turns to Hanna. "I just do as I am told."

"Berchtesgaden Valley," Robertson answers with a large grin of triumph.

"How would you know that?" Hanna snarls.

"General Williams' plane is still there."

"Who the hell is General Williams?" Skorzeny enquires.

Having been informed by Shint of his name, Hanna answers innocently. "He's the general commanding the Americans that were waiting to kill us."

"If there is a plane and we can use it, it may be our best option," Radl interrupts.

Robertson looks around, hoping he has made himself important enough to be trusted. "Our only viable option," he adds confidentially.

Lost in thought, Skorzeny pauses as his glance shifts between Radl and Robertson. "You can drive, Rumanigger."

Pleased he is part of the plan, Robertson grins, aware Skorzeny's threatening tone still has him far from being a full member. "I take it you still don't trust me, Colonel?"

"Not in this lifetime, General," Skorzeny adds with sarcasm.

***

The ambulance moves slowly through the tree-lined lanes of the Bavarian countryside with Robertson at the wheel. Skorzeny and Hanna sit at his side, relieved by the belief that they are now just a flight away from the inevitable safety of General Franco's fascist Spain. Vasteroff's Gaz jeep approaches at speed from the opposite direction noticed by Robertson, who presses the accelerator hard for the ambulance's 3.8-litre engine to splutter into action and increase its dawdling speed as they pass.

Sensing the increase, Skorzeny turns to Robertson, curious about his actions. "What's going on?"

"It's that Russian from the Berghof," Robertson relates as his eyes shift between the rear-view mirrors.

Worried the increase in speed will give them away, Skorzeny grabs Robertson's arm. "Slow down."

Realising the intelligence he is after is in the ambulance heading in the opposite direction, Vasteroff breaks hard and skids to a halt as he stares at the vehicle moving into the distance through his rear-view mirror.

Robertson keeps his eyes on his mirrors and sees the Gaz Jeep turn in the road. "He's turning to follow."

"I wouldn't worry. What is one man going to achieve against all of us?" Skorzeny said, then banged hard on the bulkhead. "Karl, we have got a tail that needs to be cut off."

"What do you mean, Otto?" Radl shouts back, preoccupied.
"There's a Russian jeep following. Cut it off by killing the occupant," Skorzeny explains impassively, to Radl's amusement.
Radl stands unsteadily and scoops up his MP40 as he makes for the doors. "It would be advisable to cover the Führer's ears, Doctor. This is going to be noisy." He cocks the MP40, which echoes around the tightness of the ambulance's tinny rear.
Dr Bergman covers Hitler's ears and winces at not having enough hands to protect his own. Opening the doors, Radl pauses, allowing Vasteroff to be near before opening fire, forcing the Gaz jeep to swerve off the road. Shaken, Vasteroff draws his Tokarev and cocks it before restarting the engine and driving in pursuit and increasing in speed as quickly as the Gaz's 3.3-litre, 4-cylinder, 50-horsepower engine will go. He leans out the window to return fire, forcing Radl back inside as several bullets ricochet off the outside. Sensing the immediate danger to his Führer, Radl recomposes himself dropping to one knee and bringing the MP40 to his eye and returning fire with significant effect as the bullets smash into the Gaz's windscreen and bodywork which forces Vasteroff to veer off the road and skid several times as he breaks hard before crashing side on into a tree with a massive thud that ends his pursuit. Radl steps back inside, closing the door, then sits pleased to carry out his duty.
"Doesn't that bother you?" Eva said solemnly as she stared at the SS major. "The taking of another man's life."
Radl looks sardonically at Eva and grins, bewildered at her naivety of a barbaric war that had raged for many years. "He was a Russian," he answers flippantly as if the death of a Red Army soldier was less than that of anyone else.
"He was a man, Major."
Years of conflict had given Radl a deep loathing of war, but no hatred was greater than that of the Red Army adversaries he had met on the cold steppes of the Soviet Union. He admired their tenacity to fight but despised their inhumanity toward the Waffen SS prisoners who were given no quarter. "He was a Russian, and as a Russian he was an enemy of Germany. Compassion is a luxury I cannot afford, Frau Hitler," he adds reassuringly. "Maybe when all the madness is finally over, I will have the time to reflect on a wasted life, or someone can explain what it was all about, and then the almighty can take his inevitable revenge. Until that day, I will continue my duty as it is laid out before me."

Eva looks away, unable to comprehend the inner turmoil a soldier's mind goes through while carrying out the duty of war.

***

Williams' C47 stands where it had landed eight days earlier, with the burnt-out remains of von Stiffel's JU 52 to one side. Not taking his task of standing guard seriously, an American paratrooper lounges in a jeep with his dirty mud-covered boots adorning the bonnet as he looks over the souvenirs looted from the burnt-out Berghof. The ambulance comes off the country road onto the valley grass, bumping across the uneven ground to everyone's discomfort. They circle the C47 and stop a short distance off. Robertson and Skorzeny alight and move to the rear doors to reveal Radl sitting in the doorway with the MP40 on his lap and Hanna sitting adjacent.

"You won't need that, Major," Robertson said, reaching for the machine pistol, but Radl had no intention of relinquishing his weapon and turned it to point. "If it means that much to you, keep a hold of it," he adds as he backs off. "But you will find it is no longer required."

Robertson moves to the paratrooper, who gets out of the jeep and salutes. Unable to hear what is being said, Skorzeny moves mistrustingly forward as he places his hand over his Lugar.

"Don't worry, Otto, I've got them covered," Radl said, turning the MP40 to point, but Skorzeny pushed the barrel to one side.

"When he dies, Karl, it will be by my hand."

"You still don't trust him," Radl said, perplexed. "Even after he's got us this far?"

Showing her opinion hasn't faltered even though she stands not thirty feet from the plane destined to fly her to safety, Hanna interrupts with venom. "I don't."

Smiling confidently, Robertson moves back to Skorzeny as the paratrooper drives off. "Get the Führer onto the plane as quickly as possible."

Believing everything unfolding before him is too easy, Skorzeny looks to see Radl and Hanna's faces telling him the same story.

"I've requisitioned the Dakota to fly an injured officer to Paris."

"And he believed you?" Radl said in disbelief.

Pointing at the two stars on his epaulettes, Robertson answers abruptly. "These don't give him the option to disobey."

Amused by Robertson's mannerisms, Radl laughs as he jumps out of the ambulance and walks off several paces before turning back, keeping his finger firmly on the MP40s trigger.

Even though the C47 has a big white star on the side, indicating that it is from the United States Air Force, Hanna's stare moves up and down it with great admiration. "It's been a while since I have flown this type of aircraft." She smiles, her passion for carrying on flying.

"There's already a pilot on board," Robertson said, straightening her face with angst. "We caught it just before it was set to take off." He moves to the C47 and climbs on board, watched by Skorzeny. "Come on, let's get on before that bastard takes off and forgets we are here."

Having instructed the pilot, Robertson sits in the cockpit when he notices Skorzeny nearing through the fuselage, checking that everyone is safely belted in. He lifts a Colt pistol to aim at the pilot as the Austrian pops his head through. "He now knows what is expected of him, Colonel."

Skorzeny sees the Colt and draws his Lugar to point into Robertson's side. "Where did you get the gun?"

Robertson nods at the pilot, then reluctantly turns the pistol on its end and relinquishes it into Skorzeny's hands before handing it to Radl. "Any more surprises?"

Robertson shakes his head slowly.

"Then we can get underway."

The C47s propellers burst into life with smoke and fire billowing out of the engine's exhausts. They edge slowly across the grass, picking up speed as the pilot pushes the throttle levers to full for it to lift safely into the air and climb over the Obersalzberg Mountains gaining altitude. After flying several miles, the pilot points to his right for Robertson to look and see a large concentration of Lancaster bombers of the Royal Air Force flying several miles to the North.

"Where do you think they are heading?" The pilot said his words hardly out of his mouth when the Lancasters bomb bay doors opened for tens of thousands of pounds of high explosives to fall indiscriminately onto the Berghof and the surrounding Obersalzberg Mountains to brighten the air with flashes of fire and concussion as the ordnance obliterates the beauty of Hitler's Mountain retreat.

"I think Ike's got his way," Robertson whispers. Hoping he hadn't been overheard, he turns to Skorzeny and opens the cockpit door fully to find the Austrian paying little attention to the outside world. "Looks like the RAF are bombing the Berghof," he said excitedly, pointing for Skorzeny to see.

***

The Avro Lancaster four-engine-heavy-bomber was developed from the Manchester bomber and was chiefly designed by Rod Chadwick. It first saw service in 1942 and carried a crew of between five to seven men depending on the circumstances of the mission and planes designation. A maximum bomb load of between 12,000 to 22,000 lbs was easily achieved with modifications to the bomb bay over its many facelifts.

***

Skorzeny looks out of the window, saddened at the sight of each explosive concussion.

"Lancasters," Hanna said excitedly at seeing a large formation of aeroplanes before realising what they were doing. "Hasn't the English Air Force had enough practice killing women and children?"

"We're not in the Berghof, and neither are your men or any women or children," Robertson defends the decision to remove its evil presence from the face of the earth.

Baffled as to how he would know such a thing, Skorzeny turns to him.

"There's more in the Obersalzberg than the Berghof."

"Property can be rebuilt if required."

"How do you know no people will be there?"

"Your men were being marched through Berchtesgaden this morning. No doubt in preparation for the bombing," Robertson answers, aware there are very few locals around the Berghof as they had all been evicted and their homes demolished by order of Bormann because they spoilt the view for his Führer.

"And the RAF isn't renowned for being on target," Skorzeny carries on with bitterness.

"Is that right?" Robertson retorts, taking offence to the apparent slur on the brave men who had carried out the terrifying bombing missions over Germany. "Maybe you should ask the captain of the Tirpitz what he thinks of their targeting abilities."

Now Skorzeny takes offence as the two soldiers face off, but the irony of their words is soon recognised and, Skorzeny turns to look out of the window, finished with their conversation.

After hours of flight, Robertson looks out of the cockpit into the fuselage toward Skorzeny, who is still staring vacantly out of the window. "Everything is going to plan," he explains, but the Austrian ignores him. "It will be dark when we land."

"That will allow us to disappear quickly."

"That won't be necessary," Robertson interjects. "Gerona has given us permission to land."

Skorzeny turns slow but menacing to face the Scotsman. "Permission to land?" he questions, unable to comprehend their situation.

"The Führer needs hospital treatment at the earliest. We won't get that without the help of the Spanish."

"Why would the Spanish help us?" Skorzeny adds, bewildered by the thought.

"We are a diplomatic flight, Colonel."

"Diplomatic flight?" Skorzeny mutters, adding to his disbelief.

"The only way to fly and land unmolested is to carry it out under the mantle of diplomacy," Robertson explains with what he believes was their only option.

Hanna makes her way through the fuselage to Skorzeny and sidles in next to him.

"You said we can land unmolested, but that still leaves us with the problem of hiding the Führer."

Having believed he had already explained, Robertson reiterates bemused. "We're a diplomatic flight."

"What does that mean?"

"We'll have no interference."

"No interference!" Skorzeny said disconcerted. "We have the Führer on board and need to get him into hiding before everyone starts hunting for him."

"First things first, Colonel. We need to get him to the hospital. The Russians believe he is dead, so no one will be looking for him. As for everyone concerned, he's an injured soldier who requires hospital treatment."

"I can't believe we have made it!" Hanna said excitedly as she took hold of Skorzeny's hand.

"I'm not sure we have," Skorzeny adds as she kisses him passionately on the neck, and Robertson smiles in the belief he is witnessing love at first-hand, but the Austrian sees his grin and kicks the cockpit door to slam in his face.

Feeling the effects of a long, cold, uncomfortable flight, Hanna leans into Skorzeny as he sits rigidly upright and wide awake. Believing he is walking them into another trap, he debates how he can prevent it from happening.

"We are coming into land, Colonel!" Robertson shouts with elation from behind the cockpit door.

Skorzeny straightens himself out, then nudges Hanna until she comes around dazed and confused. He draws his Luger and places it at his side.

"What's going on, Otto?" she questioned, distressed by the show of mistrust, but he covered his mouth with his index finger to stop her as he whispered.

"We don't know what is waiting for us. We could just as easily be landing in London or Moscow."

"After all he has done," she said, coming around to the reasoning they had escaped. "I don't think so."

Apprehensively, he looks out the window into the darkness but can't make out any recognisable landmarks. All he knows is that they are about to land, and his Luger will not protect the Führer for long. He looks down the fuselage at Radl. "Karl, are you still armed?" he whispers, and Radl smiles as he lifts the MP40. "Good."

"Are you expecting trouble, Otto?"

Aware Radl's loyalty would never be questioned, Skorzeny nods.

"I'm not sure how much help my three bullets will be," Radl said with a grin. "But they are yours to command."

***

The C47 comes out of the darkness to land smoothly on the tarmac and taxis toward the hangers, where it comes to a halt, and the engines cut out. The door opens, and Robertson looks out into the bright lights, welcoming heat and quiet of the area as Skorzeny moves up behind and digs his Luger into his ribs.

"Remember, Rumanigger," he said with malice. "You're going to be the first to die."

Closed to civil aviation and the general public, Gerona airport is brightly illuminated with large numbers of Spanish soldiers and military hardware facing away from the runway to ensure nothing can approach. An ambulance stands to one side of the nearest hanger with a full complement of medical personnel who had been fully briefed and sworn to secrecy to expect casualties.

Smoking heavily on a large cigar, General De Sancha exits the hanger as he looks around his command, pleased to see everything in place.

"Where is my old friend?" he bellows, catching Skorzeny's attention.

***

A rotund, heavily moustached, dishevelled jovial man, Capitan General Fernando De Sancha is a veteran of many battlefields spanning the Spanish civil war to the cold Steppes of Russia. Born in

Cueta on the coast of the Straits of Gibraltar in the Spanish protectorate of Morocco in 1900, his family history stretched back to the days of the Conquistadors, and he has always been one of the ruling classes. His late father, also a general, had been commander of a prison camp in Morocco that detained Arab insurgents against the Spanish occupation of their homeland. He joined the Spanish army in 1917 as a private soldier gaining a commission by 1923, and excelled through the ranks to become one of General Franco's commanders during the Spanish civil war. He entered Spain by the side of his commander in a Junkers 52 flown by pilots of the Luftwaffe Condor legion that had been supplied in Unternehmen Feuerzauber (Operation Fire Magic), the German military aid to the Spanish Nationalists which came into force five days after the rebellion began on July 17th 1936. Throughout the Spanish civil war, he fought at the front gaining general status in late 1936, but never left the front line or his soldiers, which earned him the reputation of a fighting general. After the aid Germany gave during the civil war, Spain sent the blue brigade of Spanish volunteers to help fight the Red Army on the eastern front, with him being handpicked by General Franco himself to command a small force that acquitted itself with great honour. On October 10th 1943, General Franco ordered him and his men home, but nearly three thousand stayed to fight against the Red Army and join elite regiments like the Brandenburgers, who also fought Tito's partisans in Yugoslavia. After initially ignoring the generalissimo's orders and staying with his command, he was ordered at the insistence of his premier home early in 1944 to leave his men to die on the cold Russian Steppes. Well aware of Germany's immanent collapse, General Franco didn't want his old comrade going down with the rest of the National Socialists and saved his life.

***

Keeping his confused stare on De Sancha as his eyes adjust to his surroundings, Skorzeny lowers the Luger and pushes past Robertson onto the tarmac.

"What's with the gun, Otto?" De Sancha calls out.

Skorzeny's embarrassed stare shifts to the Luger, which he quickly holsters as Robertson moves off, shaking his head playfully, aware he had been mistrusted right up to the end. Skorzeny moves to De Sancha, and they shake hands with genuine friendship embracing, with the Spanish general's gaze shifting to Hanna standing in the C47s doorway, bringing a brighter smile to his face.

"And, of course, the ever-beautiful Hanna."

Hanna steps down for De Sancha to take her hand and kiss affectionately.

"Good to see you safe and looking well, General."

Radl moves behind, and De Sancha turns in acknowledgement to shake his hand. "It's like the good old days," he said, overawed to have arrived safe and well.

De Sancha turns to Robertson but doesn't utter a word as he nods his acknowledgement of the Scotsman walking to one side.

"What brings you here, General?" Skorzeny said in awe of his old friend's presence.

"To meet you, of course," De Sancha answers pretentiously as he waves for the medical personnel to make their way onto the C47. "Maybe we should forget the pleasantries and get the Führer to the hospital."

Bemused, Skorzeny enquires with great agitation. "How do you know we have the Führer with us, General?"

"Never mind that, Otto. An ambulance waits along with the best doctors in Spain."

Believing an explanation is required to placate the Austrian, Robertson interrupts. "We radioed ahead. We had to tell them we were a diplomatic flight."

"Then the news the Führer is alive is out."

"Only a few selected people know," De Sancha explains. "And only the ones I trust personally."

Skorzeny looks around the throngs of Spanish soldiers.

"You have nothing to worry about, Colonel. The Führer's secret is safe. They believe this is the arrival of a Spanish general injured on the Russian front being repatriated."

Believing De Sancha wouldn't lie to him, Skorzeny looks at the general, who smiles wholeheartedly before beckoning over a captain with several flicks of his hand.

"Take the Americans."

Thinking Robertson now deserves a little trust and loyalty, Skorzeny calls out. "Hold on, General!"

"They are only to be debriefed," De Sancha reassures. "Once we are finished, they can go on their way, wherever that may be."

"We'll be alright," Robertson adds, touched by Skorzeny's concern even though it had come too late.

"Before you go," Skorzeny mutters, reaching into his inside jacket pocket to produce the cigar given by von Stiffel and handing it to the Scotsman. "A present from the last days in the Führerbunker." Robertson looks at the cigar and smiles, the fragility of a non-smoker. "Thank you, Colonel."

His head covered to conceal his identity, Hitler is stretchered off the C47 and loaded into the ambulance. And is followed by Dr Bergman and Eva, who both turn to Skorzeny, smiling with great relief at reaching safety.

"It's time to get out of here," De Sancha adds, determined. "The less time on the ground, the less chance the Führer will be detected. A large military gathering makes everyone suspicious, especially in Spain, with every country having their intelligence operative's intent on disrupting Generalissimo Franco's advancement."

Robertson lifts his hand to shake Skorzeny's, but remembering the first time it was offered and refused, he refrains before walking off with the captain. "Take good care of that beautiful lady!" he shouts back with a passing wave of relief.

Robertson, the pilot and the captain enter the aircraft hangar then Robertson salutes and then reaches to shake someone's hand as they disappear out of sight, leaving Skorzeny staring with bewilderment at the open door for a short time until Radl walks up behind and slaps him playfully on the back to bring him around in relief it was all over. "Come on, Otto. I need food and then a bath," Radl said with a heavy sigh. "I have six years of sleep to catch up on."

***

FRIDAY, SEPTEMBER 7TH 1945

***

Sitting on a hill overlooking the Mediterranean Sea at Punta de S'Alqueria on the northeastern coast of Spain, the church of Santa Maria glistens as the sun shines bright and hot on a beautifully tranquil day. Spanish soldiers stand alert as far as the eye can see as they guard all approaches and keep the secrecy of an event they haven't been made privy to. The doors to the church crash open for Eva, her eyes red and filled with tears of sadness, to exit with haste, followed closely by Dr Bergman who wholeheartedly attempts to give her comfort to no avail. They walk down the path through the lychgate, then off into the distance, watched by Skorzeny, Radl, Hanna and De Sancha as they exit the church.

Uncomfortably hot in the midday sun, Skorzeny unbuttons the collar of his dress uniform and removes his hat to give him instant relief. "And with this comes the end of my military career," he said, unruffled by the prospect.

"Now you can go hide in the hills," Radl adds ironically with a wry smile as he unbuttons his collar and removes his hat.

"Now, hopefully, we can all get on with a normal life," De Sancha adds. "That is if you can remember what one is."

"I can't remember it has been so long," Radl adds with a wrought-looking grin.

Hanna's glance shifts to Eva and Dr Bergman rushing into the distance. "What will happen to them?"

"That choice is theirs," De Sancha answers. "Come on let's get back." They walk a short distance in silence as all minds contemplate how Hitler's passing will change their futures. Unaware of the importance of what is unfolding in front of them, a Spanish woman and her children stand to one side of the path, having been stopped from going about their daily business by a soldier. Seeing the young children, Skorzeny stops dead as the others carry on walking as his stare shifts between the boy, aged about seven and a girl, aged about five, and his mind flashes back to better days in pre-war Austria and the memory of him playing with his young son and daughter in the garden of his middle-class home with his wife standing in the background clapping and laughing. His heart races as the uncanny resemblance of the children to the family he left back in Austria gives him an unnerved feeling. Radl, Hanna and De Sancha stop and look back, equally bemused by

Skorzeny staring at their naïve innocence. Perceiving Skorzeny as a threatening authority figure, the woman beckons her children to her side, where they cling to her legs as they stare with terror at the massive scar-faced foreign soldier staring back at them.

"Are you alright, Otto?" Hanna calls out, catching his attention which quickly rounds on her. "You look distracted."

Unwilling to explain his thoughts, Skorzeny moves off, increasing his pace as he frequently turns to stare at the woman and children he is leaving far behind.

"What's going on?" De Sancha enquires of Radl, who looks at the woman and her children to instantly notice the resemblance to his friend's family. "Karl," he insists, but Radl shrugs his shoulders, deciding not to relay information Skorzeny would consider personal and turns to follow his commander.

***

SATURDAY, SEPTEMBER 8TH 1945

***

It was almost five in the morning when Skorzeny woke with the sun rising over the beautiful villa that had been set aside and paid for by the Spanish government and the diamonds he had taken from the Kehlsteinhaus for the conspirators of the Wagnerian Assignment to live out the rest of their lives in safety and comfort. Shifting luxuriously under the silk covers with a deep desire for more sleep, he can still feel the warmth of Hanna's naked body sleeping and shuffles tightly into her buttocks.

Keeping her eyes tightly closed, she mutters without moving. "Go away, Otto."

Rolling onto his back, he considers the day ahead and growing serious; he rises to stretch out his body. Setting himself up with a smoke, he crosses the room to the window to gaze out over the beautiful scenery that overlooks the Mediterranean Sea.

Hanna opens her eyes slightly, her face radiating what only a glorious sunny morning and a night of lovemaking could bring to a happy, contented woman. "Another lovely day, Otto, don't you think so?"

His thoughts drift between the Spanish woman, her children and his family back in Vienna; he wants to answer, but nothing comes out as he keeps his troubled stare into the distance.

Hanna takes a deep breath and rises in her nakedness to walk up behind and drape her arms around his waist to cuddle him in tight. "What's going on?" she mutters, concerned by the noticeable change to his demeanour since the funeral of Hitler, and he pauses with dread.

"I've decided to go home," he mumbles, and her face emanates into a wide smile that is overcome with excitement at the prospect of returning home. "I have to get my family," he adds bluntly with words that cut into her every being.

Knowing her presence is no longer required, it takes a few seconds to register as she steps back awkwardly, realising that their journey together is coming to an enforced end.

Recognising his words had been selfish, he reaches to take her hands but she backs away from his touch. "They don't know if I'm still alive," he pleads, hoping she would understand.

Unable to hold back the tears rolling down her cheeks, she moves into the bathroom, but on hearing him nearing, she busies herself furiously, splashing cold water over her face to conceal their flow before putting her robe on.

"I'm sorry," he mutters, aware they are not the words she truly wants to hear.

Feigning a smile, she turns, keeping her composure. "I'm the one that's sorry."

Saddened that their life together had come to this, he didn't know how to reply.

"I've allowed myself to be seduced by the tranquillity of this place. I knew this moment would come, and I selfishly put my feelings first. Of course, you should go to them. I'm embarrassed I hadn't thought about it prior."

Desperately upset, he moves to take her into his arms, but she moves off and exits, leaving the door wide open for him to close with finality.

**

Reading the daily report, De Sancha sits at his desk as Radl and Skorzeny sit to one side. The briefing, as always, has gone on too long for Skorzeny as he stares vacantly out of the window, too wrapped up in his thoughts to care about the day-to-day running of his protection from the outside world.

"This doesn't make sense," De Sancha said, unaware of Skorzeny's boredom and Radl catches his attention and nodded toward the colonel. "Otto," he adds to no avail forcing him to shout. "Otto! Have you got something on your mind?"

Skorzeny turns as his vacant eyes shift rapidly between Radl and De Sancha.

"Are you alright?"

Skorzeny debates the best way of conveying what he has to say and looks around as he shuffles uncomfortably. "I've decided to go home, General."

Having waited for this day with foreboding, De Sancha knows of Skorzeny's family ties and that they would at some time be too big a draw for him, and he would want to leave but this had come far too quickly for his liking. "That's not a good idea, Otto."

"Why is that?" Skorzeny questions, oblivious to the danger his thoughts are about to put him through.

"All top-ranking Nazis are to be put on trial," De Sancha explains calmly.

Believing he is just a soldier who had obeyed orders and not a top ranking National Socialist, only being a party member, Skorzeny laughs.

"I've purposely kept the news from you, but there is to be a great victory show trial of all the top Nazis still alive. It's to be held in Nuremberg, the home of the National Socialists."

Believing this doesn't cover him personally, Skorzeny shakes his head and laughs awkwardly.

"Otto, you're not taking this seriously," De Sancha carries on. "You are on the Allies' most wanted list."

Skorzeny's laugh becomes more self-conscious. "Most wanted list. Why would they have a most wanted list, and why would I be on it?"

"For war crimes."

"War crimes!" Skorzeny repeats several times.

"Is there such a thing in war?" Radl adds naively. "Surely war in itself is the crime?"

"Not for what happened in battle, Karl," De Sancha explains. "Although, might I add, in numerous circumstances, that will be the case, but this is mainly for the persecution of the Jews."

Skorzeny coughs uncomfortably as the accusations of wrongdoing agitate his sense of honour.

"Millions were killed in concentration camps and villages all over Europe and Russia," De Sancha continues. "All in the name of the man buried with a Christian service less than twenty-four hours ago."

Agitated that De Sancha is talking disparagingly about his Führer, Skorzeny wants to argue but holds back in respect of their friendship.

"They called it the final solution to the Jewish question."

"The final solution to the Jewish question! What the hell is the final solution to the Jewish question?"

"With the end of the war came the end of the genocide."

"Genocide! You've lost me, General."

"It was a policy the National Socialists had to rid the world of the Jewish race," De Sancha explains as he grabs the small cross he wears around his neck as a sign of his devout Catholicism and conviction in a God he believes never waned for one second no matter what he had witnessed throughout his life. "Why do you think Spain never entered the war after all the Führer did for us in our great civil war? We excused ourselves as not having an army ready for action and an economy to build, but we sent brigades of men to be butchered instead. Spain lost over four thousand five hundred dead to a war that was not her doing, but was that ever enough? General Franco wouldn't have won the civil war had it not been for the resources the Führer and Germany gave, but all this was before the bad years." He slams his fist hard onto his desk. "I didn't leave the Russian front because I wanted to. General Franco ordered me home," he adds, hoping to make his friends understand.

Skorzeny gives De Sancha a cynical look of disbelief.

"Your eyes inform me of what I have worried about all these years, Otto. You thought we were cowards."

Incensed that anyone could tarnish De Sancha's good name, Radl interjects. "Never, General! We would never disparage your honour."

Radl and De Sancha turn to Skorzeny for validation, but he has more troubles in mind than the allegation of cowardice the Spaniard believes has been laid on him.

Having witnessed the general's bravery first-hand on the field of battle on many occasions, Skorzeny is well aware he is not a coward, but his thoughts at that moment are self-regarding. "I knew about camps. Prisoners of the Reich were detained in them."

Agitated by Skorzeny's naivety, De Sancha sits forward, rubbing his forehead defiantly. "You must have witnessed executions."

"We all did," Radl answers, looking around the faces gathered with the loyalty to protect Skorzeny's honour and good name.

"I had cowards and traitors executed in the field," Skorzeny interrupts. "Some were arrested, and no doubt were sent to the camps."

"Jews were deemed enemies of the Reich," De Sancha argues to Skorzeny's irritation.

"I knew of the Nazis hatred for them. It was the platform they used to get elected."

"They murdered them in the millions, Otto, but it wasn't just the Jews," De Sancha adds angrily. "They murdered gypsies, homosexuals and the infirm. Anyone who got in the way of their racial doctrine."

Unnerved at how best to answer, Skorzeny stares his awkwardness at the general.

"If you return to Austria, you will be arrested," De Sancha said solemnly. "You are a colonel in the Waffen SS and a marked man."

"I had nothing to do with killing the Jews, gypsies, homosexuals, the infirm or any other non-combatants," Skorzeny pleads with a great belief in his own words.

"Neither did I, but I accept my share of the blame," De Sancha adds, his tone decidedly guiltier. "As we fought to protect Germany, we were also protecting the animals carrying out the heinous acts and allowing them to do it right up to the end. I warn you, Otto, you will be arrested and put on trial."

"How can you take a share of the blame for something you weren't involved in?"

"We are all to blame!"

Skorzeny takes in a deep breath as his heart races to the sound of guilt. "I've just been informed by a man I have trusted that I fought for a corrupt and evil regime."

"You must have known that, Otto," De Sancha adds, exasperated by his friend's naivety.

Skorzeny stares, desperate to shout out his innocence but remains quiet.

"We were all fooled by the Nazis," De Sancha carries on. "Luckily for me, General Franco insisted I come home, and I acted on his order."

"Lucky for you, General, you got to go home," Skorzeny adds with venom. "To safety while my men and I carried out our duty."

"I wasn't recalled out of cowardice!" De Sancha retorts furiously. "I was acting under orders of my commander and chief."

"He didn't mean it, sir," Radl interrupts turning to Skorzeny, angered he would slur De Sancha's honour.

Not needing his words defended by anyone other than himself, Skorzeny stands slowly, then moves to the door, saddened at a disagreement he never thought he would have with the amiable Spaniard, then stops to look back. "You know, General, I thought I had right on my side. Now." He pauses as the war years race through his mind. "Now you inform me I didn't." He takes one last look around the room that had been just as much a prison to him as the police cell in Augsburg, convinced he had made the right decision and exits.

"Take time to think, Otto!" De Sancha shouts, aware Skorzeny is paying him no attention.

Radl rises slowly and moves to the door. "You know, General, like Otto, I didn't know of any final solution."

"That may be, Karl, but you aren't as accountable as the colonel. The Allies believe he is a war criminal and will arrest him on sight."

"Otto's a soldier, not a politician."

"He was Adolf Hitler's chief of special troops. He has little defence in the matter. You need to talk him into staying where he will be safe."

Radl had never been able to talk Skorzeny into anything after he had made up his mind, and it shows on his desolate face. "Otto didn't decide policy, General. He knows what he has to do, and nothing will change his mind."

"He won't be safe if he returns home."

Radl grins weakly, then exits.

"Somehow, I don't think ignorance will help his defence!" De Sancha shouts with genuine worry for his Austrian friend's wellbeing.

***

Skorzeny walks at pace along a corridor and then stops without reason to find he is outside Hitler's quarters. Entering for the first time to find eagles, swastika banners and flags and a large portrait of the Führer adorning the wall along with a large self-appreciating bust that stands to one side on a mahogany plinth with the date January 39th 1933, inscribed on a solid gold plaque. The day he was appointed Chancellor by von Hindenburg, and he had come to power. Recognising the signs of a Megalomaniacal personality for the first time, he takes a deep anxious breath as he moves further inside. Alone, he moves to the bedside cabinet, which is covered in all sorts of medications and looks over the photographs spread neatly over the wall that show Hitler's old days when he was the icon of German life. His mind racing, he glances around as he doubts the allegiance shown to a man who had brought the world to devastation and ruin that killed millions of innocent people. Large numbers of them were close friends and associates. His eyes shift from a shelf full of the Führer's favourite Wagnerian operas and marshal music to a gramophone player standing with a seventy-eight ready to play. He winds it up and then moves the arm gently onto the spinning record, which crackles into action for Die Fahne Hoch to start playing with its marshal music beginning, bringing an instilled pride in himself and the country he had loyally served.

***

Born October 9th 1907, Horst Ludwig Wessel joined the Sturmabteilung in May 1929. Musically talented, he played the Schalmei, a type of Oboe and founded a Schalmeienkapelle band which provided music for SA events. In 1929, he wrote the lyrics for a Nazi fighting song named Kampflied (battle song) later known as Die Fahne Hoch (raise the flag), which became the Nazi party anthem after his assassination by communists in 1930 and renamed Horst Wessel Lied in his honour. When the National Socialists came to power in 1933, Wessel had been given almost martyrdom status as the soldier of National Socialism who gave his life for the cause. His lyrics were adopted as the unofficial second part of the German National anthem, played and sung immediately after the Deutschlandlied.

***

Skorzeny listens for a short while until the realisation of the music's significant history in the rise of National Socialism comes to light as his hands shake with nervous tension that turns to violent rage, so he pulls the record off the turn table to smash off the wall. Looking at the shelf of records, he pushes them onto the floor to smash before kicking them to one side as he looks for more things to vent his anger on, but he is interrupted by a light tap on the door and quickly calms.

"Are you alright, Otto?" Radl shouts from the corridor.

Skorzeny opens the door and stands aside for his friend to enter in shock at what he is witnessing. "What do you think I should do, Karl?" he asked softly.

No matter how bad the situation that confronted them, Radl had never seen Skorzeny ill at ease, which threw him off a little. "Otto, you have never once in all the years we have been friends asked or needed advice from me, and now at the time of reckoning, I don't think I am qualified even to try. Only you can do what you think is right, but I would give De Sancha's words serious consideration. The revenge of the victor is sure to have its sting."

Skorzeny grins awkwardly at what he knows will be the truth.

"I will return with you," Radl said with a genuineness that makes Skorzeny smile as he reached out to touch his shoulder.

"That I can't ask of you, old friend. If what General De Sancha says is true, you are better off remaining here in anonymous safety."

Radl goes to argue, but Skorzeny carries on.

"This is something I must do on my own… I will get my family and bring them back here."

***

WEDNESDAY, SEPTEMBER 12TH 1945

***

GIs stand guard at a checkpoint barrier at Coccau Valico on the Italian Austrian border as masses of starving, unkempt weary German soldiers, refugees, and displaced persons pass desperately to escape the Russian military zone of influence. Having driven from Spain through Italy in an Opel Olympia, it was almost dark when the Spanish diplomatic car drives through the refugees, beeping its horn impatiently for them to stand aside in fright. Sitting in the rear, Skorzeny can only see the beauty of his country in the distance that the surrounding mountains give, making the journey pleasurable to be almost on his home soil as he pays no attention to the plight of the unfortunate people passing. As the car comes to a halt at the barrier, a sergeant callously pushes his way through the refugees having no pity or concern for them, before tapping on the car window for the driver to wind it down.

"This is a Spanish diplomatic car," the driver arrogantly blusters, believing he should be allowed to carry on unmolested, but the sergeant has other ideas in mind.

Feeling the strain of almost continuous action since the Normandy landings of June 6th 1944, the sergeant isn't impressed by the driver's arrogance. "Papers!" he hollers, showing he means business and isn't in the mood for chit-chat.

Under orders of De Sancha not to create attention toward them, the driver picks out the papers and hands them to the sergeant.

"What's your destination?"

The driver clicks his fingers impatiently for the papers to be handed back and answers, annoyed at being asked, "Vienna!"

"That's in the Russian zone," the sergeant said, bemused as to why anyone would want to go into the arms of the Red Army. "Most people are heading in the opposite direction." He looks into the rear and notices Skorzeny sitting in the shadows in civilian clothes. "Your papers."

"This is a diplomatic car," the driver retorts.

"I won't repeat it," the sergeant scowls aggressively as he lifts his M3 to waist height to cock and point.

Skorzeny hands over his forged papers, which identify him as Jose Ferrara, a citizen of Spain, for the sergeant to inspect.

The sergeant's glance shifts between Skorzeny and a captain standing some distance away. "Don't go anywhere," he orders as he moves to the captain's side.

Unnerved, the driver reaches for his Ruby revolver, but Skorzeny grabs his arm to prevent what would unquestionably have ended up with both their deaths and several civilians in the crossfire.

The sergeant and the captain walk back as the non-commissioned officer opens the rear door to point his M3 into the opening. "Step out of the car?" he orders.

The driver turns frantically to Skorzeny and glances on his revolver, but Skorzeny shakes his head as he leans forward to place a hand on his shoulder.

"Thank you for your consideration," he whispers in a broken Spanish as he pushes the chair forward, and they both alight.

The sergeant points at Skorzeny. "I believe this man is wanted, sir."

"This is nonsense," the driver pleads.

The captain takes Skorzeny's papers off the sergeant and looks them over incredulously. "Your name is Jose Ferrara?"

Skorzeny knows his appearance is Germanic, that his Spanish is mediocre at best, and that his accent will instantly give him away as an Austrian.

"This is a diplomatic car under the protection of the Spanish government," the driver ripostes, only to find the M3 turned on him.

"Can't he answer himself?" the captain said, keeping his stare on Skorzeny. "Are you sure you recognise him, Sergeant?"

"Not the name, sir, but the scarred face."

Knowing the scar had proven a hindrance since the day he received it, Skorzeny laughs.

"Until we can confirm your identification, place them both under arrest."

"You can't do this!" the agitated driver shouts. "This is a diplomatic car under the protection of the Spanish government!"

Seeing an impending commotion, GIs surround the car and cock their weapons in a sign of strength as the gathering refugees back off frantically in fright that a firefight is about to ensue.

"You will find I can," the captain calls out confidently.

The GIs harshly manhandle Skorzeny and the driver toward a waiting M3 half-track and bundle them inside.

"You've just surrendered to the United States 30th Infantry Regiment," the captain adds with pride, but Skorzeny doesn't reply.

***

SATURDAY, SEPTEMBER 15TH 1945

***

Having withheld his identity and remained quiet, Skorzeny finds himself staring through the barred window of a military prison cell in an abandoned army barracks in Graz, Austria. Annoyed with himself for walking into the hands of the enemy without putting up any resemblance of a fight, his mind races until the door opens for an MP to enter and aggressively kick the bunk.

"On your feet, Kraut!" he commands.

Skorzeny ignores the shout and stays seated, but this angers the MP, who kicks the bunk several more times before grabbing the Austrian roughly around the neck and forcing him to his feet. Not prepared to take the unwarranted treatment, Skorzeny knocks the MP back against the wall, holds him tight as a truncheon is brought to bear, and swings threateningly in his direction to strike him across the back. Furiously, Skorzeny takes a tight hold of the MPs arm to prevent the weapon from making contact a second time and swipes it out of his hand to throw into the corner.

Fraser enters smiling with the air of a victor and takes his Walther out of its holster to point at Skorzeny as Ingram follows in shock. "That will do soldier."

Skorzeny lets go of the MP, who backs off, picks up the truncheon, and drops it back into its holder as he reluctantly exits.

"I don't believe it!" Ingram calls out.

"Well, well, if it isn't Jose Ferrara," Fraser said sarcastically. "You have the appearance of a certain SS colonel I am acquainted with."

Aware he had been found out, Skorzeny laughs as he returns to his bunk and sits. "Have you forgotten my number, Colonel?"

Fraser grins, amused by his candour to Ingram's bemusement. "No, but I still require the answers I asked during my last visit. Plus a few new ones."

"So, you have forgotten."

"You know, Colonel, this isn't a game. You don't seem to understand the situation you are in."

"I've been informed I'm one of Europe's most wanted men," Skorzeny said, amused by the infamy. "Well done in capturing me. It must be the highlight of your career so far. You are going places."

Fraser cannot comprehend the sarcasm and grins weakly at Ingram, who understands the candour. "I want to know what happened to the stooge you had masquerading as Adolf Hitler," he adds as he holsters the Walther.

Skorzeny's humiliation at being captured turns quickly to bemusement as his glance shifts between Fraser and Ingram, but he doesn't answer. The cell door opens, and the MP enters to stand patiently in the doorway as he waits for the arrogant American colonel to turn.

"What bewilders me most," Fraser carries on. "Why would you have a man masquerading as your Führer? What was the reason? Did you get the real Hitler out by other means, and was this all just a way of making us focus all our efforts on a ruse? Maybe by submarine, or can you enlighten me as to how?"

Skorzeny laughs at Fraser's wild attempt at questioning, but it quickly turns to an awkward cough at the thought. "Where would he go?"

"You tell me?" Fraser said as he sensed the MP and turned agitated to see him. "What is it, soldier?"

"Sir, the general wants to see you."

"General! What general?"

"He didn't give a name, sir; he just ordered me to get you straight away."

"Do you want me to see to the general, sir?" Ingram subserviently enquires.

"No, Captain. I believe I will do that myself," Fraser said as he turned back to Skorzeny. "Don't go away, Colonel," he adds with a laugh. "You need to think about those questions. They will need to be answered, one way or another."

Once again threatened with torture, Skorzeny glares his anger as Fraser and Ingram exit, leaving the MP in the doorway staring his contempt.

"Have you got a problem, Joe?" Skorzeny said with malice.

The MP lifts his truncheon out of its holder and drops it back in an attempt at intimidation that makes the Austrian laugh.

"When you're ready!" Skorzeny snarls in the hope the MP will make a move, but he smiles as if victorious and exits.

***

Debating which general is visiting, Fraser, followed by a subserviently attentive Ingram race along the corridor toward his office as soldiers stand aside saluting, but he pays them no attention as his boots echo his impatience and frustration. He reaches his office door and barges in to find Waverley sitting behind his desk with Robertson to one side. "What the hell is going on?" he shouts, angered by their presence, as he reaches for his Walther.

"Don't you mean what the hell is going on, sir?" Robertson said annoying Fraser whom he knows through experience, is humourless. "I wouldn't do that, Colonel," he adds as he stands to come face to face with Ingram, who backs off slightly. "Nice to see you again, Major," he adds sarcastically, aware there had been no promotion.

"What's going on, sir?" Ingram enquires as he turns to face Fraser. Fraser's stare shifts from the Walther to Robertson and Waverley to see they haven't reached for their sidearms. "And why wouldn't I, Major?" he answers Robertson's question.

Waverley hands Fraser an envelope. "The prisoner is to be released into my custody, Colonel."

Fraser's hand comes reluctantly off his gun. "Prisoner? What prisoner arc you talking about?" hc said in a pathctic attcmpt to bluff.

"Colonel Otto Skorzeny," Waverley said with determination. "All you need to know is in the letter."

Fraser attempts to return the envelope, but Waverley doesn't take it. "I don't have Colonel Skorzeny here."

"I have no time to piss about, Colonel," Waverley snipes as his determination increases in volume. "You have your orders; act on them!"

Fraser glances at the door, wondering whether to shout for the MP, but he refrains as he opens the envelope and reads intently. "A nice array of signatories. Are they meant to impress?"

"They impressed me," Robertson mocks to Fraser's ire.

"You will notice General Eisenhower's is on there too," Waverley adds. "Now, in case you have forgotten, he's your boss."

"You'll find he's yours too, General."

Waverley smiles knowingly. "Sorry, Colonel, but you will find that is not correct. We play to higher powers in this game. The captain should know that."

Having heard the same speech many times, Ingram shuffles uncomfortably, making Robertson laugh.

"That's right, Major," Waverley adds with a laugh. "You remembered."

Put out by the light-hearted banter of Robertson and Waverley, Fraser's intelligence-hungry mind can't compromise the deception unfolding before him.

"Last I heard you and," Fraser said, turning to Robertson with a look of disdain. "Were under arrest."

"You were misinformed," Waverley adds, amused. "But all that is irrelevant, and as you can see, that paper orders you to hand your prisoner to us and as I have already said, we don't have the time or inclination to piss about, so we will take him now."

Fraser scrunches the letter tightly in his hands. "And General Eisenhower agrees with this?"

"Like you, he doesn't have a choice."

"I'm not happy with this," Fraser roars as he drops the letter. "I must object to my treatment in this matter."

"You don't need to be happy," Robertson said with the pleasure of having one over on the arrogant colonel. "You just have to live with it."

Not liking a subordinate officer talking down to him, Fraser glares his total hatred at the Scotsman.

"Your best course of action is to put your complaint in writing, Colonel."

"That won't see the light of day," Robertson adds with a laugh. "But it won't harm you to try if it makes you feel any better. Now step aside while we take our prisoner."

"You can take him when I have had this confirmed by HQ," Fraser said pompously as he moved to the desk and picked up the phone. "Until then, you will have to wait. Now if you don't mind, I need to use the telephone. Get me SHAEF, General Eisenhower's office," he calls out as once again he takes hold of the Walther's grip. "I hope for your case you are speaking the truth because I ain't in the mood to take any more prisoners."

Robertson and Waverley settle back for what they know won't take long.

"Captain, keep them covered. I don't believe a word of this."

Ingram draws his Browning to point, but neither Robertson nor Waverley pay the threat any attention.

***

Gripping the cell bars with desperation to rip them out with his bare hands and escape, Skorzeny stares out of the window, disillusioned and isolated. Still having the unfinished business of finding his family makes his enforced incarceration intolerable, and as the cell door opens, he turns to see Robertson and Waverley enter nonchalantly.

"Nice to see you again, Colonel," Robertson said, genuinely pleased to see his old adversary is well.

Skorzeny's betrayed glance shifts around before calmly turning to look back out the window. "I see I have been made to look the fool again."

"Hardly, Colonel," Robertson states.

Angered, Skorzeny charges forward to take the Scotsman by the neck to throw him against the wall. Believing he has the upper hand, he keeps his hold, unaware Robertson had allowed him the advantage during their tangle in Augsburg Sanatorium, but this time, he doesn't need the Austrian to feel he is in command and pushes him back against the adjacent wall face first to restrain him.

"What the hell is going on?" Skorzeny shouts in frustration as he attempts to force Robertson back but finds he is being held too tight.

"Calm down, Colonel," Waverley said to placate the Austrian, who gets into an even worse frantic state each second he is detained. "First things first, Colonel, what made you return?"

"I've come for my wife and children."

Robertson turns to Waverley shaking his head in confirmation of the misinformation he had given him.

"We thought it may have been for another reason."

"What else could it be?" Skorzeny said bewildered.

Robertson lets go of Skorzeny and steps back, allowing him to recompose himself. "I thought Hanna was your partner."

"Why would you think that?"

"The major believed you were lovers," Waverley adds, making Skorzeny annoyed.

"Don't worry, Colonel. We are all guilty of a little post-marital tension while away from home."

Although embarrassed by his wartime love affair, Skorzeny's only concern is for his family, and he is desperate not to explain his actions.

"I need to get my family out of the Russian zone to safety. If the Soviets discover who they are, they may be held for ransom."

"No need to worry," Waverley said with confidence. "Your family are safe and well in Salzburg."

Skorzeny sighs as he sits back on his bunk, his elation exhaling with the deepest breaths.

"When we realised the intelligence on you was wrong," Waverley said, turning his irritation on Robertson. "We got them out."

"I could only work with the information I had at the time, General," Robertson excuses.

"And we now know how good that was, don't we, Major?"

His bewilderment at an all-time high as to why his enemy would consider helping him on a personal level, Skorzeny enquires. "Why would you get my family to freedom?"

Having spent several days incarcerated before his superiors in Washington had him released, Waverley looks around the cold, damp cell. "We can discuss that outside in the fresh air. I'm sure you could do with some." He stands aside to allow Skorzeny to exit but pauses in the doorway.

"How did you know I was here?"

"That, Colonel, is irrelevant," Waverley said not wanting to go into greater detail. "Come on, let's get out of this shit hole."

"You still can't get it into your head you have friends," Robertson said on noticing Skorzeny's apprehension as he pushed past him to exit first.

***

Two United States Packard Clipper staff cars stand with their engines running. Jacobs sits in the driver's seat of the first with Waverley's staff car behind. Robertson, Waverley and Skorzeny exit toward the vehicles, and the Austrian turns with mistrust to face the men he believes are still pretending to be his ally.

"So, what was all this about?" he questions as his stare fixes on a window above to see Fraser staring out, red-faced with rage.

"Preventing the continuation of a costly war," Waverley answers honestly, but Skorzeny cannot agree with such a simplistic explanation.

"If the Führer were found to be hiding out at the Berghof, National Socialist fanatics would have flocked from all over the Reich to carry on the fight," Robertson explains.

"That was General von Stiffel's plan all along."

Waverley gives Robertson a curious glance.

"The Wagnerian Assignment," Robertson adds with knowledge. Skorzeny's questioning stare shifts between Waverley and Robertson on noticing their edginess. "How could you know of the Wagnerian Assignment?"

"General von Stiffel planned to get the Führer out of Berlin to hand him to us," Robertson answers to Skorzeny's ire.

"Nonsense! Why would the general do that?" Skorzeny questions but Robertson and Waverley avoid the demand.

"When the charred bodies of a man and woman were found in the Reich Chancellery by the Russians, we thought Adolf Hitler and Eva Braun were dead."

"That was part of the plan," Skorzeny adds naively. "But how could you know that?"

Waverley hesitates, but Robertson once again answers on his behalf.

"General von Stiffel was a member of the German resistance. He had been for many years."

Skorzeny steps back reservedly at the treasonous allegation of a man he believes was a true German patriot and cannot defend himself.

"He informed us about the Wagnerian Assignment," Waverley interrupts. "As long back as 1943, but he wasn't taken seriously. Then when the bodies were found, and air reconnaissance of the Berghof showed nothing, we thought the National Redoubt was a myth or just misinformation on behalf of the German propaganda machine who wanted the Allies to flood the Obersalzberg with soldiers and disregard the advance into greater Germany."

Skorzeny's stare shifts rapidly between the two. "If what you say is true, and I very much doubt it, why would you think it was misinformation?"

"General von Stiffel may have been a traitor to some," Robertson interjects. "But he died for what he believed in, as you were also prepared to do."

"He was a very close friend of mine, and let me tell you if he was relaying information to the Allies, putting my comrade's lives in jeopardy then he was a traitor, and that's unforgivable."

"He may have betrayed National Socialism, but he was a patriot to Germany," Waverley explains.

Unsure what he believes in, Skorzeny's eyes drop to the ground.

"At no time did he give information of troop movements or tactics that would result in us having the advantage during a battle. You are taking this the wrong way, Colonel."

Agitated by how he is meant to take the news that a man he admired was a traitor, Skorzeny laughs.

"Many men of the resistance had contact with us and were captured and started giving false information against our knowledge, most long after their violent deaths. The Russians had their bodies, and the fighting went to almost zero," Waverley adds. "If news got out Hitler was still alive more lives would have been lost on both sides."

Skorzeny laughs in awkward disbelief.

"We have had a close working relationship with Spanish military intelligence for many years."

Shocked and betrayed by the realisation his dear friend General De Sancha had informed on him, Skorzeny shakes. "That's how you knew I was here?"

"Don't blame the general, Colonel," Waverley adds, noticing Skorzeny's anguish. "He was acting under orders just like the rest of us."

Skorzeny sits on a low boundary wall to their side, believing he had been betrayed by two old friends and comrades whom he had trusted with his life. "Words I have not long since heard from his lips," he says as he laughs awkwardly. "Don't tell me Hanna flew you here," he adds with irony but finds the thought too much to take and puts his head into his hands.

"I haven't seen the lovely Hanna since Gerona," Robertson adds to Skorzeny's irritation. "When I left you at the airport."

Aware Hanna would never betray him, Skorzeny glares at Robertson, unable to believe a word coming from his mouth. "It's all coming back. You saluted someone as you went into the hangar."

Robertson nods toward Waverley.

"Of course. I was just a pawn in your little game all along."

"You were a vital part of a plan to get Hitler to safety," Waverley reassures. "We sent people to pick you up when you crossed the border into Italy, but they missed you."

"I had General De Sancha's driver change his route several times. I don't know why," Skorzeny adds sardonically as he glances at Robertson. "But of late, I find it almost impossible to trust anyone."

"What made you think of driving to Vienna? Surely you knew the risks of falling into Russian hands?"

"I had to get my family out. Not to take the risk would be shameful and dishonourable," Skorzeny adds, humiliated that he hadn't attempted to find them earlier. "After the Führer's death, my duty was over, and I only had an obligation to find my family."

"All that time, they were waiting for you in Salzburg," Robertson laughs. "Maybe we should have found a way of getting them to you."

"Hindsight is a great thing," Waverley adds dismissively.

Solemnly, Skorzeny turns his eyes back onto the ground and pauses for several seconds in contemplative thought. "Have you heard of the final solution to the Jewish question?"

Wondering where the question is going, Waverley's curious glance shifts to Robertson before turning back to Skorzeny. "Are you saying you haven't?"

Skorzeny looks up and his stare shifts in awkwardness between Waverley and Robertson as he scrutinises their facial expressions for the answer that they are both well conversed with. Contemplating his years of service, he rubs his face and forehead. "I witnessed it all but was too wrapped up in my duty and misguided sense of honour to give it a second thought."

Robertson grins at Waverley and shakes his head, unable to believe the words of the SS colonel.

"I've done things I was never proud of but this is the first time I have felt shame."

"The Nazi power was handed to them by the German people to commit state-sanctioned genocide," Robertson interrupts to Skorzeny's disdain. "You knew of their hatred for the Jews, but like the masses, you stood aside and allowed it to happen. It took men like General von Stiffel to stand up to their tyranny. Many Germans and Austrians were willing abetters."

"My friends and comrades killed, and for what? A political ideology," Skorzeny adds, ignoring Robertson's ranting.

"A racial ideology based on hatred and bigotry," Robertson adds.

"We all lost friends and comrades. The war affected us all," Waverley interjects, wishing he could keep Robertson's ill-timed remarks out of the conversation. "Anyone tainted with its distaste can still feel the sting and probably will until the day they die."

"My friend Ernst warned me about the National Socialists before the madness of war began. He hated them for the violence they brought to the streets of Austria after the Anschluss, but I believed they brought order and discipline. I believed in a greater Germany where all German-speaking people could live."

"Lebensraum!" Robertson snarls at the hypocrisy. "Which roughly translates into English as the ethnic cleansing of all non-Germans... Hardly a romantic notion, Colonel."

Skorzeny understands Robertson's words but doesn't question an argument he knows he could never win. "I could have had him arrested, but I knew the penalty would have been death."

"Death," Robertson interrupts.

"I'm afraid so."

"All enemies of the Nazis have died horrifically."

Waverley grabs Robertson's arm and gives it a sharp tug, hoping that he will calm down and cease his argument.

"Ernst still enlisted in the Wehrmacht in 1939 when the call came and fought courageously." Visibly shaken, Skorzeny rubs his eyes before finishing. "He joined me at Friedenthal in 1943, and I held him in my arms when he died. I left his lifeless body on the banks of the Oder on

January 14th as we fought to protect the approaches to Berlin. I couldn't even bury him… I fought for Führer and fatherland and he fought for his family." Feeling the hangman's noose around his neck, he looks into Waverley's eyes. "I understand I am wanted for war crimes."

"Now the peace has to be won, Colonel," Waverley adds to appease the tenseness of the situation. "We want you to use your connections to locate important people for us."

"I won't work for the enemy, General."

"The war is over," Robertson interrupts. "You will find it is now the Russians, not us."

"They always have been," Skorzeny said, showing his deep hatred for the Soviet nation.

"All we want is for you to find people of interest for us," Waverley adds. "The men who designed the wonder weapons, the scientists and engineers, but ultimately the choice must be yours, Colonel."

Skorzeny turns to look back at the prison, then Fraser's office window to find him gone. "Help you or go back to prison?"

"We've just got you out," Waverley said with a laugh. "Why would we send you back? No, you are free to go get your family."

"You could join the French foreign legion with the rest of your SS comrades," Robertson said, relating to the thousands of Waffen SS men who had enlisted in France's elite regiment as a way of escaping the gallows, knowing they would receive new identities and the legion would protect them even though they had not long since been enemies. Waverley moves to the first Clipper and opens the rear door. "Go back to Spain if that suits you. Take this car. Inform the driver where you want to go but take the time to think. We all need to stick together if we are going to defeat the Communist threat."

"How things change," Skorzeny says. "First, we are Allied to the Russians, then you are. Now nobody wants to be their friend."

"They only have themselves to blame," Waverley said with a humorous grin as he withheld his knowledge on the subject.

"We told the world of their tyranny, but nobody listened."

"How could the world choose between two despots? Both the Führer and Stalin persecuted their own," Robertson explains. "Tens of millions have died because of their tyranny."

Believing Skorzeny's vanity could use a boost, Waverley pronounces. "I believe the colonel will make the right choice. He knows Soviet Russia is the world's enemy of the future."

Skorzeny walks to the first Clipper and stops next to the open door. "Why didn't you just kill the Führer instead of letting him live out his last days in peace and tranquillity?"

Emotionless, Waverley ignores Robertson's glare as he answers. "We aren't in the assassination game."

Knowing of many German officers who had been gunned down under orders of the Allied secret services, Skorzeny shakes his head in disbelief. "War is war, General. I was tasked with assassinating Roosevelt, Churchill and Stalin at the Tehran conference in 1943. Unternehmen Weitsprung."

"Operation long jump," Waverley mutters, having been briefed on the plan.

Skorzeny reminisces over the complexities of such an audacious mission. "I knew it was a hopeless task, and thankfully, it was cancelled before all of my men were killed."

"Stupidity."

"I hear there is to be a great show trial at Nuremberg where the victors will seek their revenge. Why didn't you put the Führer on trial?"

"The same reason we had to get him out of the Berghof. Fanatics would have come from all over to carry on the fight."

"My advice, Colonel. Go see your family," Waverley interjects. "Spend a little time with them, relax and enjoy yourself. We'll be in touch shortly."

Skorzeny smiles at the thought of putting his military life behind him and spending time with his family and goes to get into the car, but Robertson stops him as he takes out a neatly wrapped bundle from his pocket.

"What's this?"

"Your medals, Colonel."

Visibly moved, Skorzeny grips the honours tightly in his hand and smiles with delight at their return. "Thank you, Major," he said, reaching into his jacket and tearing at the stitching to reveal the envelope he had received from Dr Bergman. "Something I believe is vital to history." He smiles as he hands it to Waverley, who looks at Robertson in bewilderment. "The Führer's last will and testament," he adds, getting into the car, and Waverley slams the door shut, slapping the roof for it to drive off.

"The Führer's last will and testament," Robertson said with a mischievous grin. "What do you intend to do with it, sir."

"Give it to the relevant powers. What else could I do with it? It's vital to history."

Robertson laughs. "What was that with the colonel? First, you tell him to go and think things over, which I believe is against your standing orders."

"We can give him the time."

"Then you tell him that we aren't in the assassination game. You know about Operation Foxley to assassinate the Führer and all the others that went ahead."

"I'm aware of Foxley and that the powers that be deemed it wrong to kill Hitler in the belief he was making enough bad decisions that would bring the war to an earlier conclusion, and they didn't want someone with half a clue on warfare taking over and turning the tables on us. With what I know about the bastard, I would have shot him myself."

Robertson and Waverley walk to the second Clipper, glancing at each other over the roof.

"Do you think he knew about the final solution, General?"

Not wanting politics to come into his reasoning. Right or wrong, he needs Skorzeny for the intelligence gathering of the future, Waverley answers. "I will leave that to his conscience."

"What about his involvement with ODESSA?"

"That's something we can use to our advantage when the time is right."

***

The Organisation der Ehemaligen SS-Angehörigen (ODESSA), which translates into English as the Organisation for Former SS members, was set up by Otto Skorzeny as an international Nazi network to aid SS officers to avoid capture and prosecution for those who chose to escape would have meant imprisonment or execution.

***

Irked, Waverley taps on the roof of the Clipper several times before pointing at Robertson. "You know what worries me most about all of this isn't Colonel Otto Skorzeny, one of the most wanted men in Europe and Hitler's chief of special troops driving off with the chance of never coming back. It's your incessant use of the word Führer."

Robertson laughs, amused. "As I said to you overlooking Berchtesgaden, I miss those days before the war."

"That may be, but don't allow the powers that be to hear about your admiration for one of the world's worst despots and their National Socialist doctrine."

"I hardly admired him or it, but if you live amongst them long enough, you take on the part a little further than your standing orders require. You see another side to them. It just became second nature to call him Führer. It just translates into English as leader, which is what he was in reality. Look at you; you soon forgot your Scottish heritage and became an overbearing pain in the arse Yank."

"I was born in America."

"That, General, is no excuse."

They stare at each other for several seconds, then smile in unified amusement. Ingram exits the barracks and races over to Waverley's side to stand as if nothing had happened between them.

"Yes, Captain?"

Ingram salutes but doesn't receive one back. "I wondered what you wanted me to do, General."

"Want you to do?" Waverley said with a laugh as he smashed the captain in the face bursting his nose as he fell to the ground. "Take that as your dismissal."

Ingram vaults to his feet and, clutching his bleeding nose, makes his way back into the barracks, thoroughly dismissed.

"Come on, Will, I need a stiff drink," Waverley said, getting into the passenger side, and Robertson gets into the driver's seat, and they turned to each other.

"I bet that felt good, sir?" Robertson asked Waverley, who nodded his agreement as he flexed his bruised hand.

"Not enough to make up for my time in that cell."

"Where do you want to go, sir?" Robertson adds with a laugh.

Waverley debates how to answer. "Just drive, and we can stop at the first place that sells Tennessee whiskey."

Robertson smiles at the thought of winging it and drives off to follow the direction of the first Clipper. "We'll probably have to drive to Tennessee, sir."

"Well, I'm getting a taste for schnapps, so whatever fits."

***

Jacobs drives along the main road looking in the rear-view mirror as he sizes up Skorzeny, who keeps his stare out of the side window, unaware of the attention being bestowed on him.

"Where do you want to go, Colonel?"

"Salzburg," Skorzeny answers.

There is a slight pause before Jacobs carries on. "So where is Adolf Hitler now?"

Skorzeny's curious glance shifts to Jacobs' reflection in the rear-view mirror, then back out of the window, ignoring his inquisition.

"Come, Colonel, you can tell me."

Agitated, Skorzeny shuffles but still doesn't offer a reply as the Clipper turns onto a country lane as he pays scant attention to their direction or surroundings. They drive a short distance before stopping in a small clearing facing a Gaz jeep.

Skorzeny looks up to recognise the Red Army vehicle but doesn't feel threatened by its sight. "What's going on, Captain?"

Jacobs turns threateningly to point his Colt revolver. "Out."

Skorzeny pauses until Jacobs pulls back the hammer to force the Austrian's cooperation, and he opens the door to step out with the realisation of being betrayed again hitting home. Noticing a shadow in the Gaz jeep behind the windscreen glaring towards him. "Who's your friend?

Dressed in his NKVD uniform, which Skorzeny instantly recognises, Vasteroff alights with arrogance, believing that he had outwitted the SS colonel, who is now his prisoner.

"Standartenführer Otto Skorzeny."

"You have me at a disadvantage, Captain."

"Apologies, Colonel. My name is Kapitan Alexei Vasteroff," he said, coming to attention, clicking his heels together and nodding politely.

"What can I do for you, Captain?" Skorzeny adds flippantly, not seeing the threat.

"My government wants you for crimes against Mother Russia, but as an amiable man, I am willing to negotiate your freedom and life. All, of course, in return for intelligence."

Skorzeny laughs at the thought of ever giving any information to a Russian. "Everybody wants something."

"What I want to know is what happened at the Berghof?"

"Hasn't the American traitor informed you?"

Vasteroff looks his disappointment at Jacobs. "He doesn't seem to know."

"I take it they don't trust you?" Skorzeny said to Jacobs' annoyance.

"Can't blame them. I have never had time for traitors personally."

"Neither does my general," Vasteroff said, attempting to make a new friend. "But they do come in useful."

Belittled by Vasteroff's scathing remark, Jacobs knows he has to impress his Soviet masters before they decide to dispense with his services. "I've just heard Adolf Hitler's name mentioned by General Waverley, Captain."

Pleased that his suspicions may be true after the long months of investigation but with no concrete intelligence to back it up, Vasteroff's stern face turns into a wry smile. "In what context, Captain?"

"Err, just about getting him out of Berlin."

Vasteroff looks at Skorzeny to see if his body language confirms Jacobs' words, but the Austrian remains rigid and silent to his annoyance. "You will tell me, Colonel," he adds, drawing his Tokarev. "One way or another, you will tell me."

"I'm not afraid to die, Captain. Far from it. People have been trying to help me on my way for many years now, but here I still stand."

"There are many ways to die, Colonel, some better than others."

***

Robertson and Waverley drive at a leisurely pace before Robertson breaks hard, forcing the car into a skidding halt with Waverley's head hitting the windscreen.

"What the hell, Will!" Waverley shouts angrily as he rubs his bruised forehead.

Dismayed, Robertson's head shifts frantically in all directions. "What's going on?"

"I'd like to know that."

"Where's the other car?" Robertson adds as he focuses on the long empty road ahead. "They couldn't be that far off."

"They must have turned off," Waverley said, perplexed as to why Robertson was so bothered.

"Why would they need to turn off, sir?"

"Skorzeny may have requested a different direction. Look at the way he got into Austria. Don't worry; he'll be back."

"He was going to get his family in Salzburg. That is why he risked his life in coming back. Last time I looked, Salzburg is in that direction," Robertson adds, pointing straight ahead.

Waverley looks around as Robertson turns the car and heads back up the road at speed. "What are you doing, Will?" he adds, disconcerted.

Robertson breaks hard to skid at the junction to the country lane and heads down, increasing his speed as they go.

"What the hell has got into you, Will?"

"Something's wrong, General, and I want to find out what."

***

Skorzeny stands with Vasteroff and Jacobs on either side. "So, you want to know what happened at the Berghof?"

"The only way you walk away is after giving me the information I require on Adolf Hitler."

"Do you take me for a fool?" Skorzeny said, unperturbed by the threat. "I tell you, you shoot me; either way, I lose."

"I also give you the choice to come back to Mother Russia and explain what happened to my superiors."

"I've been and didn't like it," Skorzeny jibes. "Far too cold for me."

"It's a lot warmer than a hole in the ground."

"I'd still rather not. Too many Russians for my liking."

Angrily, Vasteroff cocks his Tokarev and points it toward Skorzeny's face in the hope of intimidating him into talking. "I'm sorry to hear that, Colonel."

The sound of Robertson's car takes their attention as it approaches at speed, and Vasteroff turns to fire several times, forcing Robertson and Waverley to duck as bullets smash into the windscreen. Losing control, Robertson breaks hard, which causes the wheels to lock, but the car carries on tearing through the road to hit Vasteroff with great force, smashing him onto the bonnet and knocking the Tokarev out of his hand to land next to Skorzeny as the car skids to a halt propelling the Georgian across the ground into a crumpled heap. Skorzeny picks the Tokarev up as Jacobs draws his Colt, aware he had been found out and the only way for him to escape is to kill them all. Dazed and confused, Robertson and Waverley get out of their car and notice Jacobs swinging around, aimlessly pointing the Colt without picking a target. "What are you doing, Captain?" Waverley calls out, shocked, as Jacobs makes him his target and takes aim.

"He's a traitor," Skorzeny shouts as he puts a bullet in Jacobs' chest to buckle his knees and drop him to the ground.

Bloodied and dazed, Vasteroff stands, and Skorzeny charges forward, firing several times to hit him in the chest and knock him back onto the ground as he takes his last gasping breath before dying. Jacobs lifts his Colt and squeezes the trigger for bullets to miss Skorzeny as he spins around and fires off two more shots in rapid succession to send the traitor sprawling into a crumpled heap, dead.

"What the hell is going on?" Waverley shouts as Skorzeny turns fast to point the empty Tokarev at them. "It's all over, Colonel," he adds, attempting to calm the Austrian.

"Is it, General?" Skorzeny said as he shifted the Tokarev between Robertson and Waverley, unable to decide whom he could trust.

Waverley walks over to Jacobs and looks down at his lifeless body. "What the bloody hell happened?"

"They wanted me to go with them to Russia."

"They?" Waverley shouts shocked.

"Your man and the Russian. The captain was a traitor."

"Harmless, General," Robertson retorts ironically. "No wonder this Russian keeps appearing."

His face covered in shock at the thought of another member of his staff betraying him, Waverley's glance shifts between Robertson and Skorzeny.

"Do I still need this gun, General?"

"No, you don't!" Robertson shouts relieved. "You are among friends."

Reassured, Skorzeny spins the Tokarev through his finger in the trigger guard and throws it into the adjacent field, pleased to be rid of it.

"You sure know how to pick them, General," Robertson said to Waverley's annoyance. "Both your captains betrayed you."

"I didn't pick Jacobs," Waverley rants. "He was transferred to me but Ingram." He pauses, unable to understand the personal betrayal of his friend. "He'd been on my staff since 1938."

"I would want to know why," Skorzeny interrupts as he moves to Waverley with his hand outstretched. "It's your turn to refuse, General."

Waverley stares at Skorzeny's hand for several seconds before shaking it firmly.

Even though his leading role as commander of Hitler's special troops was hardly anything different, Skorzeny adds disillusioned. "All this cloak and dagger shit."

"I suppose you prefer conventional war, Colonel?" Robertson adds cynically.

"No, Major," Skorzeny answers solemnly. "I prefer peace. The sort that only comes at Christmas time."

Robertson and Waverley stare at each other in amazement at an answer they would never have expected from one of Germany's foremost soldiers before laughing.

"Why would anyone want war? I can't think of anything more abhorrent."

Robertson laughs, catching Skorzeny's irritated attention. "You see, Colonel," he adds with a smile. "I told you we would have something in common."

Skorzeny lets go of Waverley's hand to take Robertson's to shake. "At last, Colonel, we have found a mutual trust."

"That, only time will tell. There is still too much mistrust in the world for us ever to become true friends."

"What's wrong with a little mutual mistrust?" Robertson adds with ironic foresight. "Hopefully, it will prevent us from going to war again."

THE END